Dear Reader:

Here's a pitch I promise you haven't heard before: *Palm Meridian* is set at a Florida retirement resort for queer women, in the year 2067. It's a place full of palm trees and careening golf carts, where the residents are just as likely to be playing pickle ball as they are to be learning how to pickle preserves or sculpt ceramic gnomes. These women are exceptionally busy enjoying the latter half of their lives, but they are also, inescapably, in the latter half of the twenty-first century, where mail, travel, and Wi-Fi are no longer as reliable as they once were, and large-scale weather events happen multiple times a day.

Three months ago, long-term resort resident Hannah Cardin was diagnosed with terminal cancer and decided she did not want to undergo treatment. Tomorrow, she will die by assisted death. Today, her quirky, beloved cast of friends (imagine the crew of *And Just Like That . . .*, plus ten or fifteen years) will overpower all obstacles—environmental, physical, and emotional—to throw an all-night celebration of her life. As you can imagine, bittersweet hijinks ensue.

If this sounds semi-utopian to you (minus the terminal diagnosis), you're right on the money: As you can see in her author photo on the back of this galley, Grace Flahive is not ready for retirement just yet. However, like most of us, she *was* overwhelmed by all the depressing, scary predictions about the world we're faced with daily, so she decided to conjure up the future she wanted into existence on the page: A future where the inevitable effects of time, like aging bodies and global warming, haven't fantastically disappeared, but neither have they successfully extinguished the love, joy, and pleasure she wasn't willing to imagine her life without.

With its completely original mix of wit, wisdom, and tenderness, and told in Grace's singularly stylish voice (has anyone else ever described egrets as "dubious noodles the height of your knee . . . in a kind of constant, wiggling peril, stepping tentative toes across bushes and baking lawns, tiny and tipsy, like kind-spirited loops of string"?!), *Palm Meridian* is sweet spot, life-affirming fiction, aimed squarely at the book clubs, beach bags, and cozy chairs of readers young and old, gay and straight, and anyone anywhere in between who has ever had the infectious thought: What if my best friends and I could all move to a beautiful place and live our best lives together?

But don't go thinking this book is a one-note wonderland, either. Underlying the audacious concept, you'll find achingly tender portrayals of the difficulties of caring for a sick loved one, the complications of grieving someone who is still here, and the surreal impossibility of saying goodbye, even when you know you're lucky to have the chance. *Palm Meridian* is about how we become people who live lives we love *and* how we learn to love the lives we've lived, even if it didn't go the way we hoped. It celebrates the possibilities and joys of aging in ways we too rarely see, and depicts expansive versions of community, sexuality, niche hobbies, and tropical cocktails to manifest a hopeful future where there's room for all of us, dancing under the universally flattering light of a neon disco ball.

So come on in, the water's warm. Welcome to Palm Meridian.

Sincerely,

Margo Shickmanter

Margo Shickmanter
Executive Editor | margo.shickmanter@simonandschuster.com

AVID

READER

PRESS

PALM
Meridian

Grace Flahive

AVID READER PRESS

NEW YORK AMSTERDAM/ANTWERP LONDON
TORONTO SYDNEY NEW DELHI

AVID READER PRESS
An Imprint of Simon & Schuster, LLC
1230 Avenue of the Americas
New York, NY 10020

This book is a work of fiction. Any references to historical events, real people,
or real places are used fictitiously. Other names, characters, places, and events
are products of the author's imagination, and any resemblance to actual
events or places or persons, living or dead, is entirely coincidental.

First Avid Reader Press hardcover edition June 2025

AVID READER PRESS and colophon are trademarks of Simon & Schuster, LLC

For information about special discounts for bulk purchases,
please contact Simon & Schuster Special Sales
at 1-866-506-1949 or business@simonandschuster.com.

The Simon & Schuster Speakers Bureau can bring authors to your live event.
For more information or to book an event contact the Simon & Schuster Speakers Bureau
at 1-866-248-3049 or visit our website at www.simonspeakers.com.

Interior design by Ruth Lee-Mui

Manufactured in the United States of America

1   3   5   7   9   10   8   6   4   2

Library of Congress Cataloging-in-Publication Data

ISBN 978-1-6680-6545-7
ISBN 978-1-6680-6547-1 (ebook)

To Mom, Dad, Alice & Finn

FLORIDA
2067

The residents of Palm Meridian Retirement Resort were retired only in name.

Though they were formally unemployed, nothing—no force of nature, no act of God—could stop these elderly women from attacking their days with a kind of energy that would make a working person quake.

Already, at 8 a.m., the resort was a microcosm of life in all its brightness and its rowdiness, its hurry and its pain.

Some residents were roiling with orgasm, while others were fifteen minutes beyond, licking the orange, sated dust of post-coital Cheetos from their fingertips.

Some residents were waxing, others ruminating, some stricken by grief and others by IBS. One woman drank her coffee at the window, a bit of loose boob hanging from her robe. Diarrhoea threatened at the fringe, adding an element of danger.

On the main lawn, a troupe of hula hoopers shimmied and stepped, their hips and hearts hot with the motion of swirling. Nearby, the podcasters sat in the grass, headphones puffy with sound-proof feeling, sharpening their anecdotes and loosening their rapport.

Some were still awake from the night before, nursing hangovers by the edge of the pool, the chlorinated water lapping at their legs. Enjoying a cigarette, they tipped their heads back and returned to memories of the previous night: a tryst in the badminton clubhouse, the birdies bristling against bare shoulder blades.

One resident was in the bathtub, redrafting her will. She'd leave everything she owned to Esmerelda, her new dentist, who she'd met yesterday. A woman fifty years her junior. Through the suck and squelch of gums and fluoride, how could she ignore the tender care and intoxicating scent of this woman—who, it must be said, was smoking hot? She'd only gone in for a filling but had come home with a mouth full of porcelain and a heart sunk deeply in love.

Some at the resort were in decades-long marriages, their love as soft and dependable as their complementary pyjamas. They sometimes argued at the breakfast buffet about flavours of toothpaste, or their adult children, their words as hot as the soybean bacon. But at night they pressed their silent affection, with their noses, into the sleeping backs of their loves.

Others were widowed, some of them recently. Their partner's scent was preserved on a pillowcase, kept safe in a Ziploc bag. At night, their strength wavered like the palm trees in the darkness.

Some were actively single, magnetic and boastful. At the pool, they spread their bodies across the loungers, laying their charm on as thick as their SPF. They sauntered and suggested, did their best to land a breakfast date—a stack of pancakes at the diner down the interstate, the maple syrup dripping erotically.

There were tap-dance recitals and dildo debriefs, tuba lesbians, tennis lesbians and elite croquet teams. There were scheduling conflicts, too, like the *en plein air* painters who, due to allergies, were forced inside. They displaced the women of Remedial Bingo, who now dabbed with hesitance at their B4s and G39s on the lawn, in the bright of the sun.

There were unexpected changes in self-conception. One woman stepped out of the shower and considered her naked, wrinkled body in the mirror. She decided she looked like a hash brown that had been through a washing machine. Then she amended this quickly: she was a *glamorous* hash brown with a daring sense of fun.

There were the marinating scents of sunscreen and humidity, the peppermint stink of pain ointment. Old age had turned their knuckles to lumps of hardened lava, aching and volcanic. They used their arthritic hands to care for their dying friends and, at other times, to drink poolside tequila from jazzy plastic cups.

It was the second half of the twenty-first century and everything was flavoured with apocalypse. And yet—this gelato-coloured place, its rolling lawns riddled joyfully with lesbians, flush with bisexual women, blessed by a bevy of trans and non-binary people—how could you leave a home like this?"

This was what Hannah was thinking as she sped along the path in a twice-refurbished golf cart, her windbreaker rippling. The engine groaned and she pressed her sneaker on the pedal, felt the air lift her ponytail, silver and shining. She tugged her baseball cap tight to her head.

Hannah took a hard left at the food hall. How familiar was all of this? The looping paths, the leaning palms, lizards dashing across pebbled landscaping. At night, the gurgle of the swamps, hot and eternal. The gators snapping their worried teeth. The distant thundering of trucks down the interstate.

As Hannah hurried her cart towards the main lawn, the wind picking tears from her eyes, she thought how unlikely it was to be alive.

It was a feeling dramatically sharpened by the knowledge that, by this time tomorrow, she wouldn't be.

2

FLORIDA
8 a.m.

*H*annah took the hill at shuddering speed, the tyres spitting gravel. Were the cart to topple backwards now it would probably kill her, and what a colourful way to go: the overstuffed cargo hold would crack open, and Hannah would lie amidst a happy wreckage of hot dogs and ice cream and smashed crates of beer, dips slicing across the grass like paint strokes, the taramasalata and tzatziki lurching for opposite horizons.

But to die right now, and not tomorrow, would be inconsiderate, given the amount of party prep that had already taken place.

So Hannah squeezed the wheel and steeled her nerves, chugging the cart up the crest of the hill and coming to a stop beneath a beleaguered palm.

Stepping out, Hannah caught her reflection in the windows of the bar—she was like a small teenage boy mixed with an older woman. Her frame was slight, her delicate features now washed with deep wrinkles, and she was rough and loose in the way she carried herself. There'd always been a restlessness in her hands that drove her to flip things neatly in her palm when she held them, like a baton: hairbrushes, bottles of ketchup, TV remotes.

Hannah was dressed the same as she had been for the last ten years: a t-shirt, a faded green windbreaker and a pair of black shorts that stopped above her knee. Her grey ponytail was strung through her baseball cap and a pair of sunglasses caught the light.

"Morning, boys."

The egrets had once been wild but had sought refuge at Palm Meridian years ago. Their habitats had been wrecked by worsening storms, so why not move in with the nice lesbians, whose ponds were rife with frogs and grasshoppers?

About a hundred egrets lived at the resort now: white-feathered, long-necked birds, dubious noodles the height of your knee. They were in a kind of constant, wiggling peril, stepping tentative toes across bushes and baking lawns, tiny and tipsy, like kind-spirited loops of string.

A group of them stood by the door of the bar. They scattered in slow motion as Hannah approached with her stolen key. She carried the first bags of supplies in both hands, their weight making red marks on her skin.

The small building was an oval with glass on all sides, a lozenge gleaming in the morning light. By the door, in clean, Art Deco lettering: FRANKIE'S.

Inside, the sun spilled through the windows and across the bar top, which was lined with stools and stocked with napkins and wedges of lime. In the corner there were stacks of flyers for one-woman shows, Welding Wednesdays, charity fundraisers centred on birdhouse building competitions, birdhouse décor competitions, and the wellbeing of Florida panthers. Glass fridges behind the bar were stocked with a range of juices and wines, plus the medicated eye drops of patrons who tended to neglect their glaucoma after a martini or two.

Hannah put her bags down and stepped behind the bar. Coffee was forbidden thanks to her half-dozen medications, so she resolved to drink four today. She started up the machine, and soon the nutty smell of coffee beans pierced the air. She turned around, surveying the dancefloor.

Memories moved across the empty space. What hadn't it witnessed?

Not even on weeknights did an uneventful moment go by. This floor had seen marriage proposals, projectile vomit, bare feet mangled by mobility scooters, and medical insurance made void by Herculean dance moves.

Even on the quietest of evenings, Frankie's was charged with something: an undertone of flirtation, rippling hot and strong as the Florida winds.

On the far wall were tacked-up photographs taken over the last twenty years. They showed tangles of friends raising glasses, kissing cheeks, winning raffles. There were images from every occasion: Halloween, Valentine's Day. Big blow-out events where witches fornicated, and Cupid fell in the pool.

One photo was from Hannah's seventy-seventh birthday, earlier that year—the faces so close to the camera you could see their pores, the hysterical whites of their eyes, their hair dusted with piñata pieces.

In the centre of the wall, beside the photos, was an oil painting—made in jest but loved in earnest—of the bar's unofficial founder, Frankie. In the painting, she was smoking a pretzel stick like a cigarette, a wink caught in her eye.

The coffee machine hissed and drained, and Hannah took her two cups and headed back outside into the already baking heat.

The terrace was dotted with tables where, in the dim light of every evening, residents traded gossip and grandiose plans, a chorus of crickets rising up from the darkness below.

Now, though, the world was bright, the sun burning the dew off the lawns that sprawled to the horizon.

From here, Hannah could see everything: the long, low residential buildings that sat along the edges of the resort, with their outdoor corridors and tropical-pastel paint jobs. The buildings were designed in mid-century style—a label that had stuck, though they'd passed the mid-point of the next century.

Hannah could see the food hall and the welcome building, the kiosks and clubhouses. In between it all, the paths spooled out, accommodating putting greens, a pair of swimming pools, the spaces bordered by shaggy palms and yawning hibiscus flowers.

Hannah sipped her first coffee, enjoying the sharp flavour on her tongue and the quickening of her heart. Her leg jittered underneath the table. She licked the sweat from her upper lip and took off her baseball cap, letting the sun reach her scalp, feeling it sear her skin. For the first day in ten years, Hannah wasn't wearing sunscreen. Given the cremation, she figured she could afford a bit of crisp.

It hadn't always been this hot, but it had always been coming.

The resort was an imperfect refuge, a mostly okay oasis that was maintained amidst a crisis of a place. For thirty years, the south of the state had been slowly lapped up by the ocean, until there was little Florida left in those places—just eddies and islands, sopping with inevitability.

If you drove two hours south of the resort, the drug stores and nail salons and Burger Kings had been reclaimed by nature. Where there were once baseball diamonds and vape shops, there were now herons making happy homes, gators glad for the peace. The wood-panelled walls of flooded family basements were bloated and barnacled. The wind rippled disused swimming pools, thick with silt and emerald green algae.

The nearest city, Orlando, was left with the wreckage of a sprawling Disney empire, the company long gone bust. The abandoned theme parks poked their noses above the palms when you passed on the highway. Panthers stalked the grounds of Magic Kingdom. In Epcot: a ghostly, broken crystal ball.

The more northern parts of Florida had managed to hold on to civilisation—there, lush greens and sun-baked citrus trees revealed little wrong. Still, dotted amongst it all were burst pipes and rotted foundations, car dealerships gouged by storms and abandoned to time.

At the southernmost tip of the state—which moved northward every day—you could buy a square of property for forty dollars. What you were buying, though, was little more than kelp, and principle. What was once luxury was now liability.

Few tourists came through those parts these days, and the ones who did were more like prospectors, driving down in trailers with schemes and dehumidifiers, their life's savings blinking desperately behind their eyes.

The storms had become more frequent, too, and weather was unpredictable. The wind could pick up without warning, ripping through the palms, stalling golf carts on the freeway, lifting garden hoses and sending them twisting through the pink sky, rapturous spaghetti.

Then ten minutes later it would be gone. The air would go thick and hot again, smelling of swamp grass and chicken wings and the worry-burn of a hundred thousand electric generators.

By now, a third of the United States was without a reliable power grid. California was on fire more often than it wasn't. There was a generally held belief in Florida that the whole of Orlando could explode in a giant fireball, and Washington wouldn't know or care for at least a week.

Inside the grounds of Palm Meridian, the world was gentler, but not immune entirely from the hazards of the century. Phone and internet connection was shoddy at best—technology had gone backwards that way. Sometimes the power went out completely, the lights on the paths disappearing and leaving them in humid darkness, a kind of primordial force that swallowed the cheerful place they called home.

On paper, the resort promised safety, fun and community for the over sixty-fives—precious things in an increasingly tumultuous planet. These days, it delivered firmly on the latter two promises, but faltered on the first—after all, any resident could enroll in hat making class, but none could out-run a tropical storm.

Like the temperature, retirement ages had crept upwards in recent years, and so too had the median age at the resort. Now, the bulk of residents were sept- and oct- and nonagenarians, plus a handful of centenarians whose rogue, robust health made everyone else look bad. They curled their wrinkled biceps and shared secrets for longevity; frequent lucid dreaming, or one corn dog per day.

Thinking of tonight's party now, Hannah started on her second coffee. She checked the signal on her phone but, just like last night, there was nothing. For weeks at a time, they'd be lopped off the map like this, isolated from the rest of the world. It was peaceful, but precarious.

The stillness of the morning was broken by a pecking sound. Hannah spotted a team of egrets stepping across the seat of the golf cart she'd arrived in. Their worried beaks were investigating the rest of the supplies. She left her coffee and approached them gently.

"Sir—sir, I'm going to have to ask you to leave."

In four trips, Hannah brought everything from the golf cart into the bar. She'd slipped Nate's bar key from his dresser the night before, knowing that if she didn't show up early and start preparing, her friends would do it all—those loving bastards—and they'd done so much for her already.

Though they'd hired people to feed them that night—caterers who would arrive with trays of hot, delicious food, and crates of champagne—Hannah had felt compelled to contribute more, to feed her party guests personally, in some supplementary way. And so, she'd gone to the super-store down the interstate at dawn, stocking up on extra snacks, drinks and supplies.

The last things Hannah brought in were her parents. For ten years they'd sat sweetly in their urns, atop Hannah's TV stand. Tonight, she'd give them pride of place in a safe spot above the bar.

Hannah often imagined them in some yellow street-lit limbo, Montreal snow blowing through their hair. She saw her father driving his Zamboni in icy, immortal loops. She saw her mother, laughing, cracking the cardboard recycling over her knee.

Would she see them again, tomorrow? In the place where she was going? A hope rose up inside her, but Hannah pushed it aside. The end was coming, and when it did, she would know. She couldn't control it either way.

After securing the urns, Hannah checked through the various lists on a clipboard at the bar—the supplies they'd picked up, the schedule for the evening.

On the paper, circled in red:

$\overbrace{5\,p.m.\,—Guests\ arrive}$

A warm wind came in through the open door, and it rippled the packs of paper streamers, the bags of potato chips crowded on the floor. Hannah's gut swirled with the breeze.

At this time of the morning, the bar would normally be dotted with residents sipping espressos, but today they'd kept it closed to prepare for the party. There were still thirty minutes before Hannah's friends—all residents of the resort themselves—would arrive to help set up.

Feeling restless, Hannah went out the back of the bar where a second, smaller terrace looked over a slope and another sprawling lawn. At the bottom of that slope were two white plastic patio chairs, empty and turned towards one another. Pairs of chairs like this were dotted all around the resort, and at night they'd seat pairs of people who couldn't sleep, who'd trade stories of the things they'd seen. Passing a bottle of bug spray back and forth, they would return to their beds at the citrus crush of dawn, their skin oily with emotion.

Now Hannah padded down to the chairs and sat, the birds chattering through the trees. She surveyed the lawn that would be gone to her tomorrow.

It was only three months ago that Hannah had received the diagnosis. Maria's office was beautifully designed and kept very cold, goosebumps rising on Hannah's skin. Hannah had sat on one side of her wide, mahogany desk, cracking jokes about bladder leaks and a swallowed hearing aid while she eyed Maria's medical degrees on the wall.

Maria was fetching papers. Fetching test results. Fetching a glass of water for Hannah that she hadn't asked for. When she finally closed the door of the office and sat down at her desk, Maria suddenly felt so far away from Hannah. How big was this desk?

The outlook was a mixed blessing. The onset would be gradual, so there was time. Things would take hold slowly, the cells responding, the body noting a change. But deterioration would be quick, once it found its rhythm. The suffering would be great, the pain likely unbearable. Life would not be life.

You do have choices these days.

Hannah had thanked Maria, noticing for the first time the youthful glow of her skin, the shine in her hair. This woman was flush with natural collagen. She was probably thirty-three.

Hannah had left the office and walked out of the automatic doors of the hospital, which let her pass with a weighty swoosh of air. She'd taken a golf cart there, but walked past it, out of the parking lot and down the sidewalk, lined with scrub brush and palms. By the time she'd made it home, the resort was dark. The lights in the pool sent up quivering patterns that played across the trees nearby.

Medicine had advanced in the decades past, and if the unbearable could not be borne, there were a greater number of options than before, and a greater number of people choosing these ends when they needed them.

Countless nights at the diner down the interstate had helped Hannah come to a decision over those last three months. If life would not be life, then she wouldn't live it. She'd go out with a bang.

Since she'd made her decision, Hannah hadn't felt herself. Or rather, she hadn't felt like her current self. How could she explain it? Ripples of age nineteen and twenty-six and thirty-four seared through her at odd hours, skittering through her blood. Standing in the shower, or crossing the paths, everything would come up again, building under her skin like a rushing tide, rising hot to her face. An earlier part of her life would peel itself up from the past, thin as doughnut glaze, and go billowing through the sky. It would fold itself over and, with a muffled sound like a blanket falling, lay itself onto the present.

Last night, for example, standing on the carpet in her room, she'd felt anguish in her armpits, ecstasy in her elbows, felt her twenties and thirties hot and alive in the folds of her ears. Some previous motion tumbled through time and caught itself in her chest—lurching, misplaced, beautifully bewildering.

She'd closed her eyes and clenched her teeth. She'd felt paper cuts from sixty years ago rise on the pads of her fingers. Her throat flared with long-gone laryngitis and her mouth softened for kisses traded with wild-moving, long-lashed people, now dead.

When Hannah had opened her eyes, the room had been filled to bursting with sounds and shadows. The feeling sped up—it mowed through time—until Sophie was there in front of her. Sophie with her broad smile, bright eyes, dark, snow-flecked hair shimmying down her back in waves. Hannah's heart had been puffed up, hot to the touch with feeling.

The faraway crack of a golf ball across the lawns brought Hannah back to the present, sitting on a plastic chair on the grass beneath the bar, the hot breeze against her face.

She unzipped the pocket of her windbreaker and pulled out a folded piece of paper. The details of her appointment tomorrow: *Florida Grove Hospital, Palliative Care Ward, 9 a.m.*

"Hannah!"

The voice rose up from the front of the bar, startling Hannah. She stood and scrabbled up the hill, her parents' urns glinting in the window as she passed.

MONTREAL
1990

*T*he conception was not immaculate, and it featured shrimp heavily. But god, you couldn't say it wasn't beautiful.

Hannah's parents wound through the crush of the party, gleaming with youth and melted snow. One finger was hooked on one finger, their hearts tall and their knuckles hot, groins buzzing with something they didn't yet know was the future.

In the dim place, in the cigarette haze, their love made them globs of light. They were gulps of air. They were hydroplanes. They were a sweating bottle of champagne wearing a baby tuxedo.

Outside, the snow fell in soft, vicious pelts—the worst winter storm in sixteen years. The wind slammed at the windows, went somewhere else, blew up again. The cars gave up on the roads, and the street lights changed for themselves, snowbanks reflecting their red and green and yellow.

The winters in Montreal were sometimes so cold they could kill you, but everyone pretended it was fine, and so it was fine.

"Clam? Spliff? Pinot?"

The apartment was thick with their friends, warm, tipsy bodies spread across second-hand couches, others with their eyes lit up like fire.

In the centre, a point of pride, a vision of graduate student luxury: a table spread with seafood from the frozen grocery aisle, a feast poured from bulk bags the size of pillow cases. A hot mountain, stinking, delicious and bright.

"Ten minutes!" someone cried over the music, over the drunk, fishy voices and the roar of the wind.

Somewhere in the dark of this storm, the year would turn over.

With so little time remaining, every need was sharp: Must eat the shrimp. Must rescue this man whose head is wedged in a bucket—oh, it's Gary, with the two PhDs. Must lick this entire beer right into me. Don't smoke, but must smoke. Must dance like I'm the worst winter storm in sixteen years.

Must love you, must adore you—that one's easy.

Must kiss. Must fuck.

"In here—"

Two lamps were on in the bedroom they'd found, spilling a syrupy glow across everything, which was almost nothing—just some books, and some plants, a mattress, mussed sheets with the scent of coffee and weed.

The window was open and the snow blew in under the shine of the street lights and the yawn of the moon. Hannah's dad tried to slug it shut, but the thing was stuck, and the end was near—it was too important, now.

Their skin rose up with goosebumps. They couldn't feel the cold, though, their bodies hot and needing, the sounds of the party rolling through the door—a squelch of oysters, the crush of a beer can, the sucking *Pop!* of Gary's head released from another bucket.

"One minute!"

The city couldn't take this. The thickening snow was a burden on the roofs and the roads, but most of all on the electrical wires. Beneath the weight, a team of them finally snapped, the black rubberised cords sending up sparks into the sky, worming with terror to the ground. The surrounding houses dropped into blackness.

Hannah's parents pressed closer, the cold air showing their breath as the apartment surged with sound and then went dark. The voices went up, then the countdown carried on. The green numbers on the microwave blinked out, and the beers on the counter smashed, and the end was here. And on someone's borrowed bedroom floor, the gears of Hannah's life began to churn.

The nurse was giving horoscopes the night that Hannah arrived.

You have a knack for lunch meats, Libra. Stay focused and you'll pick the right bologna.

Scorpio: care for your capers.

An autumn downpour rose up outside the hospital in the middle of the night, the rain falling in sheets on the downtown, thundering onto the cars and sidewalks, the crumpled traffic cones and their dirty bureaucracy. The slicked streets reflected the city: the fluorescence of a bank lobby, a poutinerie's halo of neon and grease.

Hannah blew into the room faster than anyone had expected— reaching, howling, gnawing. Soft and unable to wait.

Hannah's parents held their daughter's tiny hands, each fingernail the size of a flake of snow.

"Virgo," her mother whispered to Hannah. "You're on the loose."

Hannah's parents were computer science graduate students, unmarried, wracked with debt. But they were also debilitated by a love for one another that hit them again—like a sweet, tender bus—when they woke up every day.

The pregnancy had been unplanned, a by-product of a lusty, fishy mania. But they had made the unwavering decision to keep it. What was a baby? Where did babies go? They would learn. They wanted to.

Hannah lived with her parents in a second-storey apartment in Montreal's Mile End, the curling stairs painted lemon-yellow, the tiny balcony populated with hockey sticks, and plant pots that filled with snow so they looked like cupcakes through the winter.

The entryway was cluttered with their boots, the cracked wooden floor stained by road salt. Their little home smelled of books and soup, wool drying on the radiator, the worn softness of second-hand furniture. It smelled of the bagels that wafted down the street from the ovens of St-Viateur, sesame-silly.

Those first winters, Hannah stayed home with her dad, while her mother finished her degree and got a job as an entry-level software developer, working downtown in a towering palace of staplers and Xerox machines.

When Hannah was older, she'd visit her mom at work, fascinated by the greyness of the office, its carpets stretching like plains, its pointed top. The city's central train station sat in the base of the building, with its cappuccinos and echoing marble hall, where trains pulled out to Toronto and New York. Sometimes Hannah and her mom would hurry to lunch there, sit contentedly eating smoked meat sandwiches, like peers, in the warren of delis and newsagents that led to the great hall.

At the beginning, though, Hannah was a baby, and she sat at the front window of their small home with her dad, in their pyjamas, the two of them eating kiwis and baby formula, respectively. Hannah told him roving baby stories, meaning nothing and everything, while he nodded and listened, sipped his coffee, scratched his beard and sketched their matching feet.

Together they watched the world go by, saw the artist with his paints dripping in the snow, the students on their bicycles, zonked on no-sleep, slush licking at their ankles. Their twenty-year-old eyes weary with cereal and possibility.

They watched the crowds that spilled from the synagogue and the church down the block, the worshippers mixing on the sidewalk, dreaming of salvation and after-prayer pastries.

At night, there were other things to see: snow ploughs passed down the quiet street with their lights like spaceships, pushing the snow into piles as high as the cars. The world was icy, lumped and blue, and Jewish prayers floated up from the downstairs neighbours.

While Hannah's dad finished his thesis, he worked as a line cook at a French restaurant in Outremont, managing salt and fat and fire. The restaurant didn't pay much, so he also took shifts at the outdoor rink in Parc Jeanne-Mance to make up the difference. Early mornings and late nights, he drove the Zamboni in the shadow of Mount Royal. The players pulled on their skates at the side, on a bench half stuck in a snowbank. There were young kids with hand-me-down helmets, students sluggish with last night's drinks, and dads whose softening bodies came alive on the ice. They waited while Hannah's dad made his prayerful loops, the hulking machine leaving shining paths behind it.

Her dad enjoyed his Zamboni work more. He smiled shyly while he did it, his nose hairs frozen and his hands turning to husks despite his gloves. But the two jobs conspired to exhaust him. He'd come home with the smell of winter in his hair, dressed in a costume of divergent parts: his long johns under his chef whites, the fabric touched with fire and ice.

Every night, Hannah's depleted parents made for a captive audience. By the age of four, all the lives that had walked by their apartment had become a part of Hannah. In the deep of winter, her parents would sit on the couch eating crackers and sipping depanneur wine, watching Hannah perform by yellow candlelight, the wind and snow raging against the windows.

Hannah, with her tiny legs and arms, was a chain-smoking cook at a diner, a mechanic making routine checks. Hannah was a property valuator, squinting at the fixtures around the house, carrying a clipboard as big as her torso. Standing on a stool, she slapped the kitchen table, said: "This place'll fetch ya six bucks," in which six bucks was a serious amount of money, and her voice warbled with respect.

Hannah was a broom sometimes, standing in the corner of the kitchen and then, when invisibly called upon, wriggling across the floor. Other times, Hannah was an electrical storm. A hula hoop. An elk, or a slug.

Every winter the storms got worse, the temperatures plunging to thirty-five below. And every winter, though Hannah's parents did their best to hide the stress of it from her, their apartment fell further into disrepair. Their ancient radiators—the only things keeping them from the lethal cold outside—failed one by one, until the air inside their apartment left films of ice on their glasses of milk every morning.

During these months, Hannah's mom would dress her in her snowsuit to watch television. Hannah would overhear her usually calm, quiet father on the phone to Georgio, their landlord, a huge man of indeterminate age who smoked cigars and avoided responsibility. Hannah was too young to understand that they had no other option, that their debt and meagre incomes meant they couldn't afford to rent anywhere else, couldn't pass up a place as cheap but faulty as this.

Hannah's parents were beholden to Georgio, this man with known links to organised crime who held their lives in his hands. He didn't care about their little girl, about her blue lips and frozen apple juice.

Hannah sat on the couch in her winter things, her breath in clouds, and heard the anger rise into her father's throat. Georgio laughed down the end of the phone and reminded him of the next rent payment.

And so Hannah's early life was characterised by frequent and sudden sleepovers—a last-minute stay at the apartment of one of her parents' friends, their three bodies snug on a pull-out couch, these cramped spaces always luxuriously warm.

Realising finally that Georgio had as little care for human life as he did charisma, Hannah's parents learned to fix the radiators themselves, and Hannah helped, her tiny hands holding wrenches with reverence. But the systems were too old, and when they still failed and the cold was too much, they would trek to Hannah's mom's office building in the middle of the night where they slept on blankets on the grey carpets, warm amidst the staplers, overlooking the city which blinked with prophecies below.

4

FLORIDA
9 a.m.

"Nate, there's been a break-in."

By the time Hannah came back into the bar with her empty coffee cups, the mountains of bags she'd placed on the floor had been unpacked and cleared away, the glasses, napkins and crates of drinks neatly ordered. It had happened in an amount of time that didn't feel possible. But Nate was like that: he walked into any space and quietly made it better. He was the sort of calm, capable person you trusted with your life.

In their years of friendship at the resort, Hannah had never before felt what she did right then: that she couldn't look at him. A gnarl of grief rose up in her throat. If she looked at Nate straight on, and saw this emotion reflected back, she knew it would overwhelm her. So she avoided Nate's eye and kept talking.

"I saw her, though, don't worry. About my height. Very sexy. *Sex pot*—I think you'd use the term 'sex pot.'"

Hannah put the stolen key on the bar and, once she couldn't avoid it any more, looked at Nate with great effort. There he was: her friend, flesh and bones before her. Time had almost, but not yet, run out. Hannah found herself smiling as Nate smiled back at her, wiping down glasses from the dishwasher, which steamed behind him.

"Nate, you're gorgeous."

He laughed, pulled a caddy of cutlery from the dishwasher tray.

"That's the coffee talking," he said, taking the key from the bar.

It was true, though: Nate was gorgeous. He'd received compliments on his appearance before he'd transitioned, too, but it was nothing like this. Growing into himself the last few years, he'd relaxed, he looked lighter. His salt and pepper hair was going strong at seventy-five. He dressed neatly, but casually; ironed a short-sleeved shirt every morning, wore a nice watch, smiled without thinking—every day—for the first time in his life. Everyone at the resort who was at all inclined towards men had admitted a feeling, or a flutter or two, and you couldn't blame them.

Nate was the manager of Frankie's, which he ran like second nature. He listened wholeheartedly, dispensed heavy drinks, helped his bar staff and shied away from praise.

For decades, Nate had run a beach-side café in Maine, rising before dawn to fire up the grill and the coffee pot. He'd kept the surfers warm on rainy days and the tourists happy in sunshine, his customers devouring lobster rolls in the sea spray. His life had been small and full and tasted of salt, the slamming waves lulling him to sleep every night in his sandy bungalow. His nieces and nephews had sometimes stayed, gulping juice and drawing adoring pictures of Nate, adorned with seagulls.

For ten of those years, Nate had been married to Evelyn, an academic, who Nate had understood innately. Though they separated in their forties, they remained close friends.

Nate had come to the resort after a heart attack had forced him to retire—clutching his chest at the café as the bacon burnt in the pan. In the hospital, he'd woke to Evelyn, fresh from California and laughing with relief.

Months later, packing up the home they'd once shared, Nate had stopped Evelyn in the doorway.

"This isn't me," he'd said, gesturing all around his body, gesturing as best he could at the entire essence of him.

"I know," she'd said.

Nate had sold the café and drove down the crumbling coast, the lightest he'd ever been.

About a year after Nate had arrived at the resort, the previous manager of Frankie's stepped down. Nate asked to take it on, the quiet joy of his café returning to him.

When not working, Nate made sure everyone at the bar was taken care of, then played cards on the lawn or phoned his family. His shyness fell away in private and revealed a gregariousness beneath.

Now, Hannah sat at the bar and steadied herself. The caffeine was still drilling through her heart. Nate nodded at the supplies, piled neatly around.

"You didn't have to deal with all that," he said.

"You didn't have to deal with it, either! Here, I've got a dish towel—"

But Nate was looking over Hannah's shoulder. Hannah turned to see Christine, who'd emerged over the slope outside like a cool vision, walking from her room across the resort. Her hair was icy grey in its ponytail, her sunglasses flashing. She stepped through the door, dressed in all black as always, her sleeveless top showing off toned arms, long legs striding in high-waisted slacks. She carried an enormous storage bag in one hand. If it was heavy, she didn't flinch.

"Chris."

Hannah had resigned herself to this feeling today: a wrenching mix of tenderness and pain. She gritted her teeth, and Christine pushed her sunglasses off her face and came to her, hugging her tight.

When she pulled away, there was a warmth in Christine's face. She spoke, and her voice was quiet, sure. "You okay?"

She asked it discreetly, with an air of shared strength, knowing Hannah might not need the question. Hannah nodded her head, thought about it. "Yeah."

Nate busied himself with the glasses to give them space, then reappeared.

"Nate, did you just go for a run or something? You're glowing."

Christine sat at a stool and leaned back to look at him. He smiled, ignored the question.

"Coffee?" Nate asked.

She shook her head. "Thanks babe, but I can't. I'm meant to be tightening my stool. Last month I was meant to be *softening* it. It's all in and out, up and down. The osteoporosis is the only thing that stays the same."

At eighty-one, Christine was in the best shape of any of them. She jogged five miles every morning, her long limbs dashing between the foliage, even on the days when the heat pressed in from all sides, when Florida seemed ready to peel off at the edges. But Christine was formidable that way. She'd worked as a *New York Times* journalist for thirty years, had met popes and dictators, reported from war zones. She had regularly appeared on CNN near the end of her career, a talking head with a steely stare.

Christine had been the first Black journalist to win the Ludowitz Prize, and the first Black recipient of the Grenadier Fellowship. She had a filthy number of air miles, and a sizeable collection of Hermès scarves.

When Christine had come to Florida fifteen years before, she'd been working on a report, travelling down for a week to investigate the climate devastation, the families and businesses who'd moved north in the state, taking refuge in slightly drier climes after losing everything to flooding.

Driving back to her hotel one afternoon to review notes from an interview, Christine had passed the sign, its letters half-hidden behind unruly fronds: PALM MERIDIAN RETIREMENT RESORT. By the open gate, a pair of smiling mascs mounted a tandem bicycle.

Ten minutes down the road, Christine had turned the car around. There was a twist in her gut as she thought of her husband, back home in New York. How long since they'd loved one another? How long since they'd looked as happy as those people on the bike?

Christine had introduced herself at the gate, was welcomed in for a coffee and a tour. Crossing the main lawn with a chatty member of staff, she'd found herself removing her short leather ankle boots and marvelling at the plush chill of the grass between her toes.

"Would you like to stay for a drink? It's happy hour. Everyone's friendly. Just mind the stand-up comedians."

The next morning, after a fitful night of sleep at her hotel, Christine had returned and asked to stay. She'd ended her marriage over the phone, and relief seeped out of them both. She'd gifted her husband their Manhattan apartment with its view of the park, traded its glassy corners for the resort's humid glow.

In the bar, now, Hannah held her friend's hand. "I was thinking about Sara this morning."

Christine smiled, breathed out—a laugh, puffed with a sadness. "What a jerk she was," she said, teasing.

"Yeah, what a jerk."

Christine had met Sara on her first proper night at the resort. Her head had still been swirling with the admin of the day: in her new room she'd been phoning moving companies, emailing friends, researching divorce procedures and Florida tax laws. She had been unwinding with a glass of Sauvignon Blanc on the bar's terrace, dizzy with the sudden change, but marinating in the evening heat.

"You look like you're having a nice time. I hope you don't mind me saying."

Sara had said this, passing by, and Christine smiled wide. She nodded hello. A moment later, she had called out to Sara:

"No, wait! Would you like to sit?"

Sara was a retired orthodontist and a not-retired gator conservationist. She was always in motion, always helping someone new. She'd travelled to all the places that Christine had travelled, but for different reasons. As they spoke, they felt the world open up in each other's eyes.

In Sara, Christine found a love she'd never imagined, and for thirteen years they had lived it, stepping into the beauty—and the new indignities—of age.

When Sara had died two years before, they'd rented a gator boat for after the funeral. The group of them had sped through the everglades, sensing Sara in the snapping teeth, as the wind pulled softly at their sadness.

"Hannah, is that your parents?" Christine asked now, gesturing to the urns above the bar.

"Yeah, they heard I'd be drinking. They wanted to supervise."

Christine nodded, then leant down to open the bag she'd brought with her.

"That's good, 'cause I brought you this."

Christine revealed a luxe bottle of wine, something so old and elegant-looking that Hannah knew it had to be important, its parchment label inscribed with elaborate script.

"Someone really special gave me this a million years ago and I've been waiting for the right occasion to drink it. I want to have it with you tonight."

"It was the president! The president gave it to her!"

This was small Eileen, shouting from the terrace door. She barrelled in, with tall Eileen behind her.

Christine put the bottle on the bar. She smiled, shrugged. "Secretary of State."

And then Hannah was crushed in the arms of the Eileens.

"Han. You're here. Knew you'd be here."

"We planned this, Eileen."

Small Eileen pulled away, looked at Nate. "Nate, you look terrible. No, I'm only kidding. Did you sleep, though?"

Tall Eileen stepped behind her wife, put her hands on her shoulders.

"Sorry about this one. She took a gummy vitamin. Been on a sugar high for half an hour."

Nate poured small Eileen a glass of water from the soda hose, nodded to tall Eileen to ask if she wanted anything.

"An almond milk, if you've got it, thanks."

When Nate served it, tall Eileen gulped it down, breathless, wiped her lip. "Just something to take the edge off."

Small Eileen sat down beside Christine, then stood up. Antsy, she paced around Hannah, who caught her by the carabiner that was hanging from her cargo shorts.

"How you feeling, Han?" she asked, held in place for a moment.

The question was a formality. Small Eileen knew—all of them knew—how Hannah felt. It was all they'd talked about for weeks. As the party, and the end of Hannah's life, had drawn closer, they'd all broken down at one point or another. They'd found one another wiping tears from their eyes in the food hall, had discovered each other dumb with shock at the edge of a lawn. They'd cried huge gulping tears, had hugged each other with a ferocity that scared them.

Then Hannah's friends had all agreed, for her sake, to put on brave faces for today. And that's what they were doing. Still, something terrible and inescapable warbled beneath it all. For today, they'd look just to the right and just to the left of reality for as long as they could. But already, their voices were higher, moods outwardly lighter than felt natural.

Hannah answered small Eileen's question with merciful normality.

"I'm kind of all right, actually," Hannah offered, and small Eileen was off again, bending and squinting to check the edge of the bar, slapping the beams of the walls as if to test their durability. She was like a dad on vacation, delegating himself as his family's security detail.

"Gotta check out the security on this place. Give it a lap."

Hannah laughed. "The party's gonna be a bunch of geriatric lesbians. What are the security risks?"

Tall Eileen considered the question seriously. "Over-ambitious fingering. Dehydration from alcohol consumption." She paused. "Misuse of ointment."

Small Eileen took Hannah by the shoulders. "You're being modest, Hannah! This thing's gonna be a rager."

She strode away, eyeing the potato chips suspiciously, and rapping on the dancefloor with her knuckles. Then she tottered out the back door.

Once her wife was out of earshot, tall Eileen confided in her friends.

"I lied about the gummy vitamin—she's actually just emotional about today. About everything. You know—"

There it was: their brave façade faltering. Hannah nodded, bit her lip, smiled strong.

The Eileens wore what they called "hike-lite," a fashion of habit left over from a life outdoors—large, practical shorts, their feet snug in walking boots. They kept their hair in functional styles: small Eileen's cut short, and her wife's tied back in one thick, grey braid. Their skin had withered from sun exposure, but their bodies were hardy, unbeatable—tall Eileen's sinewy limbs complementing her wife's broad hips and squat frame.

"I'm built like a boulder," small Eileen would say, winking and slapping her thighs. "Don't take me for *granite*."

Now in their early eighties, the Eileens had met fifty years ago, working falcon duty at a bird sanctuary in Washington State, their names the same and, it seemed, their souls. In moments of vulnerability, small Eileen would describe the devotion that had sunk its talons into her heart.

The women had married in Redwood National Park and raised a son, who had explored woods and lakes and mountains with them from the time he was a baby. He was in his forties now, and visited at Christmas, flying in from Seattle, where he'd settled. When he was at the resort, both women were calmer, softer, more at peace. They touched his wrists, and allowed themselves to be cared for, their son twice their size and twice as gentle.

Now, tall Eileen turned to Hannah, her face clouded with concern. "Have we got enough eggs for the party? Hard-boiled eggs?"

Hannah didn't know. Tall Eileen turned to Nate. "Have we got enough hard-boiled eggs? No, no—that's all right. I'll go get some. I'll be back in a bit."

And she was gone. From outside, small Eileen's voice floated in.

"These garden hoses have to go. Too many liabilities."

An ominous pause.

"I'm cutting the hoses!"

Next to arrive was Ricky, who loped in with a cardboard box and aching eyes.

Like the others, he cut straight for Hannah, dropped the box, and took her in his arms. But his hug felt different, more frantic. Ricky was young—only twenty-five—and his knowledge of death was different from theirs. Death was infrequent enough, so far, to still feel like an ancient rite to him. It did to the others too, but at their age they knew this ancient rite could happen to your friends and family at the supermarket, or in a toilet stall, or during routine surgery, the gas blurring the edges. It happened all the time, and when you least expected it.

When Ricky pulled away from Hannah, she saw love and pain buzzing in his eyes. He was wearing his staff golf shirt, the logo smudged with bingo dabber, the material thin from wear. His young face glistened with sweat, dampening the curly hair that he often pushed from his eyes but never, ever cut. It was easy to forget he was tall, because he often hunched to speak to his much older friends. He'd never been athletic, but was well-built without meaning to be, his hard work in the Florida sun creating modest muscle.

Ricky had lost his last job when the frequent, waterlogging storms and unreliable power grid had run the area's only remaining golf course out of business. He'd now worked at the resort for five years, officially tasked with moving residents and their belongings around as needed, and facilitating move-ins. In reality, his responsibilities were wide and weaving, as one of the few full-time staff. He repaired sprinklers, cleaned the filtration system at the pools, and prowled the perimeters of the resort in the security cart, checking for gators. Ricky took orders from no one but his ladies, as he called them. Mostly, they taught him things, and he soaked them up.

When a resident died, Ricky was the one who called the ambulance, then stood sentry. He held the hands of the bereaved, his soft face keeping strong. He gracefully stood in for the adult children and grandchildren who would take another six hours to arrive by plane from Delaware or New Mexico—longer, if flights weren't running that day. Their loved

ones who were scattered across the breadth of North America and beyond.

Ricky lived a mile away, where the greenery puffed over everything,
in a rented clapboard house he shared with his girlfriend, Marina. When
Marina visited, even the hardest of butches were melted soft, whipping
off their caps on the sunloungers, straightening up and smiling shy as she
floated past in her sun dress, Ricky radiating by her side. Marina taught
weekly craft classes at the resort that were always oversubscribed, regardless of the subject. Her *Working with Wicker* course was so popular it had
been repeated eight times, and her most ardent admirers' rooms were
stuffed with baskets that creaked with tell-tale infatuation.

From the moment of Ricky's arrival at the resort, he and Hannah had
fallen into an easy and endlessly replenishing friendship. On his first day,
Hannah had been collecting her mail at the check-in desk and happened
to catch his worried eye. She sensed his whirring mind, was endeared
to the goofy earnestness in the way he was memorising a map of the resort. She offered to show him around that afternoon, and on her tour she
cracked as many jokes as she could to show him the job wouldn't be so
bad. She was delighted to watch him, slowly at first, crack the jokes back.

Hannah had swelled with pride over that next year watching Ricky
blossom and catch his stride, becoming as much a part of the community
as the rest of them. Most days for the last few years, Hannah had joined
Ricky in the cart on his early morning gator patrol. Their conversation
was effortless as they rounded the boundary fence at a snail's pace, coffees
in hand and vegetation squashing past the windscreen. The more than
fifty years between them disappeared.

Ricky had been the last of Hannah's friends that she'd told about her
diagnosis, the thought of the conversation making her nauseous. Hannah had told him eventually while on a gator patrol, the air like golden
syrup around them, the stillness of the sky. Ricky had stopped the cart on
the path, quiet and calm. Hannah had willed herself to look at him and
watched as the tear stains appeared on his golf shirt.

Now, in the bar, Ricky composed himself. He gave Hannah his

signature smile. The one he couldn't help, the one he gave to everyone who approached the Palm Meridian check-in desk.

"I made something for you."

Ricky planted the cardboard box on a bar stool and opened it up.

He looked to Nate, Christine and both Eileens—small Eileen had reappeared and was carrying a pair of shears and a bucket.

"You guys are gonna love this," said Ricky, and from the box he pulled heap of tangled paper. A heavy dusting of glitter fell to the floor. The paper was cut into frightening shapes—lumps here and splices there, something gone horribly wrong.

"Someone told me that it was nice to add a personal touch to parties like this. So I made some decorations."

The paper hanging between his hands finally gave way, unravelling itself, and a garland spread out between Ricky's long arms. He nodded at each of the mangled shapes in turn.

"This is you, Hannah," said Ricky, pointing to what looked like a legume needing emergency medical care. "And this is a maple leaf, for Canada," he added, pointing to a nightmare shape.

Ricky put his garland on the floor and pulled another from the box. This one was pristine, cut evenly, in hard, lavender paper. It showed an extraordinary profile of Hannah's face, repeated, her likeness perfectly captured—the youthful curve of her nose, her eyelashes.

"Marina made this one," said Ricky, grinning, and none of them could help themselves from giving way to their collective crush. They could practically smell her perfume, looking at the flawless thing, and even the Eileens had to gush.

"Oh my god, what a talent. She is such a doll."

"Isn't she?"

Ricky put the garlands on the bar. He shrugged, laughing. "Mine are crap. But I hope you like them."

Hannah stood from the bar stool, reached her hands up to Ricky's shoulders, kissed him on the cheek. "They're perfect, Ricky. I love you."

By now, the winter sun had filled the entire sky, a haze coming down

on other residents who'd spilled out onto the lawns, their voices rising to
the bar. They were eating breakfast at small round tables in the shade,
and swimming laps in the pool. Their bodies—like Hannah's, and those
of her friends—were slightly slower now, required more maintenance.
Age had brought physical challenges with it, though not as much dif-
ficulty as generations before had experienced, as medicine plodded forward and gave them extra grace with each passing year.

Still, growing old was no joke, especially for those in their eighties
and nineties: their vision failed them, their joints went stiff, and their
sterling memories sometimes receded, leaving them stymied and swiping
at nouns. Varicose veins climbed up their calves. Every day, it seemed,
something new was growing on them: age spots appearing on the backs
of their hands, on the skin that had long-ago slackened under their arms.

Where it was possible, they adapted to the changes in their bodies.
Some residents used wheelchairs and others pushed rolling walkers.
Benches dotted the grounds of the resort, allowing respite for tired backs
and legs. Those who couldn't bathe themselves any more made use of a
lover with a loofah, or a friend who they could dub their lady-in-waiting.

Many residents could no longer bend down to pick up a sock or a
cocktail napkin, so they carried plastic grabber claws. The grabbers were
useful in the food hall, too, where a claw could extract a pizza roll from
the plate of a nearby friend.

Despite these challenges, Hannah always marvelled at how little
seemed to change with age. Their home was proof of it: all the laughing
people who were eighty-something and felt twenty-five.

Soon Ricky was hunting for tape. Christine was spooling lights from
a box by the bar. Tall Eileen was showing off a new pair of dentures to
Nate, teeth bared. Hannah stood nearby, her body vibrating with life.
With dwindling time.

Returning to the clipboard on the bar, Hannah flipped past the party
itinerary to the guest list, the pages of names, each with an RSVP beside.
Once she had decided she would end her life, and once she'd decided to
throw an end-of-life party, she'd known she'd invite the whole resort—all

two hundred teeming people. It was the usual courtesy for large events hosted on the property. After all, many residents were getting on in age and any party could, in theory, be someone's last, so the more the merrier.

With her friends' help, Hannah had distributed the invites to everyone's mailboxes, and of the two hundred residents invited, about a hundred had ticked *Yes, with pleasure*. From the other half, it was nothing personal—there was so much going on any given night, and there were whole swathes of the resort's residents who Hannah simply wasn't close to.

Beneath the list of Palm Meridian residents on the clipboard, there were two extra names. Beside the first was a *Yes* RSVP. Beside the second was a tiny white square, still empty. Hannah rubbed her thumb across the second name, lost in a landscape of the last half-century.

"Have you heard anything?" asked a soft voice.

Small Eileen had sidled up beside her.

Hannah stared at the blank space on the paper, shook her head. Then she looked up at her friend.

"She's coming, though. I just know."

Small Eileen slapped her on the back. "Well, you did the right thing. You'll never regret inviting her."

Hannah shrugged. "I won't have time."

Hannah's skin rose hot as she ran her eyes down the list of names again, always landing on the last one—that one. Her heart leapt and squeezed.

What had she thought when she'd received the invitation? And when she arrived at the party, what would Hannah say?

Ripples of terror and anticipation ran down Hannah's spine, the two feelings mixing electrically.

Hannah was still wrapped up in these thoughts when something outside caught her eye. In the distance, she spotted a faraway cart bumping manically along the paths, kicking up dust, towards the bar.

5

*T*he birthday cake that fell from the sky was shaped like a welding mask. When it hit the backyard below, it splattered cake pieces and fingers of icing—inky black and charcoal grey—across the grass and the concrete patio.

All of it was an accident. Hannah's dad had ducked onto the fire escape to light the candles discreetly, and the whole cake had slid right off the tray.

Hannah wasn't upset, she didn't cry. Newly seven, she was buoyant and pragmatic. She and her parents descended to the neighbours' yard to explain themselves, with a dustpan and a garbage bag. Hannah knew that the city's raccoons would lick up any mess that they missed, and that it would make their day.

The downstairs neighbours had moved in that morning, making this an unconventional housewarming gift. But now it didn't seem there was anyone there. Looking through the back windows, they could only see stacks of boxes in darkened rooms.

In the surrounding yards, laundry waved in the September light, other fire escapes curling down from back balconies, home to forgotten bikes and cardboard recycling. In the alleyway behind, there was the always-slap of hockey pucks on the cracked pavement.

"Was it a goalie mask?"

The boy startled Hannah's parents, but not Hannah, who'd noticed him. He'd been standing by the back door, with a long cardboard tube on his arm, up to the armpit, that he was knocking against his knee absentmindedly.

Now he removed the tube and came to help, grabbing fistfuls of icing from the sparse grass. He was Hannah's age, stick-thin, his hair unruly. Too-big ears poked out, that he'd no doubt grow into—for now, he touched them self-consciously from time to time. There was a distracted worry in the way he carried himself, but a gentleness and curiosity in his eyes.

Hannah shook her head, explained the remains of her cake. "It was a welding mask. I got a real one today. I can show you later if you want."

For her birthday, Hannah had asked for welding equipment—including a welding gun and an angle grinder—but the danger, and the expense, were of course too great. Instead, Hannah's parents had bought her a welding mask only. She'd spent her birthday morning reclined on the couch wearing her heavy new accessory, turning the pages of her mother's *Processor Weekly* with oven-mitted hands.

Georgio the landlord had died the previous year of carbon monoxide poisoning while sleeping in one of his own properties, a loss that was not widely mourned in the neighbourhood. A new landlord had since taken over, and the apartment was safer and warmer now. But the years of cold and disrepair had had an impact on Hannah. Seeing how vital they were to a comfortable life, she'd taken an interest in learning about furnaces and heating vents and boilers and radiators, so she could fix them herself if the time came again. From there, she moved on to toasters and radios, dabbling in plumbing and washing machines. She had a roving hunger to fix, to take apart, to build, to make new.

Now, in the little backyard, they asked the boy's name. It was Luke. They asked where his parents were and he shrugged, unbothered by the question and its answer. They asked if he liked his new home so far, and his eyes lit up as he described the extractor fan in the bathroom—its wide, grey face and how it could suck up fifteen litres of air every second. His shyness melted away as he spoke, excitement taking over.

Forgetting the clots of her birthday cake, Hannah sensed she'd found something important here, in this boy with his striped t-shirt and a smudge of dirt beneath his eye.

After they'd cleaned up the yard, they invited Luke to eat store-bought cupcakes on their balcony above. He accepted, ascending the stairs of the fire escape with his cardboard tube, which he bounced against his leg. He sat down beside Hannah on a folding chair. He never left.

For the next ten years, Luke and Hannah lived every day like they were being chased, like something was swiping at their ankles. Time was a precious thing that was burning up in their hands.

They were the same height, seemed driven by the same wild instinct, and managed to understand one another without speaking, though they spoke a lot—in syncopated stories and intrigue-laden news bulletins.

Together they read every children's book in the library and then made a start on the adult ones, gobbling up whodunnits, with their booming mansions and tobacco pipes, and Mediterranean history, thick with conquest and olive trees.

They always had a half-dozen projects on the go—staggering visions urging themselves into being via many mediums: papier-mâché, scraps of wood, oceans of Styrofoam. They made maps, plays, elaborate statues. They invented tiny, restless machines.

Their limbs moved in time and their eyes stared out at the same ecstatic city from twin pairs of bikes. They seemed to operate from the same brain, picking up the same signals. Luke and Hannah shared sweatshirts and hockey sticks, notebooks and winter coats.

They rode the metro end to end, taking notes on all the stations. They stayed up late on Friday nights at Hannah's parents' apartment, her mom and dad reading in the lamplight and her and Luke scheming on the carpet. Some nights, Luke slept on Hannah's bedroom floor in a fraying sleeping bag. In the mornings, they were gone, down the street—fetching a book, a piece of equipment, a snack, a clue, a collaborator. Roving insatiably towards the next thing.

Hannah had grown up in the cradle of her parents' academic circle,

a community of smart, kind people with cheap rent and salvaged furnishings. Their homes were stuffed with books, shaggy shelter dogs, red
wine. Hannah was the first kid that any of them had had, and so she'd
acted as an emotional support baby through the darkest nights of their
PhDs. Her soft hiccups and tiny yawning mouth had pulled them, momentarily, away from the stress of their research.

Sometimes, now, these friends hosted parties. Adoring Hannah
still, they'd invite her and now also Luke along. The two of them took
the parties very seriously and dressed accordingly, in matching tuxedos
bought from a Halloween costume shop. While the adults sipped their
drinks, Hannah and Luke drank apple juice from whisky glasses; per-
formed sofa-side skits for rapt, tipsy audiences; leant an elbow on a chair
and traded anecdotes, looking like tiny jazz pianists.

Mount Royal watched over all of this. It loomed on the horizon like
a benevolent giant, thick with trees. At the top, a cross, one-hundred feet
tall, was lit up electric in the night. High school students sat at the base
of it and drank beer in the dark half-wilderness overlooking the city.
Coyotes and raccoons scrabbled. Smoke rose from the chimneys, the St
Lawrence curving beyond downtown below.

At fourteen, high school changed things, slightly. While Hannah and
Luke had remained in the safety of childhood longer than most—building engines and fashioning space suits—their peers had skyrocketed to a
place of splodgy body image and fumbling innuendo. And soon Hannah
and Luke were pulled there, too.

Hannah's heart sank painfully the first time Luke confessed a crush
to her. With sparkling eyes, he described the way a girl, a classmate of
theirs, flipped her long hair over her shoulders as she turned down the
halls, and the feeling in his gut when she did. Hannah trained herself
away from this jealousy, so that each time Luke discussed a girl he liked,
or a classroom interaction he'd had, Hannah felt a dull disappointment
at best. It wasn't that she wanted him to like *her*, instead—it was simply
that he'd *been* hers, alone, for so long.

In fact, Hannah found herself drawn to these girls, too—a sensation that might have felt perilous had it not felt so deeply right. She was soon delivering her own confessions to Luke, confessions he received with the same conflicted expression she'd had. Hannah sensed, and felt Luke sensed, that by entering this fledgling romantic universe, they were losing each other and therefore part of themselves.

By sixteen, Hannah and Luke were two different sizes, Luke's skinny limbs having stretched, leaving her, shorter, below. They saw less of one another, though sometimes Luke would still appear on the fire escape, and Hannah would let him in. They'd read and speak, or read and not speak, the hours passing in a synchronised murmur like they had before.

By seventeen, the edges of Hannah were buzzing with so much energy that she seemed like a smudge of light. She worked two jobs alongside school, minimum wage feeling like riches. On weekend mornings she made espressos at a nearby café, and in the weekday evenings she scrubbed dishes in the back of a bistro on Parc, the patrons trading amorous eyes over plates of pappardelle.

Hannah got home every night, her cheeks flush with winter air, and got back to her plans in her bedroom. A school science fair the previous year had asked Hannah and her peers to solve a problem. The fair, with its glue guns and potato batteries, had long been forgotten for most. But Hannah had carried on her project and still hadn't stopped.

Having fixed their ailing radiators for a portion of her life, Hannah wanted to come up with something better—something infallible, and infallibly efficient. Cheap to use, and helpful to everyday people. And so most evenings now, she sketched and measured, studied systems of heating and cooling. She often fell asleep in a cache of papers as the sun peeked across the snow.

At eighteen, university was a broad, open plain, a place for overdue galloping. Hannah had lived amidst the school all her life, had crossed the leafy campus thousands of times. She'd heard the students' parties from her window, watched them loom and skitter through the city, young and hopeful and sometimes disturbed.

Now she was one of them. She went to engineering lectures in draughty buildings, licked the math up like syrup, riding parabolas with her eyes. New caverns of knowledge opened up in her mind and slowly accumulated understanding. Hannah thought of her heating and cooling plans, her pipes and panels and overlapping parts. Gears began to turn.

In a crush of assignments and exams, heart quaking with caffeine— still working two jobs, smelling of coffee grounds and rigatoni—Hannah was the happiest she'd ever been. Her life was flush with buzzing new personalities, her world cracked wide with new ideas, and suddenly she craved life more than ever.

She craved it as she worked in the library, a brutalist bulk with windows like warm, yellow portholes. She craved it in the Arts building, its stately dome lumped with snow.

Hannah craved life most of all at the parties, which she was now party to. She and her friends would cram into unexplained apartments, hot and smoky. Would stand on strangers' fire escapes, the smokers changing like schools of fish.

Luke was there, too, in those years. He was studying business on another part of campus, starting up his own life in distant parallel. They ate lunch together sometimes, at a coffee-stained table in the student centre, or on a bench outside the library, the paper around their sandwiches rippling in the wind. They probably looked like new friends, or like classmates brought together by a group project in a new course. They found themselves changed in ways they couldn't explain.

Hannah looked the same as she always had, wearing a woolly sweater and a pair of jeans. But Luke looked sharper, harder. He wore business suits and shining shoes, was dressed for an endless itinerary of PowerPoint presentations and business seminars. His once unruly hair was now trimmed short and gelled neatly in place, a point of pride. He'd grown into his features, his ears in proportion to his straight nose and clean-shaven jaw. He looked younger than his age, still, but with obvious aspirations to be taken seriously.

It was clear to both Hannah and Luke that they no longer shared the same mind. Hannah felt like a part of her was clogged, made inaccessible.

Luke was still there, though, Hannah knew. The seven-year-old Luke was in there, kind and curious. She could see him through the hair gel, through the new impatience in his eyes. But right when she felt ready to bring it up each time, his gaze would flit to his watch, and he'd rush a goodbye. She'd follow his thin, wavering body with her eyes until it disappeared through the campus crowds.

Luke would come back to her one day, she was certain. Until then, it was time to make space for new people. And so she did.

It was the second winter of university that Hannah met Esme, and something about that felt right. Icicles crackled and fell to the darkened street as Hannah headed towards the party, climbed the stairs and stepped into the humid fug. She passed through the groups of people, saying hello to the faces who made up her universe.

Hannah moved through the crowd, and then the crowd itself moved, and there she was: Esme, gorgeous, twenty years old. Fur coat. Red lips. Hair in waves.

Being in love with Esme wasn't original—it was practically automatic for anyone who met her. Hannah went towards her at the party, seeing the things that everyone saw: the shimmer she gave off, the mischief in her eyes, a smile always twitching on her lips. How she threw her head back when she laughed, unwilling to hold anything in.

When Esme caught your eye, you felt you'd give her anything, though she hadn't asked: a treasured secret. A home-cooked meal. The nearest lamp.

Esme was the kind of person who could barrel right through you.

Within an hour, Hannah and Esme were pressed against the wall of a dark bedroom, electricity rising up from Hannah's brain and rattling through her heart. Minutes later, Esme was kissing her quick, one last time, thumbing Hannah's bottom lip to wipe off the lipstick. Then she winked and rushed away again, leaving a bright, sunken, indelible feeling.

For almost a year, Hannah and Esme went on like this—roaring through parties around the city, Esme incandescent in Hannah's peripheral vision. Hannah pulled towards her, unable to resist. Most nights Esme shot off somewhere, with someone else, bounding back into the night. But sometimes—on the holiest of nights—Hannah found herself back at Esme's apartment, their mouths hot, bodies pitched with feeling. Later, Hannah found herself peeing in the sudden bright of Esme's bathroom, amongst her roommates' shampoos. Hannah saw her face in the mirror—bleary, giddy, flushed with beer.

Esme held some special affection for Hannah. There was an unspoken energy between them, and for months Esme gave it to her in the quietest moments—so fleeting that Hannah could hardly tell it was real. And then Esme would run off again.

One night during exam season, Hannah made plans to have midnight coffee on campus with Luke. Something about the library had reminded her of him. Of them. Maybe it was the sense of learned mania that buzzed around this place, sitting in a row of study carrels extending into the horizon. All around was the focused fritz of Adderall, sweaty pens, a city of laptops and paper. Outside, the glowing halos of the downtown. Office buildings dark in the night.

At quarter to twelve, Hannah checked her phone again—they'd made their plan via text at six that evening, but Hannah hadn't heard from him in the hours since.

Where do you want to meet? She typed now. I'm free any time.

Luke came online. He saw her message. Offline, and no reply. Hannah waited forty minutes longer, continuing her reading, midnight falling away.

Finally, Hannah's phone buzzed. But it wasn't Luke. It was Esme.

Mine?

A message like that was the least diluted form of pleasure. It cut right through and flooded her bloodstream.

Hannah abandoned her work. Within minutes she'd traversed the

library building, the size of a cruise ship, and was unlocking her bike in
the dark, her hands tightening with cold. She wound out of campus and
passed along Milton, all sleeping apartments and the odd, shouting voice.
She turned onto Parc, the mountain rising in the distance, took the bike
path.

Dizzy with life, lungs burning with cold, Hannah cycled the hill,
downtown glittering like an unreal thing behind her. She wheezed with
the effort, her thighs straining.

Where the road curved and turned back down, Hannah stopped and
rested for a moment. She turned around to look at her city—the bright,
towering bulk of the office buildings, milky-white strands of clouds laid
across the inky sky. Beside her, in the park, the ice rink shone in the
moonlight.

Hannah would arrive at Esme's doorstep with her skin slick, chest
heaving, joy coming off her like cold breath. Luke's reply in her backpack, unseen until morning:

Sorry, crashed off my bike! Ripped up my hand.
All good, though. In the Arts café now. Where are you?

6

FLORIDA
9.30 a.m.

Would Hannah have believed it, if you told her? Probably not. That's the thing with time: every day we press our foreheads against the future, willing it to let us in. But it doesn't. Murky as the Florida swamps, impenetrable as the Palm Meridian Soapmaking Society, the future holds its secrets until their time.

Now, at Frankie's, Nate tallied crates of drinks on an inventory sheet. Ricky and Christine hung decorations, pulling strips of tape from the ends of their fingers, bits of it ending up on Ricky's face. Tall Eileen and Hannah drank fresh cups of coffee and discussed the best placement for food, throughout the room. Where did people tend to cluster? How best to cater, spatially, for cravings of salty, and cravings of sweet?

Taking a break from her security checks, small Eileen lay on her side on the dancefloor, propped up on an elbow. She was a pin-up in cargo shorts. She munched on a hemp and mango cookie that she offered out to her friends, when she suddenly realised there was someone missing.

"Where's Esme?"

And as if she'd been summoned through the sexy sands of time, Esme's cart rounded the crest of the hill outside. Her long, dyed black hair gleaming, lips red, faux fur coat on her shoulders despite the heat. But for the wrinkles and the arthritis lumped elegantly across her knuckles,

Esme was the spitting image of her twenty-year-old self. The girl whose doorstep Hannah had arrived at so many times, her lungs burning with cold and desire, life roaring through her veins.

Esme botched her parking job, driving partway up a pile of land-scaped pebbles at the base of a palm. She reversed, righting the cart with a bump, and a crunch came up from behind her. She looked back to discover she'd been dragging a string of Christmas lights with no obvious origin—a kind of twinkling roadkill.

"*Feliz Navidad,*" Esme said to a passing resident, nodding sagely, her eyes closed.

Then, as she had a thousand times before, Esme rumbled brightly into the bar. She smacked her hands against her head.

"Oh, sorry! This is the supermodel convention. I was looking for the bar."

And she pretended to rumble back out into the sun-drenched morning, then turned on the heel of her boot.

The smile that came to Esme's face was convincing from afar, but as she moved closer, Hannah could see the faltering emotion in her eyes, the worried dip of her eyebrows.

"Good morning, babe," said Esme, into Hannah's hair. Their hug was tighter than they dared admit—something frantic there, a loss approaching, a sound like rushing water. They pulled away, and Hannah was struck fresh by the unlikeliness of life.

Fifty-eight years before, Hannah and Esme had torn around the icy streets of Montreal, Hannah's heart near to bursting with a fevered feeling. That all of that had happened, in the storm of their younger lives— that time had carried them on to gentler waves, had softened them into friendship, a friendship laced with something fierce, in the way of a former love. That they'd shared this humid home for the last ten years, amidst rising temperatures. The luck of it seemed too much to bear.

Three months ago, it was Esme who Hannah first told of her terminal diagnosis. Hannah had crossed the resort late at night and stood on the path outside her friend's door, suspended in a halo of lamplight and mosquitoes, until she'd found the courage to knock.

It was Esme, eventually, who'd suggested they celebrate Hannah's life with a party.

Now, Hannah watched Esme pull away from her and recompose her face. Her features moved, and all pain and anxiety vanished.

These brave faces were all around Hannah now, assembled on top of the faces of her friends. It would be easy to assume that the faces were for Hannah's benefit, but weeks of this had shown Hannah that this bravery was for *them*. The pain, her friends seemed to think, was better sipped than gulped. Hannah loved them, and so she let them look away.

Esme moved away from Hannah and chattered while she hugged her other friends one by one, moving around the room as quick as her stiff knees would allow.

"Anyways, I'm really sorry I'm late, I"—she went behind the bar to Nate, and into the arms of Christine—"I got caught in the line at the pharmacy—my knees have been killing me . . . " Esme hugged Ricky, picked a piece of tape from his eyebrow.

"Fuck me, that's good," she said, catching sight of Ricky's garland, which was now dangling from the wall. Esme reached down to hug small Eileen, who was still on the floor. She accepted a bite of hemp and mango cookie. Back at the bar, she hugged tall Eileen tightly, then took off her coat, sat on a stool.

"Sorry—the pharmacy. There was a twenty-minute line. There's a shortage of some drug for farting. Or sleeping." Then her eyes went wide, indicating the next drama. "Anyways, I finally got my stuff, but then there was an accident, on the south lawn—"

Esme described how, not far from the pharmacy kiosk, members of the cross-country roller-ski team had collided into the Polyamory Picnic. "It was carnage," Esme said, her face clouding.

The path had been too steep, apparently, and their footing not quite right, and just like that, feelings and hearing aids were scattered across the grass, newly formed throuples torn asunder, breakfast sandwiches mashed.

Esme clapped her hands once. "Anyways. Here's what I've got."

Counting on her fingers, Esme ran through the list of things she'd managed to get hold of for the party, including a now-rare tank of helium with accompanying balloons, and Hannah's favourite snacks: dill pickle chips, blueberry Pop-Tarts and pistachio ice cream.

The supply chain had staggered and fallen apart decades ago, then was rebuilt, piecemeal, the price of gas too expensive to live as lavishly as everyone once had. Things had gone backwards in many places, that way. Shipping trucks came weekly down the coast, but next-day or same-day delivery—princely—was a thing of decades past, and once-common food items were no longer guaranteed.

Electrical equipment, in particular, was increasingly hard to find. But Esme had an inescapable charm—and a network.

"I got the strobe light and the smoke machine from the raver at the pancake house. And I got the projector from the artist-in-residence."

"We have an artist-in-residence?" asked Ricky.

"Yeah, she's making teeny tiny models of all of us and sending them on a cruise in the swimming pool," said tall Eileen.

Soon everyone returned to their tasks around the bar. Their chatter filled up the space, punctuated by bursts of air as Esme started up the helium tank.

"How's Quinn?" Hannah asked, helping Esme with the balloons, a sharp *whooshing* noise accompanying each one.

Esme shook her head. "Not good. I'm worried about her."

A week ago, Esme had broken up with Quinn, another resident, who she'd dated for a whirlwind six months. It had been an often fun, but tumultuous relationship, their personalities sometimes jostling against each other in uncomfortable ways. Esme had thought about it for a long time until she finally chose to end things. But Quinn wasn't taking it well.

"I need to check on her later."

Hannah nodded. "Let me know if you need me."

Ricky tested the strobe light, its brightness flashing against his face, while Nate finished tallying the crates of drinks at the bar. Hannah was unfolding a tablecloth when Christine appeared at her side, wordlessly helping at first and then supressing a smile and avoiding Hannah's eye.

Hannah stopped, a smile growing on her lips. She waved a hand in the air around her friend. "Chris, you're giving off mischief. I'm getting mischief from this."

Christine put her end of the tablecloth down and stepped towards Hannah, bringing with her a pensive energy and the scent of Dior perfume. She started slowly. "Han, I hope you understand that your friendship, and your life, is the first thing on my mind today." Christine rubbed a thumb along the arm of her sunglasses that she'd pulled from her head. "And because I love and respect you so much, I wanted to ask your permission to do something tonight."

Hannah watched as Christine squared her shoulders and closed her eyes, steadying herself for an announcement.

"I've mourned Sara for two years. She was the love of my life, and nothing will change that. But something I've realised is that Sara would want me, now, to quit moping around and get laid again. And I'd like to use your party tonight to begin that process."

Hannah found herself laughing, pulling her friend close.

"Of course, Chris. Of course. They don't deserve you."

Christine laughed brightly.

Again, into Christine's ponytail. "They don't deserve you."

Hannah didn't deserve her either. She didn't deserve *any* of them. Not Christine, with her iron resolve and butter-soft cashmere. Not tall Eileen, who'd save them all from a burning building, probably, and not make a big deal out of any of it. Not small Eileen, whose least-intensive hobby was building outdoor bowling lanes, and who believed, stubbornly—unshakingly—that all people, ultimately, were good.

Hannah thought of Ricky, who'd resolved to read all of Shakespeare's thirty-eight plays the year before he turned twenty-five—partly for pleasure, and partly to prove to himself that he could. Growing up, he'd said, everyone had thought he was stupid. The day he'd finished, they'd all thrown him a graduation party, with a cap and gown, and he'd ended up puking in the swamps nearby, beer-y but beaming.

Hannah thought of Nate who, for years, had hosted all of them for dinner on the first Friday of every month, all seven of them piling into his neat, warm room. He'd calmly work the stovetop of his kitchenette, a smile flitting across his lips as their overlapping voices and raucous laughter filled the space, which by then smelled rich and delicious. They'd try to help with the meal, but he'd wave them away, and they'd smack a cartoon kiss on his cheek—*MWAH*. As they ate late into the evening, their conversation would clamber and spark, their friendships wild, reliable things.

Hannah thought of Esme, her wildest and most reliable thing. About her late mornings—the last septuagenarian who could sleep past noon. Some days, if Hannah was feeling lonely, she'd let herself into Esme's room after brunch and read on the armchair in the beam of light that fell through the blinds. The sound of Esme's breathing in the dim room was the same as it had been so early in Hannah's life.

As Hannah watched her friends move around the bar now, she filed each of these thoughts away, holding them tightly to her, for some fleeting safekeeping. Tomorrow, after all, every thought would be wiped away.

"Do you know who that guy is?"

They all heard tall Eileen's question and looked across the bar. Tall Eileen and Nate were watching out the window, where a figure had emerged on the terrace. They headed over to look.

Through the reflections of the bar windows, and the crowd of umbrellas outside, they could only see a shoulder, a dress shoe, a shock of grey hair, hesitating.

Nate wiped his hands on a bar towel and headed outside, the sun illuminating his face when he stepped through the glass door. "Hey man, you all right? Can I help you?"

Hannah heard the voice before she saw him, coming in on the hot breeze.

"I'm so sorry, I didn't know if—is this the right place? I just got here. I'm an old friend of Hannah's. I'm Luke."

7

ZERMATT
2014

*H*annah was shitting in Switzerland. Hannah was puking in Switzerland. Hannah's fever reached some staggering volcanic height, her body spewing out airplane food and bile and violence.

Tomorrow they could have six million dollars.

The hostel was old and yellowed, but the beds were cheap. Out the window, beyond the moth-bitten curtains, was a vista so perfect it could be a desktop background—craggy grey peaks and icy blue water, cows with bells on their necks. Who owned the cows? No one asked this. The cows were freelance. The beauty was pristine.

Hannah held tight to the sheets, and for sixteen hours she rode the wave of it: the jetlag mixing with the stomach flu, dehydration crashing its brittle weight.

Other guests came and went from the eight-bed women's dorm, and they paid Hannah no attention—she, the soggy Canadian, tucked in tight. Her bunk the site of a sweaty transfiguration.

The sun set, and the mountains were blue, and Hannah heard yodelling. Hannah was yodelling? The walls were coursing with mountain goats, braying. Now there was honking, honking from cabs. The honking was geese.

In her Swiss bed, racked with visions of surrealist Gruyère, Hannah's body flashed cold, then hot. She was mooing.

Hannah was conscious through a blazing sunrise, the light of it turning the room golden orange, the other women sleeping in their bunks.

When she woke again, there was a worried face swimming in front of hers. One of the other guests, an Italian with beautiful eyes.

"There is an angry boy outside for you," she said before she bounced away.

With great suffering, Hannah heaved her granite body to the door of the dorm. It was Luke, showered and suited, tapping his shoe.

"Hey. You ready?"

Hannah blinked. She opened her mouth, felt her hands shaking. Felt the wreckage of her insides.

"How long do we have?"

Luke checked his watch. "Forty-five minutes."

Hannah closed her eyes and summoned her strength. She felt that, if needed, she could discern a true yodel from a yodel vision. She had named all the cows, both real and imagined. She could probably not keep food down yet, nor water, but she felt happy, finally, to thirst.

She was broken, but nearly reborn.

And anyway she had no choice: today they could have six million dollars.

"I'll meet you downstairs."

Hannah kept her eyes closed in the shower, pretending she was sleeping, feeling her limbs conspire to drag her down. She washed vomit residue from her chin with 3-in-1 soap-shampoo-conditioner. Stars spun around her eyes in the hot water mist.

With the last of her energy, Hannah dressed in her business suit, with the tag still on. The bed was taunting her now: a paradise, a place to rest. She sipped a bottle of airline water, clenched her jaw, and soldiered on.

"Sorry, didn't mean to be gruff earlier," Luke said. "Just nervous."

The cab was crammed with their prototypes—heavy metal piping, digital read-outs, snaking cables. The equipment had required pre-approval from the airline, and the cab driver had frowned as they hauled it in.

"You got the noodle?"

Years ago, before they'd got this far, before they'd even made a trip to the hardware store for materials, Hannah had used pool noodles to map ideas on her bedroom floor. She'd brought one with them today—light purple, and perfect—to explain the original principles, and to add some colour to their pitch. It was an accessory to show how far they'd come. How real of a deal they were.

Look! We're not just clever—we have lore.

Irresponsibly, the airline had let Hannah class the pool noodle as cabin baggage. On her way to her seat, she'd gently socked a half dozen people in the nose, making enemies throughout economy class.

In the Swiss taxi, Hannah didn't hear Luke's apology. She simply clung tight to her pool noodle, aware of an icy blue lake down the mountain below, visible in bright clips between passing trees. She thought of nothing but her dry mouth, her beating heart, her shaking hands.

Her phone buzzed, a text from Esme, who had stepped into a much more reliable role as one of Hannah's closest friends:

Wally says good luck today! Wally doesn't
understand angel investment.

And a photo of her cat, Wally, standing on a five-dollar bill.

Soon, the office came into view through the trees—its low, sweeping windows and sharp points so familiar from Google Street View. Everything that had felt hazy and abstract before now seemed to crystallise, the present squeezing itself into being. Adrenaline raced through Hannah's brain and sweat pushed out of her palms. She willed herself, so low on energy, to walk through their slide deck.

This technology is ready to transform heating
and cooling across the world . . .

Clean. Sustainable. Twice as efficient as
current leading methods . . .

We have the science. We have the
plans. We just need your help.

In the months before graduating from university, both Hannah and
Luke had realised they had freshly sharpened skills and bursting ideas,
but nowhere to put them. Hannah had invented a technology in her bedroom—a gobsmackingly elegant play on a heat pump, that took its greatest strengths and ran with them, into temperate rooms. Meanwhile, Luke
knew how to take things to market—how to dream, to sell, to persuade.
Over soup in the student lounge, they'd realised they were stronger as a
pair. They went into business together, growing closer again, recovering
some of their old familiarity. They discovered that, in some ways at least,
they still shared the same mind.

While Hannah fine-tuned the technology and worked to create a vi-
able product, Luke had canvassed investors around the clock, making
cold calls and drafting emails and trying to impress upon lofty people
that they had something worth backing. After countless months with no
real leads, a Swiss investor had replied, out of the blue, saying the technology looked unlike anything he'd seen, and he was intrigued. Please
could they meet at his office, next week, in the shadow of the Matterhorn.
They'd have forty-five minutes.

Now, Hannah's ears were ringing so loudly, and her vision swimming so badly, that she couldn't understand the receptionist when she
asked them to take a seat.

"Hannah—"

Luke was already across the room, frowning and swiping imagined
dirt from a pristine leather loveseat. The reception area was huge, all
metal and black marble, and dotted throughout with electric fireplaces.
Floor to ceiling windows looked out across the lake, their hostel a brown
smudge below.

A TV hung on the wall by the desk, showing the Winter Olympics from the other side of the world. The televised snow collaged with the weather out the window.

On the screen, a Canadian bobsledder was zipping down the track. The captions at the bottom read like auto-generated poetry—WOBBLE, HE GOES! NOT HAPPY—and Hannah's stomach turned over. How did she get here?

A few days ago, she had been making espressos at the café in Montreal, teaching first-year seminars and washing dishes for extra cash. She'd been working on this project for years, giving it the energy and the time it had needed, while she allowed so many other things to fall away.

With a six-million-dollar investment in their burgeoning company, they could change so much in the world.

A telephone rang. A pause.

"Mr. Brunner is just coming down now."

The receptionist was smiling at them from the desk, and Luke nodded his thanks, but Hannah was drifting. She squeezed her eyes closed and, in the darkness, the cows were back. Her stomach lurched, and she swallowed hard. Grappling for something solid, she remembered the reasons she'd started fixing and inventing things in the first place: the frigid radiators in her parents' apartment, the taste of cold still on her tongue.

When Hannah opened her eyes, a burly man in an expensive suit was swaggering towards them, his shoes tapping loudly across the floor.

Luke stood with a tight smile. Hannah stood, her insides swimming. On the TV, the ski jumping final had started. An American woman took her place at the top. Soon she was shooting down the ramp, the captions confused and ecstatic:

THE FAVOURITE! CAN GOLD? ZIPPING! CAN SHE GO!

The woman was soaring, floating, amidst the falling snow. She landed, soft as anything—but. It wasn't far enough.

She was taking off her helmet and craning up at the scoreboard. A man, her coach, was livid, screaming. He crunched away through the snow, leaving her there.

FOUR MORE YEARS. NEXT TIME. MAYBE TIME.

The burly man was shaking Hannah's hand, looking dissatisfied. Hannah had to push her tongue against the insides of her teeth to keep from vomiting.

Luke nudged her, alarmed by the glassy look in her eyes. He whispered sharply:

"*Hannah—*"

She breathed deep, recovered, smiling at the man:

"It's a pleasure to meet you."

8

FLORIDA
10 a.m.

"*Hannah—*"

Hannah's past echoed into the bar as Luke's eyes found hers—once twenty-four years old, now the eyes of an old man. He was tall and lean as always. His face was still gentle, though his ears had lost their proportion again, looking big amidst his age-sunken features. He'd retained some hair, which was white, brushed neatly.

Hannah knew straight away that he'd arrived wearing a suit, and then regretted it, peeled off the jacket in the heat, leaving a white buttoned shirt beneath.

Luke came towards Hannah now, unsure, pain and apology in his eyes. Hannah hugged him close, expecting some familiar scent, but there was only the sharpness of a musky aftershave. She was startled to spot a hearing aid in his ear, but why should she be? They were undeniably old and—Hannah, at least—proud of it.

In the end, Hannah and Luke had spent their whole working lives side by side, in one way or another. But it had been years since they'd last properly spoken, Luke gradually growing distant.

After a life of business travel, Luke had retired back in Montreal, wealthy and unmarried. Hannah had last seen him on a trip home eight years ago, sharing an uncharacteristically awkward drink down the street from where they'd first met as children, amidst the carnage of a smashed birthday cake.

Maybe it had been the work that had kept them close, she'd realised that day. They'd sold the company and she'd moved down to Florida, after all. She shouldn't have expected things to stay exactly the same. She'd since made peace with this.

"I brought this," Luke said now, looking timid. He was holding an especially fancy bottle of champagne, the kind designed to impress, and he raised it, smiling, at the group. "I'm Luke. It's so, so nice to meet you all."

Hannah placed a hand on Luke's shoulder and turned to her friends, grinning.

"I've known this guy longer than I've known almost anyone in the world. And I've told him a lot about all of you."

Luke seemed to relax by the smallest measure as Hannah's friends came over to welcome him.

"You're . . . Nate," Luke said, shaking his hand, and Nate grinned.

"And you're Christine," he said, hugging her.

"This is a nice shirt," Christine said, brushing his arm.

Luke laughed, thanked her, apologised for the sweat.

"And you're—wait, I've got this. Big Ellen and Little Ellen."

"Close enough, dear," said tall Eileen as she hugged him tight.

It was only Esme who held back—the only other person besides Hannah who'd met Luke before. Who knew him intimately. The same sixty years were folded between them, the memories of their younger lives rising up.

Finally, once she was the only one left, Esme stepped forward and kissed Luke quickly on the cheek.

"Nice to see you again," she said, dryly, and stepped away, returning to the helium tank and the bags of balloons.

Confused, Hannah looked at Esme, searching for some clue about her coldness. Luke and Esme had had some prickly moments in the past, but that had been decades ago. How could any tension possibly remain?

Hannah quickly cast her mind back, trying to remember precisely the last time that Esme and Luke had been in the same room. Their fiftieth birthday parties? Surely there'd been other, more recent moments?

Luke and Esme hadn't spent a significant amount of time together since they were all in their thirties. Life got so crowded that way, and people drifted apart. But this felt personal.

"Ez?" Hannah asked. She was so happy to have Luke there, and she felt the second-hand sting of Esme's slight.

But Esme didn't hear her over the helium tank, or else pretended not to. Hannah couldn't press the issue now, not in front of everyone. Reluctantly, she made a mental note to check on things later, and offered to take Luke on a tour of the bar.

Christine noticed the coldness too, and went to Esme, as Hannah and Luke moved out of earshot.

"What was that about?" she whispered.

Esme shook her head, busied herself with the balloons. She seemed about to explain it, then held her tongue. "I haven't trusted that guy in a long time. I'll tell you later."

Meanwhile, Hannah showed Luke the photos tacked up on the wall. She felt shy, seeing her friend for the first time in eight years. She needed to work up to it, to get comfortable talking about things besides themselves, before they caught up.

Hannah pointed at the most recent photos, from the annual awards ceremony that had taken place in the bar just a couple of nights ago. The more virtuous awards came first, she explained, including *Best Performance in a Supporting Role*, given to an outstanding primary carer, and *Best Debut*, given to a newer resident who'd made an impact on the community in their first six months. Next came the prizes that were guaranteed to one person, because of their specificity—like *Oldest*—or ones that were so subjective as to be, arguably, meaningless—like *Most*. This last one, many felt, was a thinly veiled insult to the winner.

The final award was as prestigious as it was contentious, Hannah explained: *Best Extra-curricular Group or Activity*. Many residents considered this the highest honour a person could receive in their life, while others just thought it sounded strange. The use of "extra-curricular" implied a core, resort curriculum. But what could this be? Eating waffles and sipping matcha tea? Boning in the Pottery Pavilion?

"A book club won the award this year, and someone from another book club wasn't happy about it. It genuinely almost came to blows, but Nate kicked them out. He said they were giving reading a bad name."

Hannah was trying to make Luke laugh, to grasp at something of their old, easy affection. There was enough sadness in this day already— Hannah couldn't bear feeling distant from her oldest friend.

But look: he was right here, right in front of her. That was all that mattered.

"Do you want to sit?" she asked.

They settled at a small table at the far end of the room, where the windows looked over the thick of the trees, their lazy fronds swaying. Hannah fiddled with a piece of pink ribbon in her fingers before speaking.

"How was your flight?"

Luke shook his head.

"I drove down, over the last week or so. I stopped for some hikes on the way—a couple national parks. In Virginia. North Carolina."

Hannah smiled.

"The Eileens will love that. You've gotta tell them."

"I will."

A pause. Hannah thumbed the ribbon, stalling.

"Hey, I'm not mad or anything. That we haven't seen each other in so long, I mean. I know I reached out, and I know I didn't hear from you. Whatever it was, it's okay. You're here now, and—"

A dry laugh fell out of Hannah's throat.

"—and there's not much time, so . . . let's just enjoy it."

She touched Luke's wrist, finding his skin softened further with age, the hair white and wiry on his arms. She looked into his eyes, these eyes that had seen her childhood home, her parents, while they were still living. They'd seen Hannah through so many years of her life.

Luke held Hannah's gaze, and finally he smiled.

"I'm sorry. I was stupid to stay away." He hesitated. "I missed you."

Small Eileen's laugh rose up from the other side of the room—she was taping Ricky's eyebrows up on his forehead in permanent surprise. Hannah smiled, collected herself.

"How's Montreal?" she asked Luke.

He laughed, shook his head. "Wild. More extreme than ever. The snow was so heavy this year it fell through peoples' roofs. And then in July, the traffic cones melted."

Hannah felt the temperatures roll through her.

"Are you really retired for good? 'Cause I don't believe it."

Luke laughed again, sheepish this time. He rubbed the back of his neck. "After we sold the company, I managed a few years. I did a lot of golfing. Took some university courses. But then I just got restless. I did some business coaching, but it wasn't enough. So I tried to set up a new company—water filtration this time. But I couldn't manage it. I don't have your brain, for the science."

Hannah wrapped the ribbon around her finger in swirls. "You should've reached out."

Luke smiled sadly. He seemed about to speak, but stopped, rubbed the table with his palm, avoiding Hannah's eyes. Finally, he changed the subject. "How are you feeling? Physically? Are you . . . do you feel sick?"

His eyes were wet when they met hers.

Hannah shook her head.

"No. Well—yes. Something feels different. It's like my body knows what's coming. It's a kind of—there's a shift. I can't explain it."

Luke looked away, swallowed hard.

He spotted Esme, stony-faced and speaking to Nate across the bar.

Luke nodded towards her, back at Hannah. "Are you two . . . ?" He hesitated. "Are you and Esme back together?"

Hannah laughed out loud. "Us! Oh god, no. No, that's funny. It's been like sixty years. No."

Luke's face relaxed—was it relief?

"Sorry, I shouldn't have laughed," said Hannah, touching his hand.

"No, no, it's okay! That's good—I mean—good to know."

Hannah felt more relaxed now, leant back. She smiled, swished the ribbon towards him. "And you?"

Luke winced, ran his hands through his hair.

"No women for me, I'm afraid. Just too—just too busy, I guess."

Hannah didn't buy it, but she'd leave it for now and interrogate later. That was something that had never changed about Luke: he kept most things to himself. It wasn't until they were twenty-four, after all, that Luke had told Hannah the entire truth about everything—the full story of how it had been when they were kids.

Kept awake by jetlag after a long day of meetings, they'd climbed to the roof terrace of their Florence albergo, had set up camp at a little plastic table. Intending to catch up on work, they'd brought their laptops, but, relieved, closed them up when the glow of the screens attracted mosquitoes. It was 2 a.m., and there was only them and the hot Tuscan breeze, which ruffled the cypress trees silhouetted on the hills in the distance. Far beyond their little square, the Duomo was illuminated in the night.

Soon, Luke's words had begun to tumble out:

Like Hannah, Luke had been an unplanned surprise to his parents. Unlike Hannah's, though, Luke's parents hadn't embraced the surprise. They'd had him, and then resented him.

In the darkness, Luke's shoulders lifted, fell. A sad smile touched the corner of his mouth.

"Snore, I know. Not very original of me to have shitty parents. But I guess I'll spend the rest of my life trying to shake this off."

Luke explained that he was left alone a lot as a kid—that the day he'd first met Hannah, his parents had gone out for brunch and not returned till late at night. By the time he was eleven or twelve, they'd travel overseas for weeks at a time and leave him home with just a library card and cash for groceries. He was slowing them down, it seemed, and they were thrilled to leave him behind.

He'd been embarrassed to tell anyone, even Hannah, his closest friend and upstairs neighbour, so he'd come up with ways to hide his parents' neglect. He'd learned to keep all the lights on, would open the windows and play his mom's CDs on the stereo at a conspicuous but still reasonable volume. Sitting on the front step, he'd sometimes stage one-sided conversations, calling back into the empty apartment, and copying refrains he'd picked up from Hannah, from kids at school. He *didn't want to clean his room*, he'd shout, or he'd *be right there to start watching the movie*.

"When they were home, they weren't abusive. They didn't hit me. They just didn't care," he said.

Out of necessity, Luke had learned to cook from an early age, had thrown himself into books and elaborate plans with Hannah. He'd promised himself that once he was old enough, he'd make lots of money—that way, he could go where he wanted, could finally be in charge.

Hannah had listened on the Italian rooftop, memories of their childhood returning. Her throat was tight, and she knew not to say to Luke: *I know*. She knew not to tell him that she'd overheard her parents, many times, worrying for him. That her dad had confronted his dad, once, their harsh, whispered voices carrying up to her bedroom when she was meant to be asleep. That her parents had resolved to look out for him.

Sitting across from Luke at Frankie's now, Hannah felt dizzy with time, with the decades that they'd travelled through to reach this moment.

It was a silly thing to think, sick as she was, and leaving tomorrow. But it occurred to Hannah that her parents weren't here any more—so *she* would look out for him.

Luke was gazing around at the bar, out the windows. "Hannah, this place is incredible. You're really lucky."

Hannah grinned, admired her friends, their bright surroundings. Dappled light fell in through the windows and across the dancefloor, the whole space smelling of fresh coffee and the sweet scent of morning that wafted in through the open doors. The cycling team were heading out for the day, and their colourful shirts zipped downhill on the path behind the bar, their chatter and clicking gears carrying up through the thickness of the trees.

"I know," Hannah said.

They paused, and the palms swished against each other out the window.

Luke smiled, let his shoulders down. "I was nervous to come, Han. I feel better now."

A shout came up from the end of the bar, startling both of them. The strobe light was smoking, and the enormous disco ball had rolled off the table, scattering mirrored pieces everywhere.

"Sorry, I should go help," she said, standing.

"Don't apologise. Just let me know what I can do."

They made their way back across the dancefloor, Hannah's mind whirring with the strangeness and the sadness and the pleasure of having him here.

"Hannah!"

Ricky intercepted Hannah by the bar.

"Hannah," Ricky repeated, touching her arm. "Can I ask you something?"

Still distracted, she looked into Ricky's young, searching eyes. With effort, she focused her attention. "Sorry, Rick. Of course." She picked a piece of clear tape off his chin and rolled it into a ball between her fingers.

Ricky hesitated for a long time before speaking and Hannah could feel herself holding her breath.

"What are you wearing tonight? I'm just asking, 'cause I don't have anything fancy. Marina got me a tie a couple years ago, but the cat gave birth on my ja— I just don't have a jacket."

Hannah exhaled with relief, thankful that it wasn't something bigger. She shook her head, shook his worry away.

"Rick, you're a thousand years younger than anyone here. You could wear nothing but oven mitts on every appendage, and it'd look like a tux compared to us. Seriously—wear whatever you feel comfortable in. I know you'll be gorgeous."

Ricky seemed reassured by this.

"Any mail?" Hannah asked.

Ricky's face darkened.

"I'm really sorry, Han. Nothing yet."

Mail was delivered weekly, but often it was delayed, a month's worth arriving all at once in heavy bags, or never at all.

"Hey, Hannah . . . " Ricky caught her arm, as they were about to head away. He bit his lip, then tried to feign a smile. "You could always cancel."

Hannah didn't understand. "Cancel . . . ?"

"The appointment. Your appointment at the hospital. There's still time."

Hannah's face clouded. "Ricky—no—it's more complicated than that . . . "

She was thrown by the question, and searched for the right reply. But Ricky was already waving his hands, waving the whole thing away.

"Of course, of course, of course. I was only kidding. Look, I just wanted . . . " He hesitated, his eyes avoiding Hannah's, his hands waving through the air for the right words. "Just—can I steal you for five or ten minutes later? I really want to show you something."

He met her eye again, and she felt she owed it to him, whatever it was.

"Course, Rick. I love you. Just come get me."

Hannah excused herself quickly and headed for the toilets, saying offhand that she needed to pee. Really, she just needed a break.

Standing at the sink, breathing deeply, Hannah turned the tap on for something to do. She realised she could hear her friends' conversation through the vents.

"I hadn't realised things were that bad," Luke was saying, describing the washed-out towns he'd passed through on his way in, whole communities grown over with vines, abandoned to a precarious century.

Tall Eileen explained the world out here:

"You know when the president and her husband died last year? We didn't have signal that week. No one here got the news for three days."

Hannah looked at herself in the bathroom mirror, removed her base-ball cap, swiped a hand over her head to flatten the grey fly-aways that always sprouted as the hours passed. She touched her nose, where a sun-burn had already started, her skin turning a mortal kind of pink.

Two months ago, after telling the rest of her friends about her diag-nosis and her decision, Hannah had woken up early one morning and driven a golf cart an hour away, had parked beneath a derelict fast food sign by the highway, its neon body cracked and housing birds' nests. There was signal here, away from the swamps and closer to civilisation.

Hannah had stood in the parking lot of a strip mall, outside the post of-fice, and dialled Luke's number on her phone, certain he wouldn't pick up.

"Hannah."

She hadn't heard his voice in eight years—the last time he'd returned her calls, the last time they'd seen one another. She had squinted in the sun as she delivered the news, trucks heaving by in the heat.

"And I'm throwing a party."

The words sounded stupid, suddenly. After words like *cancer* and *pain*.

"If you're able to come, I'd love to see you."

Luke's voice was sure and strong. He'd come. Of course he would.

They talked for a while in a faltering way, and before Hannah hung up, she hesitated. A long, wavering pause. She was considering asking Luke for advice. In just a few moments, she planned to do something that could change the remainder of her life.

Hannah rolled the pad of her index finger over the corner of an en-velope that she held in her hand.

"Luke. Do you think I should . . . "

But she stopped herself before the words could come out. He might tell her it was foolish, or useless.

She already knew what she wanted to do, and so she would do it.

"Never mind."

When the call ended, Hannah had stood for a moment, taking in the sharp, hot smell of this parking lot, the yawning sky, haze shimmering beyond. Then she'd turned and headed into the post office, the invitation burning in her hands.

Two weeks later, she'd got a receipt from the post office. Confirmation that her invitation had been safely delivered to its intended recipient: Sophie Welch.

Since then Hannah had been feverish with waiting, the anticipation filling her days.

But she'd never heard anything back.

NEW YORK CITY
2018

*B*efore a formal investigation could be launched by the state of New York, a hundred rumours swirled as to how the fire started.

The hotel, after all, was grand but ageing. There could've been many culprits: the vintage gold chandeliers, the faulty boiler that boomed in the basement, the kitchen that catered for former presidents and foreign dignitaries, but was splattered with decades-old grease.

Some guessed that the ghost of a starlet who'd stayed there fifty years before had simply got bored that night and decided to make the place combust.

The truth wasn't ghostly or glamorous: the fire had begun in the hotel's business centre, a cramped space next to reception where the odd guest read emails on an ailing computer, and the occasional teenager dared a dabble of porn.

A guest—a novelist, with minibar Sprite on his lips and glory behind his eyes—had spent the last eleven days typing feverishly in his suite. That night he staggered down to the business centre with a chorus of angels in his ears, his thousand-page opus complete. He tested the limits of the inkjet printer, feeding it thick wads of paper from the cupboard below. Eventually, the machine gave out, a spark jumping up from its faulty wiring. The flame that tore along the interior wall changed the course of Hannah's life forever.

The charity gala was well underway by the time the fire alarm went off. The ballroom was crammed with black-tie and notoriety: the mayor of New York, a cluster of Hollywood actors—the loudly good ones, touting environmental causes—as well as prominent entrepreneurs and 30-under-30 types, those recently mentioned in *Forbes*, like Hannah, who was seated beside a prize-winning painter.

Hannah regretted her outfit—a gold satin suit that she'd bought in a hurry, the saleswoman encouraging her outside her comfort zone.

"You look exhausted," said the painter. "Your suit is gorgeous, though."

Hannah just smiled a thank you and sipped her drink.

The auctioneer was onstage, collecting bids for a lunch with a Nobel Prize recipient, when the fire alarm pealed through everyone's ears, startling their champagne flutes. The sound was sharp and unrelenting, and everyone sensed it was not a drill.

After a polite hesitation, the ballroom started to frenzy. Guests grabbed evacuation canapés while the evening's host—the crudely handsome anchor of a popular morning show—tried to corral the crowd over the microphone. Finally, he too abandoned order, jumping from the stage and jostling against film directors and the heads of NGOs.

Hundreds of them clamoured out of the building, a slow stampede on the lobby's plush carpet. The Art Deco features had started to smoke.

The street was a riot of voices and snow, tuxedos and glossy lipstick. Manhattan's buildings soared bright in the night sky above them. Sewer grates burped steam, and honking traffic moved past, turning snowfall to slush.

Soon, the voices were overridden by sirens, the lights of the fire trucks flashing against their faces. Following the fire brigade were news trucks and paparazzi, ravenous at this spill of celebrity onto the street.

"Hey, back the fuck off—"

An actor clashed with a photographer, their breath making clouds.

"I didn't mean to—I swear, I swear, I swear—"

The dazed author emerged from the hotel, stumbling in the custody of the fire department, a charred stack of papers clutched to his chest.

He would later be interviewed by news crews and given a thirty-second bit to explain his novel—a multigenerational fantasy saga set entirely inside a dishwasher, where toils for might and supremacy played out amidst hot spikes and frequent deluges. For a few days he was a minor celebrity. The fire was an accident after all, and the hotel was liable for their faulty wiring, not him for his faulty, though surprisingly spellbinding, plot.

As the fire alarm wailed on, it became clear that the gala would not resume. The auction had been interrupted halfway through, and big-ticket items were yet unclaimed. The rest of the event would need to be rescheduled.

Soon a stream of black cars arrived, and the VIPs were deposited discreetly inside them. The cars bled seamlessly back into traffic, their passengers destined for warm hotel rooms with cream interiors.

Remaining on the sidewalk was a rag-tag group of extraordinary people—community organisers, Broadway playwrights, professional athletes.

Inside the ballroom, the social situation had been carefully circumscribed. The rules implicitly agreed upon, and hierarchies maintained. There was a sense of performance to a night like this—everyone knowing when to blush at praise, when to clap for the beautiful people who were blushing at their praise. How to be powerful, but likeable. How to spectate, and earn your space.

Out there, there wasn't any of that. Loose in the night air, the snow and the thrill of emergency had stripped all conventions away. They were only people now, cold bunches of them, whose voices bounced off the possibly burning hotel.

"Could use some of your heating right now."

The voice came from Hannah's left. She turned to see a pop star winking, smiling wryly at her, as she strode past and climbed into a limousine.

Hannah waved and smiled as the girl blew a kiss and pulled the door shut.

Hannah shivered and tilted her head back, the buildings towering above her. The air smelled of ice and car exhaust, roasted nuts from a cart nearby.

Four years had passed since the Swiss investor had given Hannah and Luke six million dollars to build their heating and cooling business, to solidify the technology that would really make it stick.

The meeting in Zermatt had started off badly, with Hannah's left-over fever sending her off-piste, the fatigue turning her thoughts to clumps. But once she'd got through the preamble and onto the science of things, she'd felt the nerves rise off her body like vapour, and her sluggish brain picked up pace.

Later that night, watching TV in the rec room of the hostel—Luke working on his laptop, Hannah napping with a cushion clutched tensely to her chest—they'd received an email. They'd hugged so hard that the armpit of Luke's shirt had torn and, crying, they'd celebrated with spar-kling wine and cured sausages from a little shop nearby, after which Hannah had returned to her bed and fallen into a deep, feverless sleep.

Once back home, the two of them stayed calm and kept to their vi-sion, using the investment money to launch their technology in Canada. They partnered with small municipalities to install their panels in newly built homes, collecting data on the cost and energy savings, which were truly substantial. They used this data to capture the interest and build the trust of general consumers, offering in-home installation free of charge. Things went unexpectedly well unexpectedly quickly, and soon they were exploding into the US market and beyond.

Pop stars now knew Hannah by face and trade, if not by name. She was the heating and cooling girl, interviewed in CNN spots about green energy, profiled in science and business magazines for her revolutionary mechanics. At just twenty-seven, she led a company that was galloping across the globe.

For the past four years, Hannah and Luke had travelled the world, both together and apart, taking meetings in polished offices and scarfing hotel meals. It was perfect and turbulent. It was mind-bogglingly lucky. Hannah's younger self had raced and torn through every task she could imagine, and now her grown-up self had met her match. To keep all the Earth's people a comfortable temperature was task enough indeed.

Invitations to events like this gala came often now. Hannah was regularly invited to speak on panels, to travel to conferences, to drink champagne at the openings of research institutes and museum wings.

Hannah and Luke had accepted the invite to this charity gala gladly—Luke as a schmoozing opportunity, and Hannah because she knew the people-watching would be eye-wateringly good.

Hannah scanned the crowd of shining hair and shining teeth. Luke had excused himself to the bathroom twenty minutes before they were evacuated, and he'd no doubt torn through twenty conversations since then. Grown-up Luke had discovered he was a shaggy kind of handsome, discovered he could take his roving energy and rove the social circles of the world. That his name and success, now, would grant him access. He'd let his hair grow out again and he kept it carefully mussed, let stubble grow on his cheeks. He'd taken up running, the marathons turning his once-gangly body lean and muscular. Luke was always striding somewhere, bouncing on the balls of his feet, eyes roaming.

Hannah swallowed and felt a sharpness in her throat—the start of a cold from overworking on too little sleep.

She thought of earlier that morning in their midtown hotel, and the feeling she'd woken up to. Her body had been exhausted, mouth dry, head heavy. But there was something else, too, beyond and below it all. An unsettled energy she couldn't place. It drove her out of bed, out of the hotel, up thirty blocks of Park Avenue, where she felt herself expand, unglue.

Hannah stepped into a café on the Upper East Side, ordered a coffee and burnt her tongue as the cabs and Alsatians and fashion models rolled past the window.

Leaving the café and walking cold down East 82nd, she squinted as the sun globbed off snowbanks and parked cars.

Passing through Central Park that morning, Hannah had floated on a thick and uncanny feeling—a bright, quivering sense of expectation. Something was waiting for her.

"Shrimp?"

Hannah turned now to see one of the servers from the ballroom, a man in a white shirt and bow tie holding the tray of seafood he'd been evacuated with. He was speaking to a girl who'd appeared beside Hannah.

"Oh, yes, thank you. Thanks very much."

The girl picked two pieces of shrimp from the tray and placed them on a napkin in her palm. The man swirled away into the crowd, and Hannah's eyes met the girl's, and she took her in fully—her broad smile, bright eyes, dark hair shimmying down her back in snow-flecked waves. There was a giddiness and a sharp intelligence about her. She was Hannah's age and wore a fitted black velvet suit, the deep V of its lapels leaving her breastbone bare to the cold, though she didn't seem to mind.

The girl's eyes glimmered, but she suppressed a smile. She stepped closer to Hannah. For a few long moments, she looked around at the crowd, aloof. Then she looked back to Hannah as though she'd just discovered her there.

"Shrimp?" she asked, holding the napkin towards Hannah.

The wind picked up the girl's hair and spilled it onto Hannah's shoulders.

"Thank you," Hannah said, taking the shrimp. And they stood side by side, eating and watching the crowd, including the medium-famous actor nearby who was loudly describing a scene he'd shot on the lip of an active volcano.

Hannah stole a glance at the girl again: her striking eyes, parted lips. Her body that seemed coiled with energy, masterfully contained.

As discreetly as she could, Hannah straightened up, smoothed her hair, brushed the sleeves of her suit. She was grateful for it now, borrowing confidence from the bold material.

"I feel like I've seen you before," said Hannah.

The girl laughed. "I *know* I've seen you before. I've seen your face every day for two weeks."

The medium-famous actor was impersonating lava now, throwing his arms in the air to indicate *spew*.

"I've been at my mom's in Vermont," the girl explained, "and the vans drive by all day. Everyone in the neighbourhood's getting your systems installed."

Hannah winced, laughed. "Oh god. The logo wasn't my idea, it was Luke's. He's here somewhere."

Hannah looked around for Luke, then looked back at the girl, who was shaking her head.

"No, no, it's good. You look very trustworthy. And approachable. The baseball cap. The ponytail."

They surveyed each other's hair for a moment, then landed on each other's eyes, hovering there until they lost their nerve.

"You're from Vermont?"

The girl nodded.

"I was just on top of you. In Quebec," said Hannah.

The girl smiled. "On top of me, hey?"

Hannah blushed and looked away. She thought of the swathes of pine trees, the plains of snow, the winding roads that lay between their two homes, their borders touching, weather systems mixing.

"What do you do?" Hannah asked, regretting the mundanity of the question.

"I'm retired, technically, as of a few weeks ago. But before that I was a ski jumper."

"Jesus, that's a good answer. Where did you compete?"

"Some international competitions. A couple of Olympics."

Hannah balked, then recovered. She made what she thought was a joke: "Any gold medals?"

The girl blushed, smiled. "One actually. A month ago. It's why I've been getting invites to things like this recently." She nodded back to the hotel. "I'm meant to wear it everywhere I go."

It took a moment for Hannah to grasp that she wasn't joking. Then Hannah looked at the girl's chest and realised with panic that the medal wasn't there.

"Where is it? Did someone—"

"Oh, no, it's . . . "

The girl stood on her tiptoes and craned her neck over the crowd. She pointed out a stylish woman, about eighty years old, wearing billowing ivory trousers and a matching blouse. The woman had the medal around her neck and was showing it to the man she was speaking to, watching his eyes as he ran his fingers over the detailed design.

"It's with that woman over there. She used to be Poet Laureate. She asked if she could borrow it for a minute, to flirt with that man. She's telling him she was once in a Pepsi commercial, and she ski-jumped over a jumbo jet."

Hannah and the girl stepped aside to let a piece of the crowd pass by. Another fire truck arrived, lights flashing.

Hannah looked at the girl again and felt something inside her lift and pull. Like someone had tugged a piece of string and brought possibility with it.

"Where are you spending retirement?"

The girl laughed. "Well, lately, at my mom's. She's moving—she . . . " The girl hesitated. "Well, this is a lot, but my dad passed away recently. Right after the Olympics, actually."

"Oh god, I'm so sorry."

The girl shook her head.

"No, no—it's okay. Really. He was a pretty terrible person." She grimaced. "He was a skier when he was younger and never won anything, so as soon as he had a kid, he put everything on to me. Into coaching me. It was the only thing that mattered to him. And then I won, finally, and he died almost immediately."

She let out a little laugh. Hannah gave a sad smile.

"Don't get me wrong, I was given insane opportunities. But I've spent most of my life in training gyms and on ski-lifts. Now I want to . . .

go." She waved her hands around in front of her, as if to encompass everything. "I want to *go*."

Hannah grinned, and the girl let her hands drop.

"You must be busy lately?" she asked.

Hannah wasn't ready to move on from this part of the conversation. But she nodded.

"I feel lucky. And stressed. Mostly lucky. I'm glad we're helping people, and I'm proud of the science. It's Luke who's more into the business side of it really. He's . . . " Hannah searched through the crowd, finally spotting Luke, his eyes wide, in animated conversation with the auctioneer's assistant. "He's there. He's expanded us everywhere. He's incredible at the meetings. He always manages to create these insane opportunities for us. And he loves dressing nicely. Wearing suits. I'm never sure about mine . . . "

Hannah held out her arms in front of her, and the girl touched the material softly.

"You look good."

Hannah's pulse picked up and she lost her train of thought.

"Will you ski again?" she managed to ask.

The girl took her hand away. "Yeah, as much as I can. I'm gonna do some coaching. And some phone coaching."

"You can coach ski jumping over the phone?"

"Oh, sure. Most of it's mental. I'll show you sometime."

Hannah felt her stomach tumble over. She was about to say something—she didn't know what; some acknowledgment of this tight feeling humming between them—when her phone dinged in her pocket.

"Sorry, that might be my parents."

Hannah checked—a text from her mom:

Saw the fire on the news. You okay? Hotel
looks beautiful. Dad is making soup.

Hannah's heart twinged. She imagined her parents, warm at home in Montreal, with some music on and the snow roaring outside. Hannah's childhood drawings still tacked on the fridge, her dad's Zamboni gloves drying.

When Hannah's company had taken off, she'd offered to buy her parents a new home with all new things. But they'd insisted they were happy where they'd always been, in that perfect, worn apartment, with only the heating and cooling replaced.

Hannah texted back quickly, put her phone away.

"Sorry. I was gonna say . . . "

But a man appeared before them, his hair shining in the light of the fire trucks.

"Fucking freezing. I'm—Oh . . . "

It was Luke. He looked at the girl and faltered, looked at Hannah. He turned back to the girl and held out his hand.

"Sorry, I'm Luke."

The girl smiled, shook his hand.

"Sophie. Great to meet you."

Despite herself, Hannah stiffened, annoyed at Luke's interruption. She wished she'd asked the girl's name earlier, so she could've heard it just for herself.

"What's up?" asked Hannah, a note of impatience in her voice.

Luke's mind seemed to float away for a moment, and then he recovered. He pointed his thumb back at the street.

"I was gonna say I'm heading back to our hotel . . . "

"Amazing. I'll meet you there."

Luke hesitated.

"Oh. Sure. Well, let me know when you're heading back. I want to go over some stuff together before you leave tomorrow."

Hannah nodded. Luke shook Sophie's hand again.

"Goodnight," she said.

Luke turned to walk away, then stepped back and leaned towards Hannah.

"Do you think you'll be out long, or . . . ?"

Sophie looked away politely. But then realisation dawned on her face. "Oh god, sorry, are you two together?"

Hannah laughed loudly. Luke opened his mouth to speak, then frowned.

"No, no, no. Just business partners," Hannah explained.

Luke swallowed hard, shrugged. "It's a fair enough assumption, though. I mean, I don't have much time to date. Hannah's the only girl for me, really."

"Okay, thanks, Luke, I'll text you in a bit," said Hannah, eyes wide with subtext. Luke waved goodbye and ducked away.

It really was late though, and Hannah did need to go. She saw Sophie notice it on her face.

"Go with him."

Hannah opened her mouth to reply, stopped. Her face was hot, the freezing air forgotten. "Can I see you again?"

Hannah was halfway to the waiting cab, with Sophie's number in her phone—the cold once again biting at her skin—when she turned back.

"Sophie!"

She caught her down the street, Sophie's face turning, opening.

"I'm flying to Vegas tomorrow morning for some meetings. I'll be there for a few days. Just me. Do you . . . "

The honk of a cab.

"Do you want to come with me?"

The texture of life seemed to have changed by the time they landed in the desert. The light was different, like after a rainstorm, when the air seems sharper, gold or blue. A force that usually lay beneath life was closer to the surface, temporarily. It was letting them in on something, barely. It was letting them get some spooky, lucky sense before sinking away again.

Las Vegas met Hannah and Sophie with its wiggling haze, its glinting hotels, its gallon soda cups and extroverted water features. Everything that shone at night seemed to blink, parched, in the day, either side of the wide roads and the sandy scrub brush between.

They knew that what they were doing was strange, that it was unusual to travel across a country with someone you'd met the night before.

That shrimp, shared al fresco, was no good basis for trust. But they couldn't summon an unusual feeling about anything they were doing. Their being together on a plane, or in the hot shadow of a hotel sign, felt effortless and obvious.

That they didn't yet know about each other's lives wasn't a problem, but an impossibly generous gift. In the booming sun and in the bellies of tacky themed restaurants, they set about trading biographies, each catching the other up on how they'd spent their last twenty-seven years. Each piece of information felt like something to be savoured, a hit of pleasure pouring through them when they learned something new.

Hannah learned that Sophie was left-handed, near-sighted, and had a tiny tattoo of a microwave on the inside of her upper arm, a lukewarm attempt at teenage rebellion and a tribute to a band she hadn't listened to in years.

She learned that Sophie had been enthralled by outer space since a class trip to an observatory when she was nine. She had dreamt of becoming an astronaut before accepting she was too bad at math, so she'd settled for books and NASA videos and an unceasing sense of awe.

Hannah learned that Sophie had grown up playing every sport available and took happily to every one—but most of all to skiing. She'd skied downhill competitively from a very young age and had been on pace to compete at the highest levels, until she'd met some ski jumpers at an event when she was sixteen. Her dad, amidst a frigid divorce from Sophie's mom, didn't have the energy or presence of mind to deny her a training session with a jumping coach. From there, it was only jumping. And she was good, so her dad was pleased.

Hannah learned that Sophie didn't regret the years of training, but she regretted not standing up to her father, whose signature shouting and unrelenting pressure had been many steps too far, gold medal or not. Sophie discussed all of this regularly with her therapist, a warm-hearted woman named Janet with a Southern drawl and dire warnings about menopause. Sophie finished some sessions lighter, and others more knotted up. She accepted that this was normal.

Sophie, in turn, learned Hannah: her rough-and-tumble optimism, her sinewy wrists, the restlessness and silliness that played often on her lips and behind her eyes. The clean, powdered scent of her deodorant and the gentle, nonsensical monologues she delivered in her sleep.

So rare, before, were those moments in life where your pulse quickens and gratitude floods your limbs—in Vegas, they were everywhere. They were the fabric of an hour.

For three days, Hannah went to her meetings, which were long and dry and numerous. In a boardroom with a sweeping view of the Strip, she was friendly and thorough and did not rush. But her heart was thrumming, waiting, distracted until she could go.

While Hannah was in meetings, Sophie roamed the hotels and casinos, taking in this artificial and blinding place, beautiful in how silly it was.

One thing Hannah had learned about Sophie already was that she was open, open, open. She made friends accidentally, effortlessly—something about her way, her face. On the first day in Vegas, Sophie helped a widow buy a present for her son in a gaudy gift shop. She got laughing with a bell hop in an elevator, who she had found leaning, exhausted, against a luggage cart. She joined a family reunion by accident, was offered a slice of cake on a paper plate.

When Sophie left people, they were smiling.

After her meetings, Hannah ran to Sophie, and they caught one another up on their days in restaurants themed after outer space, or ancient Rome, gladiators duelling around them, endangering patrons with fibreglass swords. Hannah studied the soft curve of Sophie's nose, the winking defiance in her eyes. The shape of her eyelashes and the collarbones peeking out of her t-shirt.

They learned more about each other over these meals, soaking in anecdotes and habits and histories. Sophie explained the pen pal she'd maintained since she was nine, an ancient Venezuelan woman named Luisa who seemed impervious to death. They'd been matched as part of a millennium scheme designed to bring the world together. For eighteen years now, they'd traded lengthy letters, Luisa's envelopes arriving from

Caracas full of local gossip. Every March, Sophie would carefully pick out a birthday present—a book, or a sleeve of Vermont maple candy—and lovingly package it off.

For three days in this way, Hannah and Sophie roared through Vegas, one finger hooked on one finger. In the casino, the decades-long stink of cigarettes was still baked into the carpets, the light low and everything blue and maroon. They played the slot machines with oily handles, hollering as they lost ten dollars at a time. They fucked in the women's toilets—laughing, shushing—the sounds of coins in their ears.

They watched a magic show with a lot of pyrotechnics and an uncooperative cape, drank syrupy cocktails from plastic cups, with cherries floating on top. They won seventy-five bucks at blackjack and set out to buy the strangest thing they could find. They settled on a plot of land, from a guy at a faded card table, out on the Strip.

"It's out there, a few miles," he said, pointing behind him, squinting, chewing on a cigarette, rubbing his beard with his palm. "There's the coordinates," he added, tapping on the land deed. "It's one foot by one foot. It's all yours."

They considered what they could put on it, this plot of desert land that was definitely not real, that they'd never seen. One foot by one foot—they could build a lamp post. Plant a palm tree. They could take turns standing very still.

That night they ate at a fast food place and walked out past the parking lot to the desert beyond. With their phone flashlights, they went into the thick, cool gloom, exploring as far as they could before it felt irresponsible. Think of the people who would find them, who'd have to come and collect them.

On their last night, they crossed the Strip, back to the network of hotels, through the dark lobbies that smelled of metal and cologne, past the outlines of the payphones still left on the walls—they'd been ripped out and replaced by pay-per-minute phone charging points.

Hannah and Sophie took the elevator, something opening in their chests that would never really close.

They ordered room service and hunkered down, resolving to stay up all night, regardless of Hannah's morning meetings. They played movies and ignored them, tugged at the sheets, this nest with a view of glittering sprawl, their bodies hot and needing.

Hannah would have struggled to describe what was going on. Before, in her life, this feeling had been a spike and then a sinking. This time, she felt a thrill and a deep, embedded calm.

Life had expanded in size, and the desert was there to accommodate it, their newness blanketing the jackrabbits and the burrowing owls who lived beyond.

Before Hannah and Sophie left, they ate lunch by the pool, enjoyed the sun searing their cheeks. Hannah considered the palm trees, the warm blast on her skin. Golf carts bumped, unseen, across desert courses.

"When you retire again, could you imagine retiring somewhere like this?"

Sophie's sunglasses gleamed.

By the end of three days, it felt inconceivable to part. Sophie would fly with Hannah to her next round of meetings, in London. They'd figure it out from there.

Above the Atlantic, most passengers were sleeping—including Sophie, on Hannah's shoulder. In the dimness it was only Hannah and the flight attendants still awake, the hum of the plane through darkness and cold.

While Sophie slept, Hannah let herself imagine a life for the two of them, up there. Faithful, strong, Hannah would fashion them a home in an overhead compartment. Their marriage bed would be soft, if unconventional: bread rolls, napkins, life jackets prematurely inflated.

She would toil to ensure them a comfortable life. She'd upcycle oxygen masks into luxury handbags to rival the duty-free. She'd run a black-market ring of sleeping tablets and tiny bottles of wine, turning modest-quality sleep to modest-quality profits.

Each night, at the back of the plane—time zones spelunking beneath them—they'd make love instead of resting, then share peanuts in the roar of the dark. For years they would sup on Sprite and serenity, asking for nothing more than unblocked ears.

How could Hannah explain it? This love was a bewildering punch in the gut, and also wholly familiar.

Hannah felt, somehow, that their love had been there all along, and they'd only just accessed it. This feeling had been witness to every other feeling, long before they'd met. It had been watching, waiting till its time.

What Hannah and Sophie were feeling wasn't new to them. They'd simply only now found it.

Here you go—this is yours. It always has been.

Hannah rested her head on Sophie's head, the plane bumping and pitching through the dark.

10

FLORIDA
11 a.m.

*F*or all its nut butters, and its line dancing, and its resplendent vegetable beds, not even lesbian utopia was immune from conflict. Lesbians, being human, were wont to err, and err they sometimes did: rival
book clubs spoilt one another's endings, and ex-lovers drove their mobility scooters over the resplendent vegetable beds of their former flames.

Still, this time sounded different.

Hannah was splashing water on her face in the bathroom sink when
she heard sharp voices from the bar, their pain and surprise overlapping.
She wiped her face dry and hurried out, her pulse jumping.

"I don't understand it. I don't understand."

Quinn had arrived, her face streaked with tears, her voice hoarse
with emotion. Esme moved towards her, reaching gently for her hands.
But Quinn wrenched them away, anger pitched across her face. Her
voice rang through the room.

"How could you treat me like this? I'm being serious, I'm asking a
question . . . "

Shock rattled through the group of them, arranged behind Esme—
small Eileen hovering protectively, Nate watching with a bar cloth
gripped in his hands. Hannah joined Christine, Ricky and tall Eileen.
Luke sat on a bar stool, eyes wide as the drama played out before him.

"Quinn—Quinn, listen to me for a second—I don't want it to end on this feeling. We've talked about things. I thought it was okay. I thought you were okay . . . "

Esme moved towards Quinn again, body tight, face pleading.

Quinn's voice sounded like fabric tearing. "It's too late, Ez. I don't want to hear it. You broke my fucking heart."

Quinn stepped towards Esme, and Esme's face opened for a moment—a beat of hope. But Quinn only repeated, louder:

"You broke my *heart*."

Esme hesitated, stunned.

Quinn stepped back, a fire in her eyes. She licked tears from the corner of her mouth, looked around the bar for the first time, taking in the decorations, the crates of drinks at the bar.

"And you're throwing a party. Of course you fucking are."

"Quinn . . . "

Esme glanced back at Hannah, pain in her eyes. She held up her hands, explaining.

"Quinn, it's for Hannah. You got an invitation. And you know this isn't the time to be doing this. Can we *please* go speak outside?"

Frustrated tears had risen to Esme's eyes now, and the sight of them sent a bolt of pain through Hannah's throat. She left her friends and moved forward, expecting her voice to waver, but it held strong as she spoke.

"Quinn. That's enough. Go."

Quinn laughed again, slapping tears off her cheeks with the heel of her hand. "Unbelievable."

She stared at Hannah, and Hannah held her gaze, unflinching.

"*Unbelievable*," she repeated, and she walked out into the bright of the morning, scuffing her shoes on the floor as she went. "Can't wait for this party!" she called from the terrace. And then she was gone.

Esme reached for Hannah. Her words were muffled in Hannah's neck:

"Han. I'm so sorry."

Hannah held her, then pulled away. "It's not your fault. It's not anyone's fault. Let's let it be."

Esme composed herself, nodding, and slowly the tension released as they all tried to laugh about it. But the sound of Quinn's hoarse voice was ringing in their ears.

Small Eileen tried to explain things to Luke, who was faking sips from his empty water glass, and looking around for something to do. "Sorry, Luke. Things aren't normally like this around here."

Tall Eileen shrugged. "Well, they sort of are."

Everyone did their best to regroup and get back to their tasks. As Esme returned to the helium tank, Luke appeared beside her.

"That was rough. Are you okay?" he asked.

But Esme turned her head, pretending that someone had called her name. She strode away.

"*Esme . . .*"

He didn't follow her.

Esme headed for the terrace, needing a breather. Out in the sun, it took her a moment to notice Hannah standing there, grey ponytail flashing in the light.

"Han."

Hannah turned at Esme's voice, opened her arms. Esme hugged her, and together they looked out across the resort.

By now, the sun was about as hot as it could be, as hot as the freshly baked ciabatta buns just completed by the women of Loaf League. Hannah and Esme watched them emerge from the bakery clubhouse in the distance, arranging their latest creations on tables.

Beyond the bakers was the orange grove, its trees flush with ripe, gleaming fruit. In the shade of the branches, some residents reached fruit-picking poles into the air. Others, tipsy on brunch mimosas, simply slapped pool noodles up at the branches, doing about as good a job.

In the centre of the resort was the main pool, its deck now packed with oily bodies, the blue water cut up with activity. Confident breast-strokes manoeuvred around lazy breasts. The scents of citrus and soil carried across the lawns. Hannah did her best to savour them.

Esme lifted her head, rolled her shoulders back. She let out a big, exhausted breath, and caught Hannah's eye. They laughed.

"Han. I'm really so sorry."

Hannah shook her head. "Stop."

Hannah could have felt rattled by Quinn's outburst or daunted by the evening to come. But she found herself buoyed by an unexpected strength. Her body felt good. Her mind was clear. They looked out across the rolls of the resort, its lush green like gold, the palms standing sentry, the light hazing down from the sky.

It occurred to Hannah that she could speak to Esme candidly now, could ask her about the strangeness between her and Luke. But she didn't want to push her—she wanted to enjoy things as they were.

"I *am* sorry, though, Han," said Esme quietly. "I just want tonight to go well."

Hannah squeezed her friend's hand.

"Let's go inside," Hannah said.

Back in the bar, small Eileen was standing with her hands on her hips, discussing how best to form a waiting area for Christine's anticipated suitors.

"Tape on the floor is cost-effective but maybe a little demeaning. Do we have velvet rope?"

She was trying to make her friends laugh, to dispel the strange, heavy mood that had risen since Quinn's unwelcome visit.

"Nate, should I start building one of these for you, too?" asked small Eileen. "It'll save on the labour if I do them both at once."

Nate smiled from behind the bar but avoided her eye.

"What, a waiting room?" he asked.

"Yeah, for the people I see sitting at your bar every day, drooling into their Bloody Marys at you. These people are suffering, Nathan. Their perfectly good Bloody Marys are full of drool."

Nate suppressed a laugh and turned away to the counter, unpacked some more bar napkins for something to do.

Small Eileen took a seat at a bar stool, leaned over, lowered her voice. "Zoey would wait in the waiting room, Nate. I've seen the drool."

Nate turned and smiled shyly, shook his head. "No drool."

Small Eileen climbed off the stool, shrugging. "We'll see."

Around the bar, the group were chatting and working on their tasks, inflating balloons and pinning up the last of the lights and decorations. Luke was helping Christine with a flower arrangement and taking this chance to pick her brain about her legendary career. His eyes were wide as she gamely answered his questions about her journalistic trips to the Pentagon and time aboard Air Force One, about the alleged love affairs and business dealings of unsavoury world leaders.

An hour had passed when the group realised something was wrong.

"What time is it?" Ricky asked, looking up from his napkin folding, his eyes wide.

A pause, calibrating.

"SHIT!"

"Fuck."

"We have to go!"

Hannah and the others leapt into action as quickly as their bodies would allow, leaving behind their party prep and making for the door. Outside, the heat slammed against their skin.

"Luke!"

Startled, Luke was lagging behind. Hannah hurried back to get him, dragged him to the waiting carts. Esme climbed behind the wheel of one, and Ricky behind another, while the rest of them piled in.

"*Where are we going?*" shouted Luke as they tore down the path. But no one could hear him over the groaning engines, or the bullet sounds of the low-hanging palm leaves that whipped by in a blur, threatening to slap them.

At this pace, the resort was a caffeinated Impressionist painting, its colours smudged and its essence revealed: the green of the algae-stuffed reflection pools, the pink of the hibiscus flowers and the yellow picnic blankets they bloomed beside. The blue expanse of the sky, and the black-and-white face of the Giant Chequers court with its tiny, straining players.

They tore past a line of clubhouses and cut southwest, looped past the nearest residential building, its tangerine façade faded with sun. They sped past an exhaust pipe from the laundry room and the world was flooded, temporarily, by the clean scent of detergent.

They passed the food hall at top speed, turned, slid to a standstill at another entrance, laboured out of the carts and clambered for the door.

"It starts in *one* minute!" cried tall Eileen, and suddenly they were inside a clean, hushed foyer.

On one wall was a coat check window, currently closed. In the corner was a large plastic bin—the kind often used for a lost and found.

"That purple is nice," said Esme, collecting an object from the box and stepping away. They all crowded around, and Luke saw inside: it was full of formal accessories—ties and bow ties, fascinators, pairs of faux-diamond earrings.

Hannah encouraged Luke to pick something. In his panic he selected a large pair of sunglasses, the kind a socialite might wear to a fashionable funeral. Christine had pulled on a pair of silk gloves that shimmied to her elbows. Small Eileen had neatly folded a pocket square and, discovering she was wearing a t-shirt, she placed it in the front pocket of her cargo shorts.

With no time to spare, they headed towards a door with a sign above:

PALM MERIDIAN
COMMUNITY LIBRARY

The room they stepped into was breathtaking, a departure from the pastel colours outside. The library's interior was all dark wood, with endless shelves of books rising high to the ceiling. Patrons stepped along a ring of balconies above, dust motes hanging in sunbeams that fell in through vaulted windows. Study tables stretched along the main floor, dotted with oily green bankers' lamps. A pair of armchairs sat in front of a roaring fire—"Artificial," Hannah whispered—and readers were dotted around with their piles of books. A pet greyhound slept across its owner's shoe.

The library was open twenty-four hours. It was where degrees were completed late in life, where friendships were kindled and memories escaped. This was where Hannah came to read after lunch sometimes, when the heat got too much and she needed some quiet.

Now, the group of them hurried between the study tables, rustling madly through the hushed space and attracting too much attention. The sounds of their sneakers and sandals echoed above.

"Sorry!" Nate whispered to the studious people they passed.

At the other end of the library, past a cluster of shelves, about two dozen people were seated in rows of plastic chairs, arranged to form an aisle. At the front was a small table and a smiling officiant.

"Made it."

Hannah and her friends crammed themselves as quietly as they could into the back row, waving to familiar faces across the aisle. Among the people assembled were their friends, their acquaintances, their water polo teammates, the people who lived in rooms above and beside them.

A grand wooden door opened at the side of the library.

The officiant whispered:

"Honoured guests. Please stand, if you're able."

The couple were radiant. Ravishing. They walked arm in arm, as quietly as they could, up the aisle with no music. When they arrived at the officiant, no one clapped; they just sat down quietly.

The officiant, in a stage whisper:

"Thank you everyone for joining us today to celebrate the matrimony of Ruth and Celine."

From over the nearest shelf, a peeved noise:

"*Shhhhhhh.*"

Esme pulled a handkerchief from a purse she hadn't had before, and handed it to small Eileen, who dabbed at her eyes, overcome with tenderness. Christine watched the ceremony with a peaceful smile, her arm looped in Ricky's. Luke looked all around, bewildered, looked up at the ceiling, the giant sunglasses making the whole thing even more opaque.

"Why is everyone whispering?" he whispered.

Hannah leant close to his ear. She explained that this library was the resort's best-looking venue for a wedding—but weddings were a fairly frequent occurrence. The library patrons felt it wasn't fair to keep constantly shutting their space, and so everyone agreed that events could take place there, but at a library-appropriate volume.

Now the proceedings were nearing completion.

"Please will you join me in welcoming the new Mrs and Mrs Gershwin-Garnier?"

A minute later, the wedding spilled out through the grand wooden door and into the food hall, where the light and the volume increased by tenfold—like time-travelling from a medieval castle into a gay IKEA.

"Let's eat!"

While others from the resort enjoyed their lunch, the wedding guests took over a corner of the food hall. A large cluster of tables had been set up with flowers and white tablecloths, and by the far wall was a banquet table for the wedding party. Beside them, a jazz quartet launched into an upbeat number.

Luke sat down beside Hannah and took off his sunglasses. He whispered again, though noise rang around them: "Han, since when is there a whole wedding today? Won't this mess up your party?"

Hannah shook her head, sipped a glass of white wine. "Nah, this'll be over in thirty minutes."

And she was right: end to end the event was half an hour—but in that half an hour, a full-sized wedding reception was lived. By minute seven, the couple had changed outfits, returning into the hall to cheers as if they hadn't just been there. By minute ten, their meal was served. And by minute twenty-three, the best man was too drunk and gave a searingly inappropriate speech, breathing wet into the microphone.

"This is incredible," Luke said, eyes wide. "I've genuinely never seen something so efficient."

"You should see a vow renewal," said Christine, shimmying past their chairs with two glasses of champagne aloft. "We can get those done in about six minutes."

Finally, Hannah and Luke had another moment together to catch up, there in the raucous food hall. As they spoke, Hannah could feel them relaxing into their old friendship. They were nosing their way around each other's sense of humour again, spotting familiar things—like the way Luke's eyes flitted around a room, his mind moving quicker than he could speak. His younger face was transposed on his older one and she could see the warmth of him again, his curiosity—those things she'd always known. Her love for her oldest friend spread through her.

Very soon, though, Hannah was pulled away from their conversation, as other wedding guests began dropping by the table, some putting a supportive hand on her arm.

"How are you holding up, Hannah?"

"Been thinking about you this week."

"You know, my brother had the same thing as you. He let it go on way too long. You're making the right choice, I promise."

In previous weeks, these constant condolences had made Hannah feel heavy, itchy. She knew that all these people only meant well, but she often got the sense that their words had nothing to do with her—or worse, that they undeniably did. The spectre of death was nowhere and everywhere, and it left Hannah feeling knocked off her centre.

Now, though, these words didn't have that effect. In fact, Hannah felt lifted by them. It could've been the wine, of course, or the proliferating joy of the couple who'd just married. In any case, Hannah had found a sense of calm, and she settled into it.

"What was your wedding like, Eileen?"

Tall Eileen sat on Hannah's left—she was watching her wife cheer on the jazz quartet while twirling a cocktail umbrella contentedly between her fingers. She turned at Hannah's question, the memory opening her face into a smile.

Tall Eileen knew that Hannah already knew this story. That she just wanted to hear it again now, to spend this easy time listening to her friends.

"Well, we got married in Redwood National Park. We'd been camping for a week when our friends and family came to meet us. Everything had gone wrong. Eileen had been whittling a falcon out of wood, for months, in secret. She wanted to surprise me with it, but on the first day she slipped on a hike and crushed it in her backpack. The whole beak snapped off, and she cried.

"On the third day, poison oak got us on the arms and the legs—we were being careless; it was a stupid mistake. And on the fifth day, a storm flooded right through our tent.

"On the day of the wedding, we came out of the thickest part of the woods, to all these people we loved. And they were smiling, and we were smiling. I was itchy and tired. And I was the happiest I'd ever been."

Hannah enjoyed the memory as if it was her own.

Carmen, another wedding guest and co-captain of the badminton team, had sat down at their table, taking a break from the dancing that had just begun nearby, the improvised dancefloor perilously close to the hot lunch buffet. Carmen tipped her glass of champagne towards Hannah.

"Have *you* ever been married, Hannah?"

The question caught Hannah off guard. She took a long time to reply, taking a sip of wine, the sounds of the party falling quiet in her ears.

In her mind, Hannah saw Sophie's smile, heard the golden thunk of Vegas slot machines.

"No. There was a time when I thought I would be, though."

Carmen's face fell from expectation to apology. "Oh, I'm sorry."

Hannah shook her head. "No, don't be sorry. Don't be sorry at all."

"Do you still know the person?" Anna ventured, another wedding guest who'd since sat down beside Carmen.

Hannah considered the question as the past churned before her eyes. "No, I don't. I haven't seen her for more than forty years."

Hannah's last interaction with Sophie played out in her mind. She tensed her jaw, then shook any bad feeling away. The past didn't matter now—it would all be sorted out in a matter of hours.

Hannah smiled, a thrill running through her at what she was about to say:

"But she's coming tonight, actually."

Hannah felt tall Eileen tense beside her, not expecting this state-ment—Hannah and her friends knew full well that there'd been no RSVP from Sophie.

But Anna and Carmen's eyes had already widened with interest. They were hooked.

"Oh my god, are you serious? So it's like a long-lost love reunion?"

Memories rippled through Hannah like a winter wind, lighting goosebumps on her skin in the food hall. She nodded, and Carmen and Anna clapped their hands with delight at this turn of events.

"Oh my god, I can't wait to see this!"

Tall Eileen leant close to Hannah, checking her eyes for an explana-tion. "Han?"

But Hannah just placed her hand very gently on Eileen's. Her friend let it go.

The room lit up in cheers as the newlyweds hoisted a large knife and cut cleanly through their wedding cake.

"You want some cake?" Eileen asked, getting up, but Hannah de-clined, saying she'd see them in a bit. The others went off, and Hannah sipped her wine. She watched Luke congratulate the brides across the room, him laughingly accepting as one of them placed her veil on his head.

"Excuse me, ma'am, is this seat taken?"

It was Esme, breathless from dancing.

"Not for a pretty thing like you," said Hannah, and Esme eased down beside her.

Hannah poured Esme a glass of water from the jug on the table and they silently observed the party together, their friends mixing and danc-ing and forking slices of cake.

Hannah and Esme watched the brides, whose deep love radiated across the room, their joy contagious. Hannah sensed that Esme wanted to speak, sensed her working up to something difficult. She gave her time. When Esme finally spoke, her voice was quiet, private.

"I heard you mention Sophie just now. It got me thinking. I just . . . I remember getting that text, you know. From Vegas. Right after you met her."

Hannah's chest flooded with warmth and she laughed, knowing what was coming.

"You were sitting in one of those gladiator restaurants, wearing a cardboard helmet. You said, *Ez, I met this girl. And I'm gonna be with her for a very long time.*"

Hannah let the joyful noises of the room settle over her.

Was it weird to be excited on the last day of your life?

11

*A*s the taxi sliced through the city—trees and shops and the bases of skyscrapers tumbling past—it seemed to Hannah and her jet-lagged brain that the gentle stoners in university had been right: everything was in everything.

Ours was a liquid universe, all energies mixing and co-mingling. Having crossed fourteen time zones, blissfully sleep-deprived, it felt perfectly clear to Hannah that she was a cold bottle of soda in every 7/11 they passed. Equally, the cold bottles of soda were her.

Her body was a harmless illusion. She was in fact a stuffed toy, sitting in a pile of stuffed toys, awaiting selection by a silver claw in the glass box of an arcade game. She was a road stripe painted on a busy street, one pixel in a five-storey digital billboard, looming with benevolence above.

In this state, it suddenly seemed unlikely that death existed in the way people so fiercely believed. It seemed more probable that everyone simply fell asleep one day, and found themselves as beams of light overlooking a city.

Feeling lightheaded, Hannah texted Luke:

Can't promise I'll land this deal (kidding, all fine). Feeling crazy. Much to discuss about liquids, though.

?

Sorry. No sleep.

Next, she texted Esme, who now lived ten minutes from Hannah and Sophie's apartment in Montreal, with Theo, her adoring sculptor boyfriend:

Dude remind me to tell you about a baby on the
plane. Looked just like you, minus lipstick.

Finally, Hannah called Sophie, the signal wavering up to a satellite. She cracked open the window of the taxi and breathed in the sharp winter breeze, the comforting smog, the salty vapour emitted from passing ramen restaurants. It had been one year since Hannah and Sophie had met on that smoky Manhattan street.

"Thank you for calling but I already have a home insurance provider and I'm very happy with them. Thank you!"

Hannah breathed out a laugh, relaxing at Sophie's voice.

"Would you still love me if I was a traffic cone?"

The neon colours of a shopping arcade sped past the window. Sophie was weighing the question.

"Like a pointy one? Or one of the tall ones that's a cylinder?"

"Both. On different days."

"Of course. I'd adore you. I'd wash you off and put you beside me in bed."

"I wish I was still in bed with you," Hannah murmured, low enough that the taxi driver didn't have to hear.

How many hours had it been, since they'd been pressed against each other at home in Montreal? All warm skin and slow light, sleeping and waking and finding each other's lips. Hannah grasped at the calculation in her head, then let it fall away. She picked a piece of sleep from her eye that her body had formulated while flying over the North Pacific Ocean.

"I can still smell you on my sweater. Here, let me sniff . . . "

Hannah listened to Sophie sniff exaggeratedly.

"What are you guys doing today?" Hannah asked.

The previous day, shortly after Hannah had left for Tokyo, Sophie had caught the train from Montreal to spend time with her mom in Vermont. In a few days she was set to fly on to Whistler for a month of coaching work with the US Olympic team, which would be their longest stint apart since they'd met.

"It's a very high-adrenaline day here. We're going to the farmer's market for green beans and pie crust, and then we're setting up the new bird feeder out back. It's got an attachment at the front that spins so the squirrels can't cling onto it. Feels like it might just make for spinning squirrels, but we'll have to find out." Sophie took a big breath. "And *then* we're going up the forest road for a walk. And tonight, we're ordering pizza and watching a movie. It's my pick."

"Can you tell your mom I'll bring her back some snacks?"

The taxi crawled to a stop at Shibuya Crossing, and crowds of pedestrians passed across the intersection from all sides, the billboards cycling between images above them: a frosted can of Asahi, a glossy pink manicure, a boy band with perfect hair.

"Next time let's come here together," said Hannah, as the lights changed and the taxi purred through the intersection.

"Ah sorry, Han, my mom needs help in the basement. Text me when you're at your hotel later."

"I will. I love you."

"I love you."

Hannah put her phone away and took a sip of water from a little bottle left over from the airplane. She cleared her throat and blinked hard. A week of meetings with Japanese firms would start right away. The president of a large commercial real estate company had a one-hour slot available to meet with Hannah, but it required her going to their office straight from the flight without stopping at her hotel. Sealing the contract would be a huge boost—as their first deal in Asia, it would signal to the world that they were ready for the next phase of expansion. Hannah had changed into a suit in the airport bathroom, fixed up her hair, repeated the Japanese phrases she'd learnt in the last few months.

"Here it is."

The taxi had stopped in front of a formidable glass skyscraper. Hannah thanked the driver and stepped into the street with her suitcase, reminding herself that while she was a cold bottle of soda and a lick of road paint, she could, momentarily, be the articulate owner of a groundbreaking heating and cooling technology company.

The lobby was enormous, like the soaring entrance to an art gallery. Hannah's footsteps echoed on the floor. After she checked in with the receptionist, she was collected by an assistant and taken up an elevator that, after the first two floors, opened up into a glass panorama of the city, like they'd been launched directly into the sky.

Hannah was made comfortable in a sweeping, empty boardroom with the same panoramic view. She was offered a cup of green tea, which she accepted gladly, drinking down the hot liquid quickly to try to wake herself up.

The assistant left for a moment, and Hannah was alone, the city silent through the window, the sounds of the office building revealed: the anonymous hum of vents and computers, the muffled sounds of steps on carpet.

Hannah watched the cars snake through the streets below, and thought of Sophie. Dizzy with love and longing, she pulled out her phone and thumbed through her photos. There was Sophie cross-legged on the floor in their Montreal apartment last week, frowning as she assembled a chest of drawers. From last month, a selfie of Luke and Sophie, post-triathlon in New Zealand. They wore foil blankets, medals around their necks. Both were grinning, but Luke was noticeably more exhausted.

The friendship that Sophie and Luke had formed had been instant, natural. They were alike in immediately obvious ways—driven, sharp, competitive. Sophie's Olympian energy and Luke's up-all-night entrepreneurial drive aligned, and in the year since Hannah and Sophie had started dating, Luke and Sophie had taken to racing together at events around the world, competing for the better time, though Sophie always won by a generous margin.

They'd send videos of themselves hammering through a finish line in the rain, looking like they were about to be sick.

Hannah would reply: Looks awful. You're both nuts. And I'm so proud of you.

Really, it made her swell with love to see her two closest people get along so well.

Now footsteps approached the boardroom, and Hannah slipped her phone away.

"Hello, Miss Cardin."

The president was a tall, affable man, and the meeting went well, Hannah remembering her key points despite the jet lag that tugged at each thought and made her limbs heavy. The president spoke highly of their systems and was interested in having them installed in a sample of properties he oversaw, to test their real-time benefit. Hannah promised him that the energy efficiency of his buildings would nearly double over-night.

Hannah watched the skyline rush up towards her as she took the elevator back down, thinking of her waiting hotel bed, of a shower, of uncomplicated sleep.

She handed her guest pass to the receptionist, who received it, smiling.

"Your colleague is waiting in the coffee shop next door. For your next meeting," she said.

"Oh, I don't have another meeting, I'm afraid. Not until tomorrow."

The woman shook her head, smiled. "They were here just now. They're waiting in the café just here. To the right when you leave."

Hannah was sure it was a mistake, but figured she should at least tell whoever it was that there'd been a misunderstanding. She thanked the woman and headed out across the lobby, into the chill and noise. She was so tired she felt drunk, and leaned into the feeling, moving down the busy street. The café looked inviting and she was drawn by the bolstering scent of matcha and coffee beans.

Hannah stepped inside, looked around.

There, in the corner, the afternoon sun brightening her face, was Sophie, dressed in a turtleneck and jeans, her eyes smiling, dark hair falling over her shoulders.

"What—"

"I lied."

Sophie's voice was muffled in Hannah's hair, her familiar scent socking Hannah in the heart, sending her already loopy brain reeling.

They sat on the same side of the table and Sophie pushed one of two coffees towards her.

"The Olympic gig in Whistler isn't till January. I'm coaching at a camp for elite-level kids in Nagano. It's three weeks."

"But you were at your mom's—just—"

Sophie brushed her hand across Hannah's hair, laughing.

"I was in my hotel room."

Hannah wiped a tear from her eye and sipped the coffee. Staring at Sophie, she felt pelted by love, a safety and rightness, to the level of her blood cells.

Here was home, across the world.

Hannah took her meetings for a week, and on the weekend caught the train to Nagano. She drank tea in the warmth of the chalet, the ski slopes disappearing into clouds high above, while Sophie coached and laughed with the tiny athletes, who adored her.

A storm came in at night, and Hannah and Sophie were pressed together again, in their room at the base of the mountain. Their skin was hot as the snow slammed against the window, the hills illuminated outside, Sophie's ski goggles discarded on the floor, reflecting the storm.

12

*M*asturbation had not been the plan, but it quickly became the plan. The wedding reception had ended, the guests spilling towards the main buffet for seconds and thirds. Now Hannah left the food hall and its cool, hash brown smell. She broke out into the sun, its heat bearing down on everything, the air hazy, liquid, obscene. Like running into a wall, it knocked the breath out of Hannah, and she walked faster, her heart trilling. Sopped with sweat, her calves straining, she felt suddenly, gravely, deliriously *embodied*.

Death was coming, so why shouldn't Hannah? If life would leave her body tomorrow, it would riot in her groin today.

This yawning, insatiable feeling was the same one Hannah had felt dozens of times before, in her twenties and thirties and forties. She'd spent years typing emails and taking meetings in coolly bland hotel rooms and then, at the end of the day, easing into the pleasure of exhaustion. She'd leave the hotel and join the noisy street of a new city, feeling her spine stretch, feeling the evening seep into her eyes. There was an expansiveness to everything, the buzz of possibility in an unfamiliar walk, her pulse waking up again.

Now, the sights were familiar, but the effect was the same. The resort

spooled out before her and she savoured the look of it: the shaggy palms
and the sometimes-neat, sometimes-shaggy landscaping, which followed
the whims of the volunteer gardeners.

As the wedding reception wound down, Hannah and her friends
had agreed to reconvene at Frankie's in two hours, leaving them time to
rest and shower and change before the party. Christine and Esme had
headed off together to compare their final choices of party outfits. Ricky
had headed back to the welcome building to look after some things at the
check-in desk, and Nate had returned to Frankie's to confirm the bar's
staffing for the night. The Eileens were still at the food hall, sitting side
by side, sipping iced tea and speaking quietly. Hannah had checked on
Luke, who said he was tired from travelling, running his fingers through
his grey hair. She'd made sure he knew his way back to his guest room
for a nap.

Now Hannah left the path and started across the main lawn, which
was quieter than the morning. A breeze blew through the palms, knocking the occasional chestnut onto the grass. Some residents clustered in the
shade, and the sound of their chatter, their spoons and teacups, rose up in
the air, mixing with the faraway splash of the swimming pool.

This time of the afternoon had its own atmosphere. It was a lull each
day, a time that moved slower and with its own light, when many residents were napping, retreating from the heat of the day into the cool dark
of their rooms. Even if they couldn't sleep, there were comforts to be
found there, antidotes to racing hearts: recorded television, filtered water,
crunchy snacks, bleached sheets.

Hannah turned up the path towards her building. Some residents
sat outside their rooms, beside their partners. Hannah saw a pair of them
now, and a part of her wanted to shout out: *I'm dying!*

But they were probably dying, too—it was nothing special, was it?—
and so she left them to watch the lizards lick through the grass, to feel
time drip like the palms after a storm.

Hannah's room was on the ground floor of the northernmost building, its exterior path flanked by thick vegetation. She unlocked the door

and stepped inside, unable to ignore the fact that her room smelled differently now it was empty—already less like her and more like carpet
dander, like the mulch and leaves outside her window. Florida, right-
fully, had begun to creep back in.

Hannah's room wasn't big—none of them were—but without any
belongings, the spaces between the furniture felt expansive. Hannah
switched on a lamp and considered the space: a double bed, two night-
stands, a chest of drawers, a kitchenette, a round table and two chairs.
All of this in the same mid-century style of the exteriors. The walls she'd
painted a deep green in her first year at the resort, when arthritis still allowed.

Hannah noticed the two faded ovals her parents' urns had left on the
top of the TV stand.

The shelves that had long been packed with well-thumbed novels
and coffee-stained notebooks were now bare apart from a cluster of empty
prescription pill bottles, their orange plastic catching the light sometimes,
so it seemed they were burning. Hannah made a mental note to collect
these and bring them to the designated bin tomorrow morning. Depend-
ing on the day that plastic was collected, it was upcycled by industrious
residents into rain-catching barrels, or melted down and fashioned into
lawn furniture for the egrets.

In the bathroom, Hannah gulped down a glass of water, then peed.
She'd planned to shower and start prepping for the party now. But she
did neither and instead went to the bed, lay down.

The sweat on her body had dried now and she shivered, unzipping
her shorts and pushing her socks off with her heels. Her underwear was
black and plain, her pubic hair a coarse grey. Where her skin had been
smooth and tight before, it rippled now, her flesh soft and geological. She
was a field of lava, brightly veined.

Touching herself, Hannah felt she could run ten miles if she wanted
to. That she could run straight across the lawns, out the gates, down the
interstate, could circle the swamps. She could run to Georgia and not notice it, could cross the whole continent, in fact—a vast thing tangled with

towering conifers, leaping freeways, desert flowers, packed parking lots, flags and lakes and open space.

The doctors said she'd be blind in a month. The cancer was aggressive. It would spread to vital organs soon. Managing the pain would be the key goal of treatment. Things would become unbearable, and fast.

Now, on the bed, Hannah felt the last fifty years rush through her, the pleasure redeeming everything, as if no time had been lost at all. She felt Sophie's body against hers, felt the heat of Nevada and the power of a Japanese alpine storm. All that hungry fucking rose back up in her, their wet lips and shuddering bodies, their breath catching in their throats.

A lightness built in her, tightened, and broke, and in the crash of it, Sophie was there, her bright eyes on a snow-piled street, in a desert swimming pool, her hand reaching for Hannah in the warmth of the night.

And then quiet.

The birds flitted through the palms outside. The swimming pool splashed, far away. The women in the room above woke, and their footsteps padded across the carpet.

In the dim light, Hannah was still, her heart slamming, the heat of it fading away. Goosebumps rose on her naked stomach.

She was so near the end, she could see her whole life plainly: the taut moments, the wadded-up spaces, some places brittle and bare. None of the hard things, the bad things, mattered now. The love redeemed it all—that staggering love that had held her together. The love of her family, her friends. The love that Sophie had given her in ecstatic moments, quaking beneath their skin.

Having that love, and losing it, had been the honour of her life. And yet—

And yet the grief of losing Sophie's love was still there, as fresh as it had been forty-three years ago.

Hannah touched her arms, running a thumb along the tiny hairs on her forearm, ending at the bones of her wrist. She touched her stomach, its soft allowances. She felt her heart slowing in her throat.

It was this body—this same body—that had lost Sophie.

It was enough to make Sophie feel close.

Time to get ready.

The bathroom filled up with steam as Hannah peeled off the rest of her clothes, her joints crackling, her lower body fluttering with leftover orgasm.

She stepped beneath the water, sucked in a tight breath at its heat. She waited, and felt her body relax, the water coursing in tight streams down her back. She washed her hair, savoured the feeling of shampoo suds rushing down her body. Something weighty slid into place as she realised: she'd never enjoy a shower again.

Back in the bedroom, Hannah dripped on the carpet, holding a towel against her as she laid out her outfit: a black fitted suit, a white silk shirt. She planned to leave the top few buttons open to show that she still had sex appeal despite the parasite that had entered her body. She fastened a simple gold bracelet on her wrist, and slipped on a pair of shining black loafers.

Hannah dried her hair in a hurry and it fell in soft, white wisps down her back. A slick of deodorant and a splash of cologne, a slug of toothpaste and she was ready. But there was more to prepare. Just in case.

She changed the sheets, stuffing the sweaty ones into the laundry basket. On the far bedside table, she arranged a drinking glass, a fresh toothbrush. For a month, Hannah had saved her best pillow, and she brought it out now, puffing it up, and placed it at the head of the bed, beside her own.

She went to a drawer and pulled out a brown folder. With careful fingertips, she extracted a small piece of paper: a deed for a plot of Vegas land costing seventy-five dollars.

She placed the deed in an envelope, along with the letter she'd written the night before, in the warm breeze of the evening. The envelope was addressed with the curl of an "S." She placed it in the zipped pocket of her windbreaker, which now hung on the wall.

Looking smart in her suit, Hannah stood back and tried to take the room in through someone else's eyes. Anticipation rumbled through the core of her, upsetting her stomach, lifting her heart. Her body was tight with nerves.

What would happen when Sophie was standing here later? Would they sit? Would they know what to say?

They might find their voices had changed with age. That they were old, and things were different.

And what if it was worse?

A pain flashed behind Hannah's eyes when she thought of it.

What if they sat on this bed and the years joined up again—the beauty and the pain recovered—and they felt nothing for each other?

Hannah's thoughts scattered everywhere, making it hard for her to focus on the tasks of right now. She stumbled on a chair, searched for her sunglasses.

There was a knock at the door. It was too soon, surely? Too soon for the final party of her life.

Esme stood on the path, framed by a pair of palms, looking spectacular. Her hair shone down her back, her lips bright as they always were, a red dress dazzling with sequins and fringe, fit for a celebration.

When Esme opened her mouth, Hannah expected a big, grand line, maybe a troupe of accompanying dancers.

But no, it was just her friend, there to collect her. Esme's smile was soft, her eyes wet, maybe. Then she shook her head and any trace of it was gone. Her voice was gentle, with a hint of signature boldness.

"You ready, darling?"

Esme drove them back to Frankie's with one hand on the wheel. The cart bumped off the path and she righted it, knocked her sunglasses off her head and down onto her face.

As they drove, Hannah tipped her head out from beneath the roof of the cart. She closed her eyes and felt the late-afternoon sun on her skin. The day was still alive and bright.

Since her diagnosis, most people Hannah knew had asked her some form of the question: Are you ready to die? The truth was, of course, that she wasn't. But for three months she'd kneaded her grief into a manageable texture. She'd softened it, touched it to her tongue.

Death was difficult to fathom, but so was the alternative. If Hannah stayed, things would only get harder. Her body would go. Her spirit.

Palm Meridian was a wonderful home, but it wasn't exempt from pain or protected from suffering. On those plastic chairs at night, amidst the Jurassic vegetation, air thick with the earthy funk of willow trees, all the residents felt it sometimes. Grief. Insomnia. The sharpening of love to a white-hot point, watching a partner with dementia fade away.

On those nights, the sound of crickets rose across the dark lawns, filling a host of lonely spaces. And when power outages rolled through, and the night went from dotted orange to inky black, the noise of it filled the air, and passed: electricity powering down. Energy failing.

Now, as they zipped past residential buildings, Hannah spotted people getting ready. Energy was not failing them at all. They moved back and forth along the corridors, half-dressed, their hair wrapped in towels, borrowing shoes and deciding on earrings.

"Sophie's heart's gonna fall out her ass when she sees you in that suit, Han."

Hannah was grateful for Esme's faith. That her friend was hopeful, just like her, made Hannah feel stronger. She noticed her pulse racing under her skin, muscles strong beneath her suit.

Esme pumped the gas, taking a corner smoothly, and the bar appeared on the horizon.

The countdown had begun.

13

VERMONT
NEARLY 2022

*T*he diner was closed, but the owner was drunk, her apron tied around the back of her head like a veil. She was splashing whisky into everyone's coffee, a dozen customers scattered around the booths. Lamps above each table spilled a dim, golden light. Snow blew across the deserted road outside and the dark pine forest beyond.

"Only eighteen minutes till midnight! Eighteen minutes!"

The ticker at the bottom of the TV screen relayed disasters around the world: forest fires ripping up jagged coasts, whole towns plucked away by floodwaters, cyber-attacks placing ransoms on normalcy.

"Why wouldn't they tell me?"

Hannah's throat was tight and hot. She and Sophie sat on the same side of a peeling vinyl booth, one leg folded on the seat to face each other. They'd shared pancakes, eggs and bacon, and the sticky remnants lay on the plate, unappetising now.

"That's what parents do," Sophie said softly. "They protect you from things."

Sophie wasn't speaking from experience, of course, or at least not from the experience of her fairly shitty dad. But she didn't say this. In terms of childhoods, Sophie found it easier to speak to Luke, who understood less-than-ideal families first-hand. There was a shorthand there that Hannah—lucky for her—just didn't have.

"But I'm thirty-one. They don't have to protect me," said Hannah, a bitter laugh breaking through as Sophie wiped a tear from her cheek.

Hannah and Sophie had arrived home to Montreal in late November, after nearly six months of constant travel and work. In the morning they'd gone straight to Hannah's parents' apartment, its familiar yellow staircase powdered with snow. Right away, Hannah had known something was wrong.

Hannah had sat on the couch with her dad—the same couch she'd spent her childhood on, drawing and reading and planning.

Hannah's dad had sat down, his beard grey and thinning, his eyes pale, his big, calloused hands in hers. He told her he'd got the diagnosis months ago, and started treatment right away. They'd caught it early, and chemo had been effective so far. In fact, there were just a few more rounds and he'd be done.

He said they hadn't told her because they didn't want to worry her while she was travelling around the world.

Hannah blinked through tears and saw her mother watching from the kitchen table, her face older and more beautiful than Hannah remembered it. Sophie sat beside Hannah's mother at the table, holding her hand.

"I know I work a lot," Hannah managed, with quavering breaths. "But nothing is more important than this, Dad. Than you."

Hannah had no way of knowing, then, that the same cancer would one day blossom in her own body, bringing her close once more to her father, in nature's cruellest way.

Hannah and Sophie had spent that next month in Montreal, cooking and shopping for Hannah's parents, going for walks around the neighbourhood when Hannah's dad had the energy, passing slowly through the snow. Hannah drove him to his hospital appointments, waited in the oncology wing with a lump in her throat and the smell of disinfectant on her clothes.

On Christmas Eve there was heavy snowfall and, like so many winters before, Hannah and her dad went down to the sidewalk with their shovels. They all insisted that he sit inside and rest, that he not strain himself. But he laughed and assured them he needed it, that shovelling snow was an essential pleasure. That night they ate a huge meal and went for a moonlit walk through the twinkling winter gloom.

On Boxing Day, Hannah had allowed herself to leave her dad's side for the first time in weeks. Esme and her boyfriend Theo were hosting a potluck, and Hannah and Sophie trekked through the snow, arriving with tin-foiled pans of turkey and sweet potatoes. The apartment was full of drowsy, happy people draped in tinsel.

Esme greeted them with arms wide, her hair and her dress shining. Once they'd got drinks from the kitchen, she pulled Hannah aside, and asked about her dad, squeezing her shoulder and topping up her still fresh glass of Prosecco. Esme's friend Frances was visiting from New York, and she swirled over, *Long time no see*, her red hair spilling from her head, her arms delivering a hug that Hannah didn't know she needed, but when she received it, made her feel like she might cry.

Luke was already there, his lips stained red with wine, his grey suit immaculate. His face lit up when he spotted Hannah, like a decade had passed. But it had only been a month—they'd spent every moment together until so recently; spent weeks taking meetings in Copenhagen and Barcelona.

Sophie touched Hannah's back as they crossed the room, whispered in her ear, teasing:

"It's like that boy's in love with you."

Hannah laughed.

"He's only drunk," she said, and took Luke in her arms, wishing him a merry Christmas.

After dinner and gifts and more red wine, Hannah found herself deep in the couch beside Luke, the room swimming pleasurably, her brain content to watch the party pass. It had been so many weeks since she'd felt calm.

Luke's fingers were twitching on his knee.

"I met someone," he told her, turning suddenly.

He explained that she was American, that they had been speaking online for months as he travelled. That he felt optimistic about it, even though they hadn't met in person yet. He was heading to New Hampshire to meet her for New Year's Eve.

Hannah hugged him close, feeling sloppy with love for her oldest friend.

"I'm so happy for you, Lukey boy. That's so fucking wonderful."

Around midnight, Hannah and Sophie hugged their hosts goodbye and ducked out the door, taking the long way home to pass Hannah's parents' apartment and check that the light in their bedroom was off, her dad resting his battle-worn body.

Earlier that month, Hannah and Sophie had made plans to spend time in Vermont with Sophie's mom in the days after Christmas. Now, Hannah felt superstitious at the thought of being away from her dad, certain he would disintegrate as soon as she left him. But Hannah's mom pulled her aside and insisted she go. Staying in one place wasn't natural to her, and the change would do her good.

On the twenty-eighth, Hannah hugged her parents and climbed into the car with Sophie, driving through wooded landscapes, across the border and to Sophie's mom's door.

"Girls, you're like magic. You're in your thirties and you look about eight years old."

Sophie's mom was sharp, funny, sarcastic; stopped to chat to every neighbour they passed. The three of them spent a couple of days doing jigsaw puzzles, smoking weed at Sophie's suggestion and walking the dog through drifts of snow. They played cards late at night in the light of the kitchen, drove to Dairy Queen and got the biggest sundaes they had.

The new year would bring more work and travel—something Hannah normally craved, but now dreaded. Sophie had sensed this. Without telling Hannah the details, she'd arranged somewhere special for them to stay for New Year's Eve—something out of time, just to pause for a while. Leaving Sophie's mom, they drove for two hours, the yellow winter light as fragile as glass.

The woods were thick around the cabin, maple syrup taps in the nearby trees. The snow was as high as their waists, only cleared for the paths that hikers trekked in summer.

Feeling equally wired and depleted, Hannah and Sophie had lazily ravenous sex on the creaking single bed, grateful for one another's surety. When dusk fell, they were hungry for something else: dinner. So they drove to the diner by the forested highway.

Now, Hannah leant her head against the back of the diner booth and focused on the bluster of the wind against the windows, the sleepy sounds and smells of the place: a soft clatter of cutlery, the fug of grease, the news on low—comforting chatter with apocalyptic contents.

The owner appeared at their table, offered more whisky for their coffee cups. They accepted gratefully and she poured, then pranced away, her apron-veil swishing.

Hannah sipped the coffee, feeling the sharpness of the alcohol on her tongue. She wanted to enjoy this night, but she couldn't stop herself from thinking about her father.

Her thoughts returned, as they often did, to the once-cold home she'd grown up in. To how much love and care she'd been given.

Now, she had the power to care for people around the world.

Sophie kissed Hannah's eyebrow, then picked up a stray piece of bacon and tugged at it with her teeth.

"I want to install our systems for free," said Hannah. "On a huge scale."

Sophie was listening.

"We're working all the time to expand the business. We're making all this money from it. We have enough."

Sophie watched Hannah's mind working.

"I'm gonna call Luke."

Hannah picked up her phone and Sophie hesitated, put her hand on Hannah's to stop her.

"He's in New Hampshire, babe. And you're drunk. But it's a good idea. You guys should talk next week."

Hannah moved to put her phone in her pocket, but it started buzzing in her hands. Like he'd heard them: it was Luke.

Hannah put the phone to her ear.

"What's up? How's the date going?"

His voice was defeated.

"She didn't show, Han. I—"

He shouted over the sound of passing traffic, the swish of cars on a highway.

"Sorry, I'm just getting gas. She didn't show, Han. It's just really made me feel like shit. Can I come meet you?"

Sophie could hear his words through the phone and her face was clouded with worry. Hannah hesitated, but Sophie mouthed, shook her head: *It's okay*.

"We're in Vermont, Luke."

On Luke's end there was a long pause, a shuffle. A car door slammed and there was finally quiet, as he got comfortable in the driver's seat. "Sophie's with you?"

Hannah was taken aback by the question. But she heard the needing in his voice and didn't say what she was thinking: *Of course she's with me, she's always with me, and it's New Year's Eve.*

Instead, she asked: "Where are you?"

Luke sniffled, cleared his throat. "Hanover. Probably a couple hours from you. Maybe less."

Hannah nodded at Sophie, and Sophie rubbed her arm. Hannah acquiesced.

"I'll drop a pin. We're at a diner."

Luke let out a long breath. There was the sound of a car engine starting. "Thank you, Han."

"*Two minutes!*" the owner of the diner cried as Hannah put down the phone. Every patron in the room—even the beleaguered truck drivers with their backs like hulks—perked up.

"He shouldn't be crashing like this," said Hannah. She was rattled to hear her friend upset, but resented her evening alone with Sophie being encroached upon. She wanted a break.

Sophie's friendship with Luke was uncomplicated—they went to the gym together, Luke learning about fitness from Sophie, Sophie learning about business from Luke. She wanted to take her coaching global one day, make it a bona fide business, and Luke was happy to help.

Hannah didn't want to rain on Sophie's party, but her own friendship with Luke was more complex. They worked in high-stress environments together. Much like in childhood, they spent days on end together. Unlike in childhood, though, they were often exhausted and in close confines—airplanes, trains, hotel meeting rooms. Lately, Luke got on her nerves more often than not.

Sophie saw the agitation on Hannah's face.

"I love you," she said, kissing Hannah's cheek. "Come on." And they pulled themselves out of the booth and headed to the counter to join the others.

The TV was turned to Times Square, its glittering ball and bantering celebrities. Hordes of people jostled in plastic hats, looking like an orgy, or maybe a brawl. Across the bottom of the screen, more matter-of-fact disasters: cataclysmic explosion. Oncoming drought. Human rights sucked up as if by the Teletubby vacuum.

"Great hair," said Sophie to a trucker, whose mullet gleamed impressively in the light of the diner. She said it with a sincerity that he clearly hadn't encountered in a while, and his eyes opened wide with joy.

Outside, a lone vehicle went past on the dark road: a white van with Hannah's face, in green—her slightly younger, but nearly identical, cartoon self: a baseball cap, a ponytail, a smile.

"One minute!"

Hannah wrapped an arm around Sophie's waist.

Her phone dinged, and she pulled it from her pocket, thinking it would be Luke again. It was Esme. A photo of a thick gold band, in a ring box.

About to pop the question to Theo. Think I might throw up.

A joyful laugh escaped Hannah's throat and she showed the photo to
Sophie, whose eyes lit up.

"Oh my god!" she laughed.

Then a text came through from Luke:

I'll be there in 90 min.

Hannah texted Esme back—a breathless string of encouragement
and exclamation marks—then put her phone away and tried to bask in
her friend's good news, in the nearness of Sophie. As always, she thought
of her dad, and her throat tightened again.

The crowds undulated on the TV screen. The night sky was lost in
the holy, blinding light of Times Square, ads for mascara showing fashion models' faces, their nostrils two storeys tall.

In the diner, the owner raised a toast, and they all raised their voices.

"Ten! Nine! Eight!"

Hannah squeezed Sophie's waist, imagined the year coming towards
them. Nosing its way across the time zones, sliding, mammoth, above the
pine forest. A billowing curtain in the sky.

14

FLORIDA
4 p.m.

Esme overshot the bar and drove up the side of a sunlounger, jostling her and Hannah and leaving the golf cart on a diagonal.

"Esme, if you're trying to euthanise me, I've actually already hired someone for the job. But it's very sweet of you."

The metal made a crunching sound as Esme tried to reverse.

"*Lounging* over here, *lounging* over there. The people in this place could do with being vertical sometimes," said Esme. She stopped trying to reverse and nodded resolutely. "Got to go over," she said, pointing forwards, and she put her foot on the gas. Like a kind of slow-motion monster truck rally, Esme drove the golf cart over the sunlounger, and another one beside. The sound of crunching metal upset a pair of picnickers nearby. Esme waved.

"They owed me money!" she called, and the golf cart thumped down on the other side of the wreckage. Esme looped the cart slowly around a palm and headed back towards the bar.

"I'll repair those," she whispered to Hannah.

It was late afternoon now, and a golden haze fell over everything, over the grassy corners and shaded groves of the resort that spread beneath them. Guests were set to arrive in less than an hour.

Esme and Hannah left the cart and stepped across the terrace, which had been transformed since the morning. Hundreds of lights were strung from above, ready to glow. The tables were laid with candles and ashtrays. A sweetness wafted towards Hannah, the air picking petals off nearby flowers and settling them in the grass.

"Eileen," said Esme quietly, pointing out their friend. Small Eileen stood on a ladder across the terrace, adjusting a string of lights, carefully tightening the bulbs and shining each one with a cloth. She turned her head when she heard them coming; beamed.

"Watch this," she said, and flicked a switch. A galaxy of bulbs went on above them, burning in the afternoon light. Their bar had never looked this nice.

Eileen turned the lights off and stepped down from the ladder. She shrugged. "It'll be better when the sun goes down." Her normally bold, booming voice was gone for the moment, replaced with a smaller one that betrayed the afternoon she'd had.

She hugged Hannah tight, stepped away, thumbed a tear off her cheek. She tried to laugh it all away.

"I didn't want to get dressed, Han. Getting dressed meant things were really happening. I sat in my underwear for half an hour."

Hannah wanted to look away from the wetness in her friend's eyes. Instead, she pulled her close again. "I love you, Eileen."

Like the terrace, the inside of the bar was unrecognizable from the morning. Caterers had arrived with their steaming silver trays. Long tables on either side of the room were heaped with buckets of drinks, riotous flowers. The DJ booth had been assembled. The walls were covered in lights and hanging decorations, and the back windows were open. The afternoon sun streamed in, the dancefloor shining.

Hannah said hello to the caterers, who were carrying in supplies from two carts out the back of the building. When she was sure they had everything they needed, she stepped behind the bar to fetch a bottle of champagne. A bit of liquid courage would not go amiss.

"Fucking lethal outfit, by the way, Eileen," said Hannah, pouring out flutes and handing them to her friends.

Small Eileen thanked her, laughed, leant an elbow on the bar. She was wearing a dark blue crushed velvet tuxedo, the tailoring hugging her hips.

"To Hannah!" said Esme, raising her glass, and they clinked their glasses, taking long, grateful sips.

An egret had wandered in, thin and wavering, and small Eileen picked it up and tucked it beneath her arm. She cleared her throat, rolled her shoulders. She was revving herself up again. There was a sombre energy creeping in, and she'd taken it upon herself to help melt it away.

"Here they come!"

One by one, their friends emerged over the slope towards the bar. As they entered, small Eileen took it upon herself to provide live fashion commentary, speaking into the top of the egret's head, like a microphone.

"We have young Ricky here, sporting a crisp summer shirt. His legs are complemented by a pair of slacks. He is radiant. He is divine. He is slightly soiled—babe, you've got some dirt there—"

Next, Christine stepped inside, outdoing herself in a black satin jumpsuit and tall heels. Her hair was scraped high on her head, her earrings sparkling, lips bright. She was devastatingly chic to an even greater degree than normal.

"Here is Christine Williams, looking to make Slip "N Slides in the ladies' trousers tonight—"

"Too far!" laughed Hannah, but Christine threw her hand in the air. "I'll allow it!"

Nate appeared, looking handsome in a crisp white shirt and tight grey dress pants. Sensing the catwalk situation, he tugged at his cuffs, ran his hand through his hair, then shook it all off, laughing.

"This is not Nate's first rodeo," explained small Eileen into the egret's feathers. "He is actually magnetic and alluring on a daily basis."

Next to arrive was tall Eileen, wearing a forest ranger uniform from her time in the service. It was her form of ceremonial dress.

"Here we have a goddess with a perfect rear, dressed smartly in a short-sleeved forest green uniform top with matching shorts and a shining belt buckle. She is wearing a complementary brown felt Stetson and is ornamented proudly with a National Park badge, issued by the state of Washington. Her last name is stitched across her breast in brown lettering, which is so hot, I can't even explain it."

By now, Hannah was in conversation with Nate behind the bar, so she didn't see Luke arrive, in a fresh suit. It was probably for the best, because Esme intercepted him before small Eileen could announce him and his outfit. They spoke in hushed voices by the door, more heated than earlier in the day. Esme's expression was stony. Luke raised his hands in defence. Finally, he sighed and nodded, though both of them came away with sour faces. A moment later, Hannah turned, hearing Luke settle onto a bar stool.

"Hey man, would it be okay to get a G&T?" Luke asked, and Nate nodded, coming right up.

When Luke saw Hannah, he stood and hugged her.

"Han. You look beautiful. Seriously—just . . . wow."

Small Eileen had spotted him by now, and overheard this. She called out, teasing:

"Flirting with your friends—a classic queer move, Luke! You're learning quickly!"

Luke blushed deeply, and Hannah laughed, waving her friend's comment away.

"You look amazing, Luke."

"Oh—I have something for you . . . " And Luke hurried back outside. A minute later, he was striding into the bar again, with an enormous covered tray in his hands. He heaved it onto the nearest table, waved Hannah over.

She watched as he lifted the cover, revealing a cake, its icing inky black and charcoal grey. A welding mask.

Hannah's mouth fell open.

"How did you . . . ?"

But Luke just laughed, and she hugged him close.

"I'm so glad you're here."

Luke sensed they were running out of time before the guests arrived, so he put the cover back on the tray. "Here, I'll put it away. We'll all have it later."

There was the noise of the caterers finishing their set-up, and the house music that tall Eileen started, low, through the speakers. The electronic beats didn't help much though—everyone still seemed spooked, distracted. The smiles on their faces didn't reach their eyes.

"Nate. *Nate*." Christine was stage whispering as she took a seat at the bar, one leg folding gracefully over the other. Nate was drying glasses and he turned, his expression slightly despondent like the rest of them.

Christine leaned forward, knowing gossip was a powerful balm.

"What's going on with you and Zoey?"

"Hmm?"

Christine repeated herself: "Zoey. You guys seem crazy about each other."

Nate turned away, a smile rising on his lips. "I don't know a Chloe."

Christine laughed, slapped her palms on the bar. "Nate, you *have* your hearing aid in."

Nate busied himself with the drying of one very small glass, eyeing his friend evasively.

Zoey was a newer resident. Mid-seventies, she'd arrived a few months ago from Tennessee with a killer smile and a statement wardrobe—all cowboy boots and hip-hugging flares. She'd sat at Nate's bar on her very first day, and stayed for three unexpected hours, the two of them drawn bashfully together—like powerful magnets trying to be polite.

I must be keeping you. I'm sorry. You've got unpacking to do.

No, you're working—I'm a bother.

They kept giving each other excuses to leave, which clearly neither wanted to take. Since then, Zoey had returned to the bar almost every day, their conversation easy and unceasing. These days everyone at Frankie's watched their interactions like it was reality TV—a romance budding right before them.

Now, Christine sat up straight, enjoying her investigation. "Nate, I saw you make a virgin mojito for Zoey the other day. You made it take about forty-five minutes. How much mint can one person *muddle*?"

Nate hadn't dated much recently—a speed date evening here, a dinner there. He was savouring the peace he'd found since he transitioned and enjoying the company of himself and his closest friends. But lately he looked forward to seeing Zoey every day. It was a feeling he hadn't seen coming—a new and deepening thrill.

Christine was still waiting for a reply.

"Zoey's just nice to talk to," Nate shrugged, licking his lips to cover another smile.

"Nate, I was not born yesterday. In fact, I'm very old."

Nate laughed, held up his hands like he couldn't help her. "I don't think she's into me."

"Nate, that woman is nuts about you. *And* she wants to climb you like a tree."

"Who's climbing trees?" asked tall Eileen, coming round with fresh champagne.

A few minutes later, Hannah had joined their conversation and was admiring tall Eileen's National Park badge with Luke, when Ricky appeared beside her. His young face was clouded with worry.

"Hannah?"

Distracted by the busyness of the bar, Hannah didn't register the emotion on his face.

"Rick! Any new mail yet?" she asked.

He was thrown for a moment, then shook his head. "I'm really sorry, Han. I checked again after the wedding ceremony, and on my way here. I'll keep checking."

Hannah nodded. "Thanks, Rick. I appreciate it."

Ricky hesitated for a long moment, and Hannah's roving eyes finally took him in him properly. It was clear: something was wrong.

"What's going on?"

He avoided her eye, lowered his voice. "Han, I was gonna wait until later, because I didn't want to get in the way of everything, and the party.

I just . . . " He fought to get the words out. "Look, do you have a minute now?"

Hannah nodded, feeling suddenly unmoored. Ricky whispered his thanks, said he'd be back in a moment. He dashed behind the bar, and came back with a backpack.

Taking Hannah's hand gently, he led her across the room, away from their friends and the caterers. They settled at a corner table, where a tiny vase of flowers and a tea candle had been placed in preparation for the party.

Dappled light fell through the window and across Ricky's face, and Hannah saw fear, but also certainty in his eyes. She considered standing back up again, telling him gently that whatever this was, she didn't want to know. She wanted to be back across the room, making silly conversation, drinking champagne. But she forced herself to stay.

"What's up, Rick?" asked Hannah, her body tense, her voice faltering.

From the backpack, Ricky pulled out a ring binder, which he placed between them. Ungracefully, he scooted his chair around so that he and Hannah were sitting side by side at the small table, their elbows touching. Hannah considered their hands: his large and rough and weathered by sun, hers softened with time and dotted with liver spots.

Seeing the morning sun playing on Ricky's features, it was easy to forget he'd been born into disaster. Growing up in south Florida, his family had been forced northward a half dozen times before he started high school. He sometimes described the storms that had ripped through every soggy neighbourhood they moved to, how the wind had smashed the windows of parked cars and sent them shuddering down the street. He'd recall the nights they'd been evacuated to higher ground, sleeping in churches and school gymnasiums with a hundred others, the scent of damp and squeak of sneakers. It always made Hannah think of the nights she'd spent with her parents on the hard carpet floor of her mom's office building.

Her disasters had been personal, not global. Ricky's were both. She admired him more than she could say.

"Han, I want to show you something."

It was a great struggle for Ricky to find his next words, and when he did, they all came out in a tumble.

"First, I have to say that your choice is your choice. One hundred thousand million percent. And the last thing in the whole world I want to do is disrespect that. In fact, I wasn't sure if I should show this to you at all. But today I realised I couldn't live with myself if I didn't, and—well, let me just show you."

Bracing herself, Hannah held Ricky's arm as he opened the binder. He flipped slowly through dozens of pages. It was medical research, and detailed plans of care. News articles about possible breakthroughs, and clinical trials of new medications. Exceptions to the rule. It was a costing sheet showing carefully projected expenses for ten years of at-home care.

"Rick, when did you . . . ?"

Ricky kept his eyes on the binder, flipping through page after page.

"I started the day after you told me. I felt crazy, and then I realised there was something I could do. I could look into things. Han, I'm not a doctor, but—"

"No, *you're not*, Ricky. I don't know why you'd think this would be okay." Hannah's voice was harsh.

"Everything okay over there?" Esme called from across the bar. She was only half listening, in conversation with Christine by the terrace.

Without turning around, Ricky and Hannah called back in unison: "Yeah!"

The blood had risen hot to Hannah's face, but she found herself reaching across and turning the next pages of the binder herself, burning to uncover more. Soon she landed on something that stopped her. It was a sketch of her room at the resort—a mock-up, showing a hospital bed where her normal bed had been, mobility handrails and a couch for visitors. Ricky had drawn flowers in vases all around the room, and an egret in the doorway. Her parents' urns were on the TV stand where they'd always been.

"Rick, you had no right to do this," Hannah said, but the conviction was gone from her voice, her eyes scanning across the page.

Ricky sniffled, nodded his head. "I'm sorry, Han."

Hannah pulled the binder closer to her and flipped through the remaining pages, her eyes scanning medical papers and daily schedules of care. His research had been put together painstakingly. It was carefully thought through. Ricky only wanted to help her, like he'd helped so many residents in times of suffering and emergency. Holding their hands at the quaking end—he'd done that dozens more times than anyone his age should have to.

Sitting there in the bar now, Hannah got his message loud and clear: If she wanted to, she could stay. She could live.

Ricky snuck glances at her face, trying to get a read on things. When she didn't say anything for a long while, he spoke, cautiously.

"I'm sorry to show you, Han. And I don't want to spoil the party. I just wanted you to know that we could do it. We would take care of you. I've done it before. It's rough. But it can also be really beautiful."

Dazed, Hannah flipped back to Ricky's drawing of her room, letting its meaning linger in her mind. She was aware of her friends' laughing voices. A humid breeze rushed in through the window, fluttering the paper beneath her hand.

"Thank you, Ricky," she said.

He shook his head. "I'm sorry, Han."

She pushed the chair back slowly and stood up. She was about to walk away, but stopped herself.

"Can I have this?" she asked, touching the drawing.

"It's yours," he said quickly, popping open the rings of the binder and lifting it out.

Heading back across the bar, Hannah reminded herself of the many reasons she'd come to her difficult decision.

She discreetly folded Ricky's drawing, and slipped it into her suit pants' pocket.

"You okay? What was that about?" Esme asked.

"Oh, nothing. Thanks. All good."

As time ticked down, everyone checked their outfits, fixed each other's hair, chatted to the caterers. Small Eileen let go of the egret, but it didn't want to leave, so she picked it back up again. She gave it a tour of the bar, showing it where the toilets were and recommending the margaritas.

Esme was filling up their glasses. Ricky was wiping his shirt. Christine kept a precautionary eye on Luke, though Hannah didn't notice.

Standing in the centre of the bar, Hannah took a deep breath. Her heart fluttered with a sudden reality.

Nate checked his watch.

"Couple minutes to go."

The resort shone out the window. The sound of hairdryers came across the wind. Residents were putting their shoes on, closing up their rooms.

The sky was golden. Air sweet. Palms bristling.

The party was about to begin.

15

MONTREAL
2022

Sophie woke with a newness in her heart and a nipple in her nostril. She lifted her head from Hannah's sleeping chest.

The pale light of the street lamp cast shadows on their bedroom wall. Outside, the winter street was silent—inky black and frosted white and dark blue.

Hannah had stripped in the night as always, her body restless and warm and needing to be bare. Now her lips were parted on the pillow, hair mashed against her forehead, armpit hair like a neat, coarse rug.

"You smell good," whispered Sophie, and Hannah murmured back, pulled her closer.

For a minute, Sophie lay awake, feeling a stirring in her body she couldn't account for—a sense of lifting or beginning. She tried to place the sensation as she watched a pair of passing headlights scrape across the dark ceiling. In the winter stillness that followed, there was Hannah's even breathing, her sleep-scent of skin and night sweat and yesterday's shampoo. Then the coffee machine clicked on in the kitchen and moments later the sharp smell of ground beans reached their room.

At thirty-one, Sophie knew that life didn't begin just once, but over and over and over again. Maybe today, a morning in February, was one of those beginnings.

The shower door clouded with steam and revealed Hannah's phone number, where she'd written it backwards last week with a finger, sitting on the toilet while Sophie was washing her hair.

"Call me, really. I've got a great ass. And I'm very good at identifying tree species."

They had some of their best conversations in that small, green bathroom. After their separate days, they'd arrive home late in the evening, thrumming with anecdotes and plans and gossip, with new understandings of the architecture of their lives.

Soon one of them would be in the bathtub, the other flossing her teeth or undertaking a blackhead investigation in the mirror and, roaming between life's big and small things, they'd confer, process, rehash. They were up too late, like always, but they felt they could speak for the rest of their lives and still not reach the end of everything they had to say.

In many ways, these bathroom conversations felt like the meat of life, to Sophie—giddy time spent for its own sake, unrehearsed, un-replicable.

"You do have a great ass," Sophie would say, peeing on the toilet directly behind Hannah, who'd be brushing her teeth at the sink. Sophie would lean forward and rest her cheek on Hannah's pyjamaed tailbone, feeling symbiotic and quietly, happily wild. Then they would finally go to bed.

Now, Sophie showered, letting the heat relax her muscles before switching to cold to wake her up. In the kitchen, she drank her coffee and peeled an orange, waving at the squirrel on the still-dark fire escape who was watching her with curiosity. It scrambled away, poking at their recycling bin. Atop the pile of dismantled cereal boxes were Hannah and Luke's take-out cartons from the night before.

Hannah and Luke had worked till well after midnight at the kitchen table, eating egg-fried rice and sipping energy drinks as they reworked a legion of spreadsheets. They were planning their first non-profit projects, the ones Hannah had envisioned less than two months ago in the diner on New Year's Eve—offering their heating and cooling systems free of charge to hospitals, schools and care homes.

As they brainstormed at the table, Luke had folded post-it notes into origami shapes and gifted them to Hannah. A menagerie had built up at her elbow—an elephant, a rooster, a rhinoceros.

He had been folding a heart when Sophie came into the kitchen in her pyjamas, rubbing her eyelids, ready for sleep. She smiled when she saw Luke's latest shape.

"You trying to steal my girlfriend, Lulu?"

Luke blushed and crumpled the paper, but Sophie laughed, pouring a glass of water at the sink. She leant down to kiss Hannah, who was absorbed in formatting a document and had missed the whole thing.

"Love you. And you too, Lulu. I'm up early tomorrow, so I'm gonna go to bed."

"I love you," said Hannah, leaning back and stretching her arms above her head, smiling upside down at Sophie. "We'll be quiet."

"Really quiet," added Luke, and seeing the exhaustion in his face, Sophie regretted teasing him.

Luke had recovered admirably, in the end, from being stood up on New Year's. But the past two months had been stressful for all of them—Hannah's dad was continuing chemo, which was going well, but worry for him was always present. Sophie was more in demand than ever, coaching in-person and over the phone, travelling away for a week at a time to Aspen and Alberta. Luke was never not working, always on the phone or hypnotised by the glow of his laptop, a frown line growing at the side of his mouth.

The three of them had become a kind of family, and like every family, they had their dysfunctions. Feeling overwhelmed with work recently, Hannah had tearfully explained to Sophie that she was jealous of the easy friendship that Sophie and Luke shared.

"You guys have so much fun, doing your—*deadlifting*, and all that stuff. But when I'm with him, working, he's like my annoying brother. And I don't get to have that. I feel like you two are having a good time, and I always have to be the bad guy."

Sophie said she heard what Hannah was saying, and since then she'd been more mindful of the group dynamic—trios, after all, were often weird, and hard.

She didn't tell Hannah that she, too, felt left out sometimes, felt keenly the twenty-year head start that Luke had had in knowing and understanding Hannah. The two of them could communicate with just a glance sometimes—some telepathy left over from a childhood spent constantly side by side. In those moments, Sophie was sidelined ever so slightly, had the impression she was third-wheeling her own relationship. Her worst instincts told her to compete for Hannah. Her better instincts told her she didn't have to. And so she'd breathe deeply and, as best as she could, move on.

Now, Sophie rinsed her coffee mug and packed a backpack for the day, her gold medal gleaming in its case on the wall behind her. In the blue-dark of the bedroom, Hannah's limbs had retreated under the sheets, cold without Sophie's warmth.

"A kiss?" came her voice, muffled from deep beneath the duvet.

Sophie collected her phone from the bedside table and climbed on top of Hannah, who opened one eye, blinking up at her.

"Now I'm turned on," said Hannah, her hair splayed against the pillow.

Sophie leant down and kissed her hard, grinning into it. "See ya later."

Sophie took the speed bumps at speed, enjoying the lightness of her bicycle beneath her and the bite of the icy air on her face, how it stiffened her nose hairs.

This winter had been drier than most, the snow coming in periodic squalls, rather than its usual blanketing. Now, the frost on the parked cars glittered in the street lamps. Road salt had left cloudy white stains on the pavement.

At 6 a.m. on a Saturday in February, the neighbourhood was sleeping, and Sophie was free to admire the city. Everything Hannah had told her about it had been true: something unexplainable and good was going on here.

Everyone could tell you: Montreal had a way of tucking itself behind your breastbone and not dislodging itself your whole life. Wherever you went, you'd carry this icy place around with you, to faraway cities and tropical climes.

For two years, Sophie had felt the city seep in. She knew it would never leave her, either.

At St-Viateur, Sophie locked her bicycle and walked into the bagel shop. The warmth and softness of the place—its malleable dough, the red glow of the ovens—was a contrast to the sharpness of the world outside. She returned to her bike with a hot paper bag and two tubs of cream cheese, slotting them carefully into her backpack.

On Parc, the twenty-four-hour places were open: a laundromat that burped clean-smelling steam from its vents, a depanneur where an unseen attendant changed the channels on a tiny TV. Out of habit, Sophie practised her vocabulary whenever she stopped at a street light, reading and translating every French sign she could see.

She read the signs pasted in supermarket windows—deals for clementines and Black Forest ham—and the signs outside the copy shop, whose cheerful yellow mascot was an ink cartridge with lips. She was proud of the progress she'd made, of her increasing ease.

Hannah was an Anglophone Quebecer by birth, but spoke very good French through a lifetime of exposure. Arriving in this bilingual city, Sophie had been determined to keep up.

She'd enrolled in twice-weekly French lessons in an office building downtown. The teacher was a small, impatient man named Arnaud, who squinted through enormous glasses, the fluorescent lights reflected in the lenses in thick, white lines. Their ragtag class of ten adults was forever falling short of his expectations. He was blunt and cold and should have been unlikeable, but his thorniness was endearing, his disgust for them some backwards kind of charm.

"This is a conversation? To me, looks like a funeral. A funeral where nobody speaks French."

"You were drunk, yes? When you conjugated this? Very drunk."

Within the first few weeks of classes, Sophie had been wordlessly voted the leader of the students, not because she was the quickest learner—she was terrible—but because her natural kindness and confidence made the difficult lessons more bearable for them all. The more timid students expressed their gratitude with their eyes when Sophie intervened in a tirade from Arnaud, cracking a joke or asking a purposefully stupid question to attract his attention instead.

Pointing to *l'avocat* on her page:

"Arnaud, I don't think I'm drunk, but the man in this story is going to law school to become an avocado."

Arnaud would slap his hands to his eyes in cartoon horror, and the other students would be spared.

Leaving the office building twice a week and spilling back onto the street, Sophie had felt surprised at how much those French lessons affected her, at how deeply satisfying she found the homework, even as she struggled through. She left each lesson with her eyes burning from the fluorescents, lips dry from the office's recycled air. But she smiled every time.

The French lessons made her feel light and energised, not because they helped her understand the language, but because of the very fact that she had *chosen to take them*. She'd entered a new phase of life, one where she had time to give to things that weren't training or competing, things that weren't prescribed by tournament schedules or the toxic spite of her dad. She could pick goals that suited who she was and what she wanted *now*.

"Soph?"

On a tree-lined street off Parc now, an old Olympic teammate of Sophie's was also locking her bike in the dark of the morning. They laughed, and hugged the puffy hug of winter jackets, then took the curling stairs to their friends' door. Inside the apartment were a dozen pairs of shoes, and a dozen happy voices rang out when they announced their arrival.

In the living room, friends of Sophie's from a previous life were piled on the couch and across the floor on cushions. They were Canadian,

American, Czech, Slovenian, all of them former skiers of some kind—jumping, alpine, cross-country. They were settled in Montreal now, in love with its beautiful strangeness and at home in its prayerful snow.

Sophie hugged every one of them, and sat by the coffee table.

"Bagel?"

The cold had tightened Sophie's skin, and now it thawed. On the TV screen was the Olympic broadcast from Beijing, thirteen hours ahead of them, the evening sky dark and the spectators pelted with thick flakes of snow.

The women's ski jumping final began, and the friends' voices rang out through the living room—laughter and disbelief and teasing rivalries, all of them holding their breath as each athlete sliced through the air. Sitting cross-legged, heart racing, cream cheese salty on her tongue, Sophie understood it. *This* was the reason for the newness. *This* was about to change.

Sophie had once been one of those athletes, a gnawing in her stomach as she ascended to the jump. Eight years ago, Hannah had watched her unknowingly, dizzy next to a TV screen in the reception of a Swiss office. And four years ago, Sophie had won it all, her skis landing flat and sure, a weight lifting from her shoulders as the heft of her gold medal was placed around her neck.

Thus far, she'd lived her life in Olympiads, slices of time that demarcated meaning. Now, warm and floor-bound in Montreal, she prepared for the end, and a beginning. In a few moments, when the Slovenian athlete on the screen returned to earth and became the new champion, Sophie would be free in a way she'd never been before in her life.

Her friends erupted in cheers around her or fell back on their cushions in defeat. But Sophie simply felt lifted, a new calm spreading through her.

Her phone buzzed in her pocket a minute later. It was Hannah:

Just saw the result. She deserved it!
But I still love you the most.

PS the birthday boy says hello. He showed up on the
fire escape with his own tools and starting cleaning
our gutters. I told him he didn't have to do that.

Attached was a selfie of Hannah and her dad in the kitchen, smiling
with identical mouths. Hannah was wearing Sophie's hoodie, her bright
eyes full of sleep. Her dad raised his hand in greeting. A toque kept his
hairless head warm.

Sophie texted back:

You're both gorgeous

See you guys at 12 for lunch

On the TV screen, the snow fell harder, the champion's tears sparkling in the floodlights.

Flush with relief, Sophie savoured the feeling. A few minutes later,
she sent another message:

Han, where do you think we'll be in four years?

16

FLORIDA
5 p.m.

"Hold onto your bean dips. Here they come."

At two minutes to five, the landscape changed. It was subtle at first: a stirring of motion around the tranquil palms, a lifting of the breeze. Then, as if on a timer, whole swathes of green came alive, as residents spilled from their rooms and clubhouses, stepping across the lawns towards the bar.

In carts and mobility scooters, in chattering groups and pairs, they took the paths and started the party.

"It's never been better to see you, Han."

"How're you doing? How are you feeling?"

"Babe, you don't know how much you'll be missed."

Every person who arrived hugged Hannah, or kissed her cheek, or shook her hand. Many gave her gifts—but when would she use them? She heaved a blender in her arms, modelled a hand-knit sweater with her name in green yarn across the chest.

Many told her they'd said prayers for her, that they'd baked cakes for her, that they'd been at the bedsides of loved ones when they died, and they were certain there was something everlasting in it all. They offered comfort and companionship.

Hannah hugged them, one after the next after the next. They were her neighbours and her table tennis teammates, her library friends, her poolside companions. They were fellow members of the Small Machines Repair Club. She was overwhelmed by their tenderness and generosity.

Soon, though, she was happy to give herself up to lighter feelings.

"Let's get wasted," winked a friend, raising a flask in toast.

The space that had felt so big and so quiet all day was now full of people in smart shirts and smart shorts, in suits and dresses, plus the whole baseball team in their brand new, handstitched uniforms.

The captain of the Palm Meridian Pomodoros showed off the kit. It featured a logo of a determined-looking tomato, grasping a clock and leaping into the sky.

"Couldn't get these folks to practise for more than twenty-five minutes, so we leaned into it."

Bright voices filled up the bar, and the terrace was crowded now too, laughter piercing the warm air. The sound of popping corks and music drummed underneath it all.

The newlyweds from the library came in, triumphant, to raucous applause. Hannah stepped through the throngs to greet them and pour them the freshest champagne.

She passed a cluster of people discussing how to get out of a marital rut.

"Jen and I here, what *we* do is: if we haven't had sex in a month then we get naked and we both get into one pair of underpants. Now it has to be a big pair of underpants, but not *too* big, you see—and we step into the underpants, facing each other, and then we sort of wiggle around a bit, get the blood flowing, you know, some wiggling . . . "

"And that does the trick?"

"And that does the trick, I'd say, seven out of ten times."

Hannah's friends were like veteran cast members; special delegates who knew what needed to be done and did it. All around the bar, they helped, they soothed, they fielded questions from guests who did not know Hannah very well, but had come "for the drama."

"I heard her ex came back from the dead, and she's coming to perform tonight. A medley."

"No, I think it's her sister, and it's more of a showdown type of thing."

"Is she dying *at* the party?"

Nate dispelled these rumours with a smile, while Esme fetched plates
of food for everyone with limited mobility.

The Eileens made it their job to make sure everyone knew where the
fire exits were, the scooter parking, and the wine. Ricky stood by the terrace door, fawned over by guests who missed their grandsons and were
happy to divert their love to him. This day, of all days, he needed it.

Hannah was in high demand. A small, winking woman was making
advances—"I won't be your first, Hannah, but I can be your last"—and
Christine shooed her away.

"Have some ham. Have some ham." Christine slipped Hannah some
slices of prosciutto from the buffet, slapped her on the shoulder like a
boxer. "You okay?"

Hannah nodded her thanks, chewing on the prosciutto. She felt
giddy with the noise and the attention, found it surreal that all these people were here, that the party was actually happening. So far, it felt like
flying down the track of a steep rollercoaster—not altogether unpleasant,
but certainly intense.

Christine had spotted something across the room, and Hannah followed her friend's line of vision. It was Zoey—Nate's Zoey: she'd just arrived, grey hair shining, wearing a show-stopping deep purple suit with
silver rhinestone cuffs.

"God, that's a cool outfit," said Christine. Then her voice turned con-
spiratorial. "She's gonna ask Nate out tonight, you know. I can feel it."

Hannah thought so, too, but didn't want to jinx it.

"He hasn't spotted her yet. I'll go tell him she's here. I'll see you in a
bit," said Christine.

Hannah squeezed her friend's hand, and she was gone.

Hannah turned back to the tumult of the party. She'd hoped to stay
by Luke's side for a while, to introduce him to some of her other friends

and make sure he was settled in. But he wouldn't allow it—not on her big night—and insisted he was happy, he would mingle, he was fine. And he did indeed look fine—she spotted him now, listening excitedly as the captain of the baseball team described a recent grand slam. But Hannah's attention was pulled away by a new arrival.

"HONK HONK. SMALL BABY."

A ripple ran through the room, gaining in force. It was the kind of hysteria that could only be set off by one thing: a grandchild.

"TOOT TOOT. BABY BUS."

The baby was an instant celebrity, carried by her grandmother, Gwen, a woman who lived a few doors down from Hannah. Just shy of a year old, the baby was a natural performer. With one chubby hand she blew kisses to the passing crowd, like she was the Pope or the Beatles. In her other hand she clutched the string of a helium balloon.

"Is this for me, Sam?" Hannah asked, accepting the balloon and taking the baby onto her hip. "Has anyone ID'd you tonight, Sam?"

Sam nodded soberly, with her eyes closed.

More guests streamed towards Hannah, towards the bar and the buffet tables. Their words were overlapping, wired and bright.

"How's your film coming along? Is it *The Shrimp in the Blimp*?"

"No, *The Loom of Doom*."

"You spent *two hundred bucks* on a bug hotel?"

"The bugs are under a lot of stress, Maureen."

"Lesbians don't move on, darling, they *embed*. They *incorporate*."

Hannah passed the baby back to Gwen, and new guests took their turns greeting Hannah.

While she rolled between conversations, Hannah became aware of a topic popping up in circles all around her. She'd forgotten how quickly gossip got around.

"What time do you think the ex is coming?"

"Do you think they'll find they've grown apart?"

"I don't know Hannah very well, to be honest. But I heard what was going to happen tonight and I *had* to come see it for myself."

Hannah's face flashed hot. She suddenly wished she hadn't mentioned anything at the wedding reception. Feeling the sharp excitement of the guests all around her, she realised she'd brought everyone in on this private thing that should've been hers alone.

Passing through the party, swallowing a sinking feeling, Hannah spotted Luke by the door to the terrace. He was only half-listening to the captain of the baseball team at this point, one eye flitting back to Esme, who was welcoming guests at the door and matchmaking them as she went: "Hello! You're single? Do you like beekeeping?"

Luke stepped away from the baseball player and touched Esme on the arm, speaking urgently into her ear. But she simply waved him away.

Hannah felt a stab of anxiety, seeing this. Another mistake, she thought. She should've spoken to Esme before the party, should've asked what was up between her and Luke, before all these people arrived. It could've been sorted out, and she could've enjoyed herself without this question buzzing in the back of her mind. She made a mental note to deal with it as soon as she got the opportunity.

"Good night so far, Hannah?" a face loomed, friendly but startling—someone who lived a few doors down from her.

Hannah faltered, smiled.

"Yes! Fun. Intense."

As Hannah moved through the crowd, guests reached out to say hello, to trade kisses, condolences. Sliding past on Hannah's left was Quinn, wearing sunglasses to hide the rawness of her eyes. She was clenching her jaw and craning her neck over the throngs of people—but in the busyness, Hannah didn't see her.

The light outside had changed again, the sun casting an evening glow on everything. Hannah felt drawn to the terrace—to the fresh air and the vantage point it would give her.

Standing outside, she looked over the lawns and down the paths, especially the ones that came from the entrance gates. More guests were coming, crossing the resort and climbing to the bar.

The air was buzzing with voices, with heat and anticipation. Clips of conversation rose out of the party.

"Do you think heaven has a smell?"

"I've got half a gallon of holy water. Just in case we need it."

"It's all making me a bit uneasy, you know?"

17

LAKE HURON
2023

*I*t felt like a baptism, though hornier than most.

They left the stones of the beach behind and crashed into the water, the cold of it knocking the breath out of them and licking at their sunburnt skin. Hannah caught a glimpse of Sophie against the sky—a freckled back, the curve of a shoulder—and then ducked beneath the water. Its green glug was in her ears, down there with the guppies and the rocks slick with algae below.

The thick heat had made them crazy, the sun spooling down from the sky and liquefying everything. It evaporated all thoughts and left only feelings—the dizzy pull they felt towards one another.

"How are you *going* so fast?"

Hannah's laughing voice sputtered out of her throat, calling towards Sophie, whose Olympic body was already fifty yards ahead, arms cutting through the water.

They reached the breakwaters—huge boulders that shielded the shoreline from the slamming waves of storms—and scrabbled up, feet scraping on the hot stone.

Hannah's heart was racing from the cold and the effort of the swim. She collapsed next to Sophie, with an arm bent over her eyes to shield them from the sun. She looked up at Sophie—hair slick down her back, lips and nose and eyelashes dripping—and joy raced through her.

"Come here."

Hannah pulled Sophie down towards her, the two of them smiling wide as they kissed. Their bodies were scalded by the dry parts of the stones, and chilled by the water that sloshed up and spilled over their legs.

Eventually they sat up, knees to their chests, and looked back towards the shore. The lake sparkled madly in the sun, the head of a diamond dancing on the crest of every tiny wave. Their friends were small on the pebbled beach, moving around in their clumps on their towels. Their voices reached Hannah and Sophie faintly, with a delay.

To the left of their vision, the shoreline bent and disappeared into pines and scrub brush. To the right, it curved, meeting the harbour faraway at the centre of the small town. A pier extended out into the lake in the distance. A Canadian flag rippled on a flagpole, tiny from afar.

Behind them was the expanse of Lake Huron, so broad you couldn't see the other side. At its deepest point, this lake could submerge a sixty-storey building—some skyscraper that would spill out its Xerox machines and Ethernet cables and office chairs into the water.

On this side of the lake was Canada, and on the other the United States. This morning, and every morning, North America was deafeningly large.

Hannah and Sophie squinted back at the beach, where Esme, in her striped bathing suit, kicked her way down the beach like a showgirl, one sultry step at a time, towards her fiancé Theo. The sun gleamed off his broad chest as he grinned from a towel. Esme stepped right into his arms and he pulled her down onto him, the two of them a tangle of warmth and skin.

Theo was the only person they'd ever known who could keep up with Esme, really—his wit was as sharp as hers, his charm as generous, his search for fun as relentless.

Tomorrow, Esme and Theo would get married at the edge of a public park overlooking the lake. The marriage would last two years, and both would later remarry. But in many ways, they would do what they vowed, and love one another forever.

"He looks happy." Sophie nodded towards the beach, referring to Luke, not Theo. Luke sat in a cluster of their friends, wearing a pair of swimming trunks and sunglasses, a broad smile on his lips. He sipped a beer, looking relaxed, which was a rarity.

Lately, Luke had been drinking less caffeine, sleeping more. He'd been signing onto increasingly ambitious hikes with Sophie, days-long trips in the Laurentians of Quebec, where he did his best to keep up with her.

Hannah felt a swell of love watching Luke on the beach. She'd sometimes grown impatient with him in recent years, but on a glorious day like this, it was easier to remember what she loved about him. They worked well together, and they'd created something wonderful in their years of hard work. Without his belief in her abilities, and his passion for their company, they wouldn't have got anywhere at all.

There were other precious people who had believed in her from the start, too.

"Can you remind me to call my parents later?"

Sophie nodded and kissed Hannah's shoulder.

Hannah's parents were in Quebec City, touring the cobbled streets in their hiking boots with an audio tour in their ears—their first vacation in twenty years. They'd booked it after Hannah's dad was finally cleared of cancer, the relief of it making their family dizzy.

The day they'd received the news, they'd popped champagne at the top of her parents' yellow staircase, their cheers ringing up, and her dad dropping a glass from his shaking hands that smashed on the sidewalk below.

"Should we have sex out here?" asked Sophie now, running her knuckles up and down Hannah's waist.

"Are you flirting with me?" Hannah asked.

Sophie beamed, lazy with sun, and pulled Hannah towards her, the taste of the lake mixing in their mouths.

"No sex on sharp rocks."

"No sex on sharp rocks," Sophie nodded.

Hannah looked at Sophie, at her smiling eyes, at the faintest beginnings of fine lines peeking at the sides. The same ones Hannah had. They were both thirty-two.

Hannah ran her thumb over Sophie's knuckles, swished her toes in the waves.

Further down the beach from their group, towards the centre of town, a family was setting up a picnic, their umbrella rippling in the breeze. Twin toddlers stomped around their parents, wearing tiny wetsuits and tiny bucket hats, completing tasks with a baby solemnity.

One toddler wielded a plastic shovel and squatted to collect wet sand from the water's edge. Her twin brother put a flip-flop in his mouth like it was the most delicious thing.

The question rose to Hannah's mind as they watched quietly. She wavered, then spoke.

"Do you think we'd be good at it?"

Sophie grinned, looking away from the babies and back at Hannah. The breeze picked up strands of her hair and danced them around.

"I know we would be."

The waves sloshed in the gaps of the rocks and Hannah kissed Sophie. They made the swim back, and soon they stepped across the beach towards their friends, leaving dark marks on the stones from their dripping bodies.

Above the beach was a narrow road that hugged the shore. Across the road was the cottage that Esme and Theo had rented, half hidden by pines. It had white wooden slats that peeled in the sun, window screens to keep mosquitoes out, and a porch with thick wicker furniture. Other cottages sat either side, obscured by their own pines and leaning hedges.

Hungry from the heat, they all headed up there now, climbing the rocks away from the water. The road burnt their bare feet and they hurried onto the grass. They set up for lunch on the lawn, a long table laid with hamburger buns and potato salad, sweating bottles of beer. From there, they could see the breadth of the lake, still glittering. The screen door slapped, the barbecue hissed, and cicadas screeched on the wires above.

Hannah found a fresh towel and wrapped it around herself, feeling the tightness of sunburn coming on. She hugged Sophie from behind and wrapped her into the towel, too, smelling shampoo and algae in her wet hair.

Esme and Theo were working the barbecue, and Esme's laugh rose into the air. Her silk neckerchief and huge sunglasses looked glamorously out of place and entirely perfect in this tiny town. They flipped the hamburgers, and held each other, anticipation gathering for tomorrow.

There were about twenty of them altogether now, passing paper plates across the table.

"Are you Hannah?"

Hannah wiped ketchup from her fingers and shook the woman's hand. She had a broad, kind face, and looked to be in her late forties. She wore a pair of ripped jeans over a one-piece swimsuit, sunglasses pushed onto her head.

"I'm Mina. I'm a cousin of Theo's."

Mina said she'd long been following the news around Hannah's business, and so admired the work that she and Luke were doing. They chatted for a while, and Mina told Hannah about a friend of hers, in Florida, an older woman who'd worked in education all her life and who'd become restless in retirement. She had no children or family to leave her money to, and so had decided recently to buy a downtrodden plot of land that had once been a golf course, in a part of Florida where property values were plummeting, the market anticipating the climate disasters to come.

"I know she'd love to speak with you, even for ten minutes on the phone. She's looking to develop a retirement community down there. She's got the whole vision, but she needs to figure out the logistics. It's really, brutally hot and humid, and so she's got to make it liveable somehow, on a budget. I thought you might have some advice."

"I'd love to help. What's her name?" asked Hannah.

Mina smiled.

"Frankie."

The sun's rays bounced through the trees that ringed the property. The lawn was noisy now, conversation filling the air. It was so far from the quiet of this morning, when Hannah and Sophie and Luke had arrived via country roads, passing farms whose fields reached yellow to the horizon to find a strip of blue.

Groups of them sat on the lawn, on their towels, drinking and picking wet bits of grass from their feet. Hannah passed between them with a dry t-shirt and a pair of shorts in her hand. She spotted Sophie and Luke cross-legged by the base of the porch stairs, laughing and twirling long bits of grass in their fingers as they talked. Without stopping what she was saying, Sophie reached for Hannah's hand as she went past, and Hannah squeezed her fingers, blew a kiss and carried on.

The inside of the cottage was dark and cool. It was an adjustment from the heat, and it sharpened Hannah's senses, made everything feel stronger: the scent of leftover sunscreen, the coarseness and chill of her damp hair scattered through with sand.

The noise of the lawn was muffled here. Luke and Sophie's conversation was tinny with distance.

The little home was gritted with sand and furnished with knitted rugs and heavy wooden furniture, knick-knacks and framed photographs of the lake. On the kitchen table were the grocery bags they'd carried in that morning, the makings of a summer barbecue bought from the superstore, out where the country highway met the edges of farms.

Hannah spotted a discarded silk neckerchief on the counter and went to the base of the worn wooden stairs.

"Ez, is that you?"

A cackle, a toilet flushing from upstairs. "Han! One second!"

Esme came out of the bathroom and padded down the stairs, sweeping her hair up in a ponytail.

"How're you feeling about tomorrow?" Hannah asked.

Esme took a deep breath, let it out, giddy. "Good. Shitting myself. And good."

Hannah handed Esme her neckerchief. "I'll meet you back out there," she said, holding up her dry shorts and t-shirt and climbing the stairs. "I'm just getting changed."

Esme stepped out onto the porch and the humid air arrived lazy, cushioned, on her skin. She took a deep breath and tried to clear her head—the anticipation of tomorrow was proving overwhelming. A little walk would help.

Noting two empty towels at the base of the stairs, Esme crossed the lawn—past her chatting friends, past the table now littered with gouged hotdog buns and soiled paper cups.

The sun ducked behind a cloud for a moment, and the leaves overhead shivered in a gust of wind off the lake. Esme moved across the grass, past the hedge, to the road. The concrete was warm beneath her bare feet. Before she climbed the rocks up to the beach, she couldn't see the waves, but she could hear them, rushing and receding, on the shore below. She was drawn towards the water.

She climbed up through the scrub brush as the sun reappeared and heated her face uncomfortably.

Walking along the top of the rocks towards town, Esme saw bits of driftwood and the charred logs from campfires down below, tangles of kelp and parts of fish stinking between purple wildflowers. In the distance, families punctuated the sandy parts of the beach—tiny figures skipping rocks into the water.

Esme was lost in thought about the following morning, her head clouded with nerves and excitement, when she heard their voices.

"No—absolutely no."

"Soph—"

"Luke, I don't think you know what you're doing—"

"Soph, I'm serious. Consider it. *Please*. Just consider it."

Their tone instantly set Esme on edge. She stopped short, unable to tell where the voices were coming from, before spotting Luke and Sophie on the rocky shore below.

Luke was sitting, his elbows on his knees, and Sophie was standing up, turning away from him. He reached out a hand and swiped at her wrist, but she pulled away.

"Sophie, I love you. It's been *years* I've tried to hide it. You've got to believe how serious I am. It could work. *We* could work."

His voice was rasping, pleading.

Esme opened her mouth to speak, but she couldn't react fast enough. Her brain flashed uselessly and before she could figure out the right thing to do, Esme watched Sophie stride away. Luke hung his head between his knees, the scrub brush obscuring his expression.

Esme was frozen, heart pounding, only partly obscured by the weeds. Luke stood heavily, and Esme tried to move in time, but he turned and saw her on the rocks. Panic registered on his face. They regarded each other, the breeze pulling at their hair, and Luke seemed about to speak, but thought better of it. He turned in a hurry and continued along the beach, towards the town.

Esme rushed back towards her friends. Towards Hannah.

Hannah stepped out of the cottage, the screen door slapping behind her. The lawn was a happy mess, but amidst it all, there was no sign of Sophie.

Hannah wandered towards the water, savouring the smell of wild-flowers. She climbed the rocks, and the lake rose up before her: a silver, shimmering disc that fit perfectly against the horizon. Squinting down the shore towards town, Hannah couldn't see Esme coming down the road, dazed and looking for her.

Hannah's phone buzzed in her pocket. Her mom:

Can you talk now?

Hannah sat down, tufts of weeds scratching at her legs. She held the phone to her ear, its signal wavering far above.

As she waited for a connection, she noticed the piles of clouds that had gathered along the horizon. They were grey against the blue sky, like the hulk of a mountain. The same kind of comforting hulk as Mount Royal, that had watched over her most of her life—permanent, kind and right.

The phone rang, and Hannah spotted Sophie coming up the beach towards her, staggering on the stones, impatient to reach her.

Sophie had something to tell her, but she never would, because just then, the call connected:

"*Hannah.*"

Her mother's voice was shaking, far away.

"It was sudden, Hannah. The doctors didn't expect it. It happened quickly. He felt no pain."

18

FLORIDA
6 p.m.

*I*t was fitting that at 6 p.m., when the bar exceeded fire capacity, the resort looked like it was burning.

As the sun began to set, the sky was shot with hazy wisps of the brightest orange, red, purple and pink. The light flooded into Frankie's and set the urns above the bar ablaze with colour, their shine giving them a supernatural kind of life. Frankie herself winked from her painting on the wall, looking like she might step out from the frame, laughing, and crunch that pretzel stick between her teeth.

For twenty minutes, the lawns were psychedelic, the rows of golf carts glowing. The world was unreal and the effect was unsettling. Hannah felt she needed to reach out and touch the things around her—the sleeves of her friends' clothing, the glass and metal of the table, the feathers of the egrets who stepped nearby, hoping for buffet debris.

"You okay?" asked Christine quietly, sliding in next to Hannah at the large terrace table populated by their friends.

Hannah nodded, dazed, squeezing Christine's hand. But she couldn't shake her senses, couldn't escape the physicality of the things around her: the cigarette smoke drilling from nearby nostrils, lips wet with beer, cheeks and temples licked by age spots. Hannah felt the solid and the liquid parts of her body more keenly than she ever had before, imagined the squish of organs, the stretch of muscle, the hearty knock of bone.

They'd uncorked Christine's stately bottle of wine with a ceremonious cheer, and Nate had poured a small glass for everyone. Meanwhile, the Eileens had shuttled a vast amount of food from the buffet to the table, determined to overfeed their friends. Huge plates were now heaped with plant-based ribs and roast potatoes, with corn cobs and corn bread and green beans and steak. These overlapping scents filled Hannah's nose. She picked up a rib and licked it—an experiment—and discovered she was ravenously hungry.

Hannah ate, doing her best to simply listen to her friends' conversation. To forget about femurs, eyeballs, wrists, breasts and ears.

Luke had given up trying to get Esme's attention. He was seated across the table, eating a corn cob and speaking earnestly to Nate. He'd had a couple of drinks by then and had apparently gleaned enough from the day so far to know that the resort was something special.

"I really, really think you should consider franchising. This place does so much. It's got so much—*appeal*. There's big money in growing something like this."

Nate sipped his glass of beer and chimed in proudly, gesturing around at the resort. "Sure. I mean, imagine having a place like this in every state."

Luke's eyes flashed with energy, his younger self coming alive in his older body. "Let's talk about it, man. Let's talk about it."

Small Eileen returned to the table again, carrying a pot of stew the size of her torso. Ricky stood and helped her heave it onto the table.

"Eat up, kids. The night's not even begun."

As they ate, a flush of new guests arrived, including the road cycling team, fresh from a trip to the coast. They clomped onto the terrace in their Lycra and cleats, their grey hair plaited down their backs. They shook Hannah's hand, traded water bottles for vodka tonics, kept their sports sunglasses on to watch the technicolour sky.

A group played boules in the grass below, with glasses of champagne in their hands; their shouts rang up to the terrace.

Zoey passed by with a friend, laughing brightly, and Nate's head turned towards the sound, his posture straightening up. His eyes followed Zoey until she was out of sight.

"You haven't talked to her tonight?" asked tall Eileen quietly.

Nate frowned. "No, I have, I said hello. I said—*Nice suit*. Like this . . . " He held out his hands, his fingers splaying like a magician proclaiming: *Tada!* "I said: 'Nice—suit!'" He put his hand over his mouth, realising how badly he'd fumbled it.

Tall Eileen leant towards him, her voice full of love.

"Ask her out, you jerk."

Nate's eyes swam with fear.

"I'll shit myself."

"You won't."

Luke noticed that Christine had headed off to speak with a friend, and he took his chance to slide into the empty space beside Hannah.

"Hannah. Hannah, Hannah, Hannah."

She was grateful to see him and slipped her arm around his neck, pulled him closer.

"Luke. What's going on? What's all of this?" She waved her hand around at the people on the terrace. She was laughing while also looking like she might cry.

"You threw a party, Han," he said.

She took her arm off him and slapped him on the leg. "I'm glad you're here," she said.

Hannah had remembered Luke's cake and had fetched it from the fridge behind the bar. She'd cut it into slices for their friends and placed the pieces on plates around the table—thick, fluffy squares with their grey, sugary sludge.

"Hannah . . . " Now Luke picked up a fork from the table and thumbed it nervously, searching for the right words. "Han, I'm really sorry. For everything. For everything I've ever done to you."

Hannah's face tightened, confused. "What are you talking about?"

"Han, I've been horrible, sometimes. I haven't—"

But Hannah put her hand on his arm, firmly. "Luke, please, respectfully—just shut up. Let's enjoy tonight. I already know you're an idiot. But you're really, seriously, one of the best people I know."

Luke sucked in a breath, ready to say something more. He stopped himself, put the fork down on the table.

"I just—I really care about you, Hannah."

Esme, who'd brought over drinks for her and tall Eileen, overheard this and rolled her eyes. "Jesus," she muttered under her breath, putting Eileen's drink down beside her and walking away. Hannah was about to call after her, to finally deal with this, when someone spoke beside her.

"Guys, is it just me, or is this party bigger than expected?"

This was small Eileen, who'd stopped spooning meatballs from a serving plate to marvel at the number of people packing into the space.

And she was right: a hundred residents had RSVP'd—but this seemed like more than that. There were lines at the bar, and the terrace was packed, the guests kissed with that day's sun.

Nate stood, wiping his mouth with a napkin, looking warily into the bar. "I'll check on the staffing," he said, and headed off.

Small Eileen followed him, switching into action mode: "I'll check the stockroom for more drinks!"

Hannah looked around at the crowds. She recognised most of them as her friends, or friends of friends, but there were many less familiar faces. She got the sense that almost the entire resort was here, and that a feeling of curiosity was hanging in the air. Was it paranoia? No—even brand-new residents, near-strangers, were discreetly pointing her out, nodding in her direction. The gossip of her "long-lost love" must have attracted them.

Knowing Sophie could arrive at any moment, Hannah kept brushing a hand over the flyaway hairs around her face, kept running a finger over the corners of her mouth in case of a stubborn crumb of food. She scanned through the party, hoping her eyes would land on Sophie's features, on Sophie coming up the slope. Any second now—she could be just there—

"Hannah!"

There she was: dark hair, bright eyes, broad smile. Looking young—how so young? Looking twenty-seven, like the day they'd met. Arms wide to wrap around Hannah.

Hannah's brain caught up.

"Marina."

Disappointment spread through Hannah's body, but was quickly tempered with affection. She hugged Marina tight, comforted by the earthy scent of her perfume, the easy strength of her younger arms.

"Marina, you promise you'll look after Ricky for me?"

Marina nodded. "I promise, Han."

Ricky had told Hannah about Marina in one of his first weeks at the resort. His mouth had smiled around his words as he described how they'd first met, working together at a flood supplies store south of Orlando. Marina had made tarps and sandbags exciting, had got weary and heartbroken customers smiling. She'd brought an impossible, uplifting beauty to a cramped space full of suction hoses and mould remover.

Hannah recalled her first instinct: envy. This young man, with his fresh, unencumbered love. In time, the envy had been tempered by gratitude. How good—how right!—that these two wonderful people had been given a chance at each other. Here, at what often felt like the end of the world.

Now Marina stepped back, taking in Hannah's suit, her shining hair.

"You look fucking incredible, Han."

Hannah laughed and returned the compliment. Marina was a pillar of youth in her flowery summer dress, her tanned arms shining, a bracelet glinting on her wrist. She attracted party guests like infatuated moths to a flame.

"Can I get you a drink, Marina?"

"Marina, I brought you some ribs."

"Here, have my seat."

Marina, laughing: "Ash, *sit down*, you just had knee surgery. How'd it go, by the way?"

As a show of respect for Hannah, Marina had cancelled the next couple of weeks of craft classes. Hannah had insisted they should go ahead, but Marina had waved the idea away.

"I'll be a wreck," she said. "And anyways, macramé can wait."

Now, Hannah made space for Marina beside her.

"I brought some things, Han. They're only little."

Marina pulled a wrapped box from her bag and placed it on the table in front of Hannah. Hannah ran her hands along the patterned paper, then unwrapped and opened the box carefully. Inside was a stack of identical photographs in hand-made frames: the whole group of them, last summer, lying in a laughing pile in the grass.

"One photo for each of us," said Marina, as Hannah lifted the top frame out and ran her eyes over the picture. On a picnic blanket, surrounded by picnic fixings, Hannah's head was back, eyes squeezed shut with laughter. Nate and Esme's legs were kicked up in the air, Ricky waving a tub of hummus, Christine punctuating a sentence with a whole baguette. Marina was keeled over on her side, hair splayed across the lawn, while the Eileens did charades in front of them, attempting to convey *spork* through crying laughter.

Hannah's throat was tight again with tears.

"Marina, they're perfect. Thank you."

But their quiet moment couldn't last very long.

"I'll see you in a bit, Han. Just gonna say hi to Ricky, and check if Nate needs any help."

Marina stood and started stacking some of the dirty plates from the table, while they all shooed her away, but she insisted. As she headed inside, one of the bolder residents, Maya, went straight for it:

"Marina, will you marry me?"

Marina's face lit up. "Maya, I'll have to speak with Ricky about it, but if you ask me, that sounds great. I'll meet you in the library in an hour!"

Now Hannah and the others finished eating, passing napkins over one another's heads and checking their teeth for bits. Back inside the bar, Hannah manoeuvred through the crowd, looking for Esme, or Ricky, or both. She wanted to speak to Esme, to understand what was going on with her. She had enough on her mind already, waiting for Sophie's arrival. She wanted whatever was happening between Esme and Luke to be resolved.

But Hannah spotted Ricky first.

"Rick!"

Ricky was holding a chihuahua whose collar read *Kevin*. Kevin's owner was rummaging through her purse for a tube of lipstick. She found it and applied it with bravado, smacking her lips, and Ricky passed the dog back with a half-hearted smile.

"Han. You okay?"

Hannah nodded, but her head was buzzing suddenly. She felt flushed.

"Marina's here," she said, though that wasn't what she'd wanted to say. She was stalling.

Ricky gave another tired smile. "I know. She just came by."

Hannah squeezed her eyes shut, opened them quickly. She only had to ask the question. "Is there any news about the mail?"

Ricky's faced was pained. He shook his head, and Hannah's heart sank.

"That's okay. Thanks Rick."

It was time to accept it, she knew: she wouldn't hear from Sophie by mail—either she hadn't replied at all, or her reply had been lost in transit. There was still no signal in the area, either—nothing for close to twenty-four hours now.

"Rick, do you mind keeping an eye on the check-in desk a bit to-night? Just for any unexpected, you know . . . arrivals?"

"Of course, Han. I'll be checking all night."

"Thanks. I'll keep an eye on it too."

It occurred to Hannah that Ricky might bring up his plans again now, might ask if she'd thought at all about the contents of the binder from earlier. She hesitated, lingering. Strangely, she found herself hoping he would say something, that he'd open up this conversation again. But he'd already turned away.

"HANNAH!"

Luke's voice came like a roar from behind her. Startled, she spun around. His eyes were wild and he took her hands. "Sophie!"

Hannah's pulse tripled in speed. "What?" She frantically cast her eyes around at the teeming party. "Where is she?"

"What? I don't know, Han . . . "

Luke's face was bewildered. Hannah faltered, then her heartbeat drummed slower, duller.

"I don't know," he repeated.

Hannah settled back onto her heels, and the room returned to her. She'd misunderstood. "You fucking scared me, Luke—I thought you meant she was here. I thought . . . "

Luke's face was close in front of her, his eyes stormy with something—what was it? Pain? Confusion?

His voice was quiet when he spoke again. Fragile.

"I overheard someone talking about it, just now. You didn't tell me you'd invited her. I didn't know—I didn't realise that . . . "

His eyes were roving over Hannah's face, trying to understand.

She sighed, shook her head. "Maybe it's stupid. I haven't seen her in, like, forty-something years. But I got her address from a friend of a friend of a friend. It took me a couple of weeks. I figured—well, fuck it. I'm *dying*, Luke. Why not try?"

Luke looked past Hannah, some inscrutable calculation taking place in his mind.

Hannah continued. "Anyways, I know the invite got delivered, but I never got a reply. But I just know in my bones that she'll come, you know?"

There was a long pause, and Hannah realised she was waiting for reassurance.

Luke was looking straight in Hannah's eyes now. He touched his throat, coughed roughly.

"Sorry. Excuse me. Just need some water . . . "

He ducked away to the bar.

"Hannah?"

Esme had appeared behind Hannah, and Hannah turned.

"Ez."

"You okay?" asked Esme, holding her friend by the elbow.

Hannah nodded, though this answer wasn't strictly true. She'd deal with one thing at a time. First, Esme.

Hannah licked her lips, which were suddenly dry.

"Ez. Talk to me."

Esme frowned. "About what, babe?"

"Ez, you *know* what I'm talking about. You've been completely bizarre to Luke all night. Maybe it's none of my business. But I don't want you guys to be in a bad place, especially when I'm not here any more. And to be honest, I don't really get it—you haven't seen each other in forever. Did something happen in Montreal, or . . . ?"

Esme looked away, and opened her mouth to speak. Her words took a long time coming.

"Hannah, it's nothing. Seriously. Luke and I had some prickly moments when we were younger. He can be a big personality, and I guess so can I. It's behind us now." Esme adjusted the bracelets on her wrist, and looked back at Hannah. "I only want you to be happy."

Hannah searched her friend's eyes for the truth, sensing she was leaving something out. Was it worth pushing? Did she need to know everything on her very last day?

A shout cut through the crowd, sharp and firm, and they both turned:

"Esme! It's your time with the mic!"

This was Tina, the resident sound engineer. She wore a black t-shirt, black jeans and an oversized headset. She was the backbone of every resort event.

Esme composed herself quickly, turned back to Hannah. "Do you want me to wait? For Sophie?"

Hannah shook her head and forced a smile. "When she turns up, I'll let you know."

Esme nodded; hesitated. "Han, I just want you to have a good time tonight. I want you to *laugh*."

Hannah pushed her smile wider. "I'll be laughing, Ez."

Esme squeezed her hand and disappeared into the crowd.

The moment Esme was gone, a voice in Hannah's ear made her jump.

"*I* know why she doesn't like him," Quinn said, her words thick with bitter feeling. She sipped her drink, shaking the ice in the glass. Hannah's face was tight, untrusting.

Quinn leaned close. "Esme told me a lot of things while we were together. Things she's never even told you. Love does that—it makes you tell secrets."

Quinn smiled meanly. Hannah suddenly felt cold, uneasy. She wanted to tell Quinn to stop talking, to just leave her alone, but a morbid curiosity stopped her.

"Look," Quinn continued, "all I'm saying is, I know she seems like a really great friend. But she doesn't tell you everything."

"Quinn . . . "

But Quinn just swirled away, looking smug. Hannah didn't have time to interrogate any of this, though—the electrical buzz of an amplifier cut above the party, followed by the knocking sound of a microphone being plugged in.

"Hello, everyone. Check, check. Barracuda."

Esme's voice came loud over the bar, even though she was out of view. She was holding the microphone close to her mouth and her voice was breathy, full of spit.

"God, who do I think I am, Mariah Carey? Tina, is the volume okay?"

The crowd mainly ignored this, caught up in their own conversations. Hannah craned her neck to see Esme, but the room was too full.

Esme's voice again:

"Tina, you ever heard the one about the fart who had a really good office job?"

A faraway shout, unintelligible, across the room.

"Excuse me, Riz, are you heckling me during a fart joke?"

Hannah ran her hands through her hair and took a deep, shaky breath. She decided to leave the issue of Quinn alone for now. She'd ask Esme about it later, would sit her down and sort everything out. It was only 7 p.m.

Finally, Hannah spotted the top of Esme's head at the far end of the dancefloor, by the small stage that had been set up there. Christine reached Hannah in the crowd, touching her elbow, with Ricky and Marina beside her. Together, the four of them began to snake their way through the chatting bodies.

"Should we do karaoke? Should I start? Okay, you convinced me."

A long pause, then:

"*Hoooome on the raaaange . . .*"

Esme sang like a Southern belle, drawing out her vowels.

"Okay, no more messing around. I'm going up there!"

Esme stepped up onto the stage, hiking the hem of her dress as she went. You could hear the slightly hysterical energy in her voice—happy, nervous and sad.

"Hello, everyone," said Esme, as sultrily as she could manage.

"Hello, Esme!" shouted Christine, Ricky and Marina, plus a couple of tipsy party guests nearest the stage. For the most part, there was no response. The room buzzed on with music and conversations.

Esme looked to Tina the sound engineer: her foil. "Tina, I'm starting to think they don't like me."

She tried a different tack, in a slightly louder voice. "Everyone, this is just to announce that the frozen yoghurt machine in the food hall is being permanently removed, due to widespread misuse. You're a bunch of animals, basically. Also, the golf cart with licence plate LB-342 is currently on fire and will be pushed into the swimming pool, as per safety procedures. The final announcement is that this month's birdhouse fundraiser is cancelled, due to a shortage of modelling glue."

Gasps. The crowd was immediately quiet, startled whispers floating around.

Esme lifted her hands—guilty. "All right, obviously none of that was true. But now that I have your attention . . . "

Hannah spotted the Eileens pulling up to the front of the stage, across the room. They winked and waved. Nearby were Luke and Nate. Luke was finishing a drink, his head tilted back to catch the last drops from the glass. Nate was glancing around the crowd to make sure everyone was looked after, then sneaking a look at Zoey on the opposite side of the bar.

Now the noise had died down, Hannah was able to overhear the whispers of those nearby.

"Do you think they're announcing the big love thing now? Is she gonna run through a banner, like a football game?"

"That's so unsafe."

"Do you think they'll kiss? I'd kiss, personally, in that situation."

"I heard the woman hasn't shown up yet. Imagine getting stood up on the last night of your life."

"What was Esme saying earlier, about farty business people?"

Hannah tuned them out, looked up at Esme, who was holding the microphone close to her nose.

"Thank you, everyone. Now, I'll let you all get back to the party very soon, but if you'll humour me for a couple of minutes, I have a few things to say about my good friend Hannah."

Esme looked down to Hannah, and everyone cheered. Hannah felt her face go hot, feeling shy suddenly.

Esme may have looked calm, but her insides were quavering madly. She'd planned this speech with love for weeks, but now she felt on the verge of breaking down. She breathed deeply, put on a smile.

"Now, I know most of us at this party live here, in Florida. And here, everything is either burning or melting or being swept away in a hurricane. And even in the storms, the rain is warm now, somehow. But Hannah was born in a very cold place, and so was I. And when I first met her, we were there, in the snow and the ice, in thirty below. And that was normal. In fact, that was great."

Esme's eyes were wet as she continued.

"There isn't such thing as a *season* here in Florida, really, not any more. But where Hannah and I come from, in Canada, a season is—well, a season is a holy thing. And when I got thinking about Hannah, and the things she's loved the most in this life, I thought about *myself*, obviously."

She paused for a laugh.

"And the friends and the family who have loved her back. But one thing I couldn't forget was a *season*. Let me explain."

Hannah held tight to Christine and Ricky's hands, feeling her face burn with emotion, feeling the whole of the bar's eyes on her. The moment was surreal and sharply real, simultaneously.

"One Saturday morning when Hannah was nineteen and I was twenty, we woke up in a pool of sunshine in my bedroom—don't ask why, I won't tell you. It was March, and the streets were still covered with snow. But the sun was the brightest it had been since November. From bed, you could hear icicles cracking off the street lamps. Water was rushing down everyone's drain pipes and into the street. It was winter. But suddenly it was spring."

Esme looked to Hannah, laughing.

"Friends, you would have thought the girl had won the lottery. The simple fact of that season—the change in the air, the yellow quality of the light, that tiniest scent of soil cutting through the snow—Hannah was high with it. She pulled me out of bed—again, won't say what was going on there—and she took me out into the morning, in our pyjamas and our boots, and we stomped through the neighbourhood until I was high with it, too. And it wasn't just then."

Esme paused, took a breath.

"When spring turned to summer, Hannah kept her window open every night, even when bugs and squirrels were getting in. She said she wanted to smell the change in the air, that kind of sweetness that comes with summer, especially at night. She wanted to hear the trees swishing around while everyone slept. Those trees that were dressed in all their leaves, out in the street lights, because it was almost summer.

"In autumn it was the same. Hannah went absolutely crazy for it, riding her bike everywhere. And to be fair, Montreal in the fall really hits you in the gut. The whole mountain is orange, and the city is full of university kids, and everyone is rained on and crispy and the street is coated in matted leaves, and everything feels new, while it's dying."

Esme was crying openly now, and she wiped her tears with her thumb.

"And then, the best of them: winter. You have to understand that Hannah's dad, who's here tonight, as well as her mom"—Esme gestured to the urns at the back of the bar, and everyone cheered—"that Hannah's dad drove a Zamboni for a living. Our whole city was covered in snowbanks taller than cars for what felt like half the year. And the nights were like living inside a glacier. The smell of ice, to Hannah—Hannah, if you don't mind me saying—is home."

Hannah was crying too now, and laughing. Christine took her arm, threaded their fingers together.

"Even in winter, though, most people like to be warm—including Hannah. But it's not always that easy. And so when Hannah realised that the technology just wasn't cutting it, that the whole system needed a fix, she was so fucking smart, she invented *an entirely new way of doing things*. Don't ask me how it works—I don't get it, but I don't have to. She made it so that anyone, any average person, could be warm or cool, and never have to worry."

Sniffles rippled through the crowd. Esme bit her lip.

"What I'm *trying* to say, with all of this, is that Hannah is one of the most grateful people I know. Someone who, all her life, has been smart enough to be thankful for the changing of seasons. And I speak for a couple dozen of us in this room when I say that Hannah has, in a couple dozen different, wonderful ways, helped us through the winters of our lives."

The crowd murmured, moved.

"I know, good metaphor, right?"

Hannah looked to the Eileens, who were watching her and holding one another. Nate was smiling, and Luke was standing beside him, his face unreadable.

"Hannah has always been there for us. I know we all have stories. Mick, I heard she helped you out of a washing machine just the other day."

"Damn right!" Mick called out from the crowd.

"Eileen and Eileen. She stayed up with you two all night, two nights in a row, when your boy was in the hospital in Seattle after surgery, and you couldn't get a flight out because of the storms."

The Eileens tried to call out, but their voices broke, and so they just cheered, with tears in their eyes.

"She built a humidifier for me from scratch last year when I had a sinus infection," said Esme.

Hannah called out: "It set on fire, Ez!"

Esme shrugged. "It worked before that!" she replied. "What I mean to say is: Hannah has always been here for us. And tonight, we're here for Hannah."

By now, most of the light had left the sky, but across the resort the lampposts and spotlights switched on, illuminating the palm trees and the swimming pool, the curves of the paths. The night-time smelled of earth and finger food.

Inside, a charged air.

"I'd like to raise a toast to Hannah," said Esme.

A whisper in the crowd:

"Is this where the girl will come in, do you think?"

"I'm sure they've practised the choreo."

In the grip of it, Hannah looked around at the faces of her closest friends, the faces of friends who were just friends, the faces of people she didn't know but who she loved, now, with the same force as all the rest. Why not? There was nothing to lose.

Esme lifted her glass.

"To Hannah!"

For a moment it was deafening: everyone clapping and cheering. Esme came down from the stage, and Hannah wrapped her arms around her. Life was full, impossibly full.

How had she chosen what she'd chosen? How could she fathom leaving these people—leaving her body—behind?

Hannah stepped away from the crowd, friends clapping her on the back as the music started up again. She kept a smile on her face as best as she could, but wisps of doubt flicked up her throat. A low, quiet terror settled over her. As politely as she could, she squeezed through the crowds, tensing when she spotted Quinn slinking around the edge of the room. But she didn't spot Luke, who was heading out the back in a hurry.

Hannah was grateful for the fresh air of the terrace once she reached it. She breathed in and moved away from the bar, towards the trees, where she could take a private moment. A group of latecomers was heading towards the party, and Hannah couldn't help but check their faces, their gaits, from afar. Couldn't help but hope for Sophie in every moment, every movement.

What would Hannah do, if she saw her there? Taking the path to the bar, fixing her hair, smoothing her dress, her familiar face softened with wrinkles. Her smile would be unmistakable—nervous, maybe—as she searched the terrace for Hannah's face.

Would they race into each other's arms? Would they falter?

Would it feel like being made new?

Hannah watched the last of the light fade from the sky, realising it was the last sunset she'd ever see.

19

MONTREAL
2024

The sperm was in the house.

They spoke about it as if it were a president. Like it had arrived in a parade of armoured vehicles, flags rippling on the hood, security personnel jogging alongside. They whispered about it—*Oh my god! Have you seen?*

The future was unfolding, they felt, as the vial reached room temperature on the kitchen counter. The future was unfolding, they knew, as they took the vial in their shaking hands into the bedroom—hearts sizzling, bodies fumbling.

The conception was immaculate, in a way. The donor absent, some strapping man in the world somewhere, probably grocery shopping or driving, shampooing, maybe, while Hannah and Sophie became very sweaty—how so sweaty?—while being very careful—don't spill—gross—no, not gross, *miraculous*—and pulled the future into view.

Afterwards, Sophie lay with her legs up against the wall. Hannah lay beside her, her legs on the wall, too, just because, and they imagined what they'd done. What they hoped they'd done.

Their child would be a tap dancer. A pilot. A prize-winning gardener, grinning beside a pumpkin the size of a car. Their child would co-found a disco revival band, the music sounding ancient and important to their ears. Their child would go to space, if they wanted to. They'd frequent water-parks. They'd live quietly, or they wouldn't shut up. They'd feel pain—wouldn't we all—but the pain would be tempered with other things.

Hannah, already lying down, was knocked back by the strength of this feeling. By the love she already had for this child who did not yet exist. She held Sophie's hand and they watched the ceiling, their skin coursing with heat, their love generating energy. Hannah's body was ready to watch and shield and keep safe.

Since losing her dad, Hannah's understanding of death and of life had changed dramatically. She wasn't certain any more, as she'd once been in a Tokyo taxicab, that when we died we simply fell asleep, waking as beams of light overlooking a city. She wasn't certain that her dad was in the things around them, either—that her dad was a lamp, or a tulip, or a clod of dirt.

But she was certain of love. She was certain that, in the calculus of things, creating a life and filling it with love must mean something.

For now, they just had to wait, though. It was March, and Montreal was thawing, the sun warming the crusts of the snowbanks. There was the sound of rain on the streets and the chill that still came in at night.

Hannah and Sophie followed every rule, prepared every meal stuffed with every vitamin and mineral rumoured to ensure success. Hannah moved things around their apartment, fixing, adjusting, coordinating. They walked over to Hannah's parents' apartment, now emptier without her dad, and picked up her mom for lunch. The three of them walked to the park, ordered sandwiches, sat at a table flanked with birds, the slightest suggestion of buds in the trees. The warmth was coming back to Hannah's mother's face, Sophie's voice rising with the leaves.

Luke hadn't been around as much lately—he was on a new self-im-provement kick, he'd told Hannah over the phone. He was taking medi-tation classes, was learning Mandarin and Spanish simultaneously. That sounded like a nervous breakdown, she told him. He only laughed, loud and long.

Sophie hadn't seen much of Luke either—she wanted to focus on Hannah, and on starting a family, she said. She didn't have as much time for gym dates or global triathlons. And so they kept their life small.

At night, Hannah and Sophie watched movies in the warm dark of the apartment, layering their nest with socks and blankets. They watched Sophie's stomach as if it might start to speak, their hearts fluttering. They looked at the actors on the screen, but their heads were full of other things.

On the tenth day, there was peeing to be done. Hannah, feeling restless, woke up at dawn and slipped out the door. The supermarket wasn't open yet, so she crunched through the slush and the weirdly warm air to the depanneur on the corner, the one with the cat who seemed to know what you were thinking, and what would become of you.

Water would do just fine, of course—pee is pee, it all becomes pee— but Hannah wanted Sophie to have options. She wanted Sophie to have everything she could've ever dreamed. And so she bought a bottle of every juice they had in stock, and milk, sparkling water and a ready-made smoothie. She paid, the owner sleepy, the cat wide awake. Its paw swiped at the beef jerky—salty, delicious, auspicious.

Hannah carried her liquid bounty home, climbed the stairs with their curling details, let herself into their warm home. She found Sophie still sleeping, her arms splayed, her hair shining on the pillow. The slap of pucks in the alley below. A sweet spring smell coming through the window.

Later, the peeing. Then, the waiting. The future shuddering, loading up.

They sipped six different juices, tropical flavours exploding on their tongues. But in their nervousness, they tasted nothing, their minds roving through the almost-there.

Is it? Are you?

I am.

20

FLORIDA
10 p.m.

*B*ehind the bar was a liquid bounty, and the party guests were having their fill: espresso martinis raced through their veins and tequila soured their lips. For an extra thrill: smelling salts pilfered from the medical kiosk.

The space was deafening, the bar overcrowded. For now, at least, things remained under control.

Hannah had just left Marina and the Eileens in conversation on the terrace, and was moving through the crowds, on the lookout for Luke. She hadn't spotted him in more than half an hour, and wanted to make sure he was doing okay. In the increasing frenzy of the night, she felt drawn towards the person she'd known the longest.

As she accepted hugs and handshakes from the people she passed, Hannah kept her eyes trained on the sea of faces around her. Though she was looking for Luke, she was also waiting for that other glimmer of recognition—for Sophie's face to appear before her eyes.

Now, the mic squealed over everything. It was Tina, the sound engineer, with her headphones around her neck.

"Everyone, we have a few housekeeping items to address before the evening continues. Just a reminder to please take any pills that you would normally take at this time, as many of you would normally be heading to sleep at this hour. Also, we have a drunk person who has found her way to this chair"—Tina pointed politely to a woman who was happily slumped in a chair and waving to the crowd—"she says she's someone's wife. If this is your wife, could you please come collect her."

"I'M SO SORRY TO INTERRUPT! BUT I HAVE SOMETHING I NEED TO SAY!"

There was a scuffle of movement at the side of the room, and then Nate stepped out of the crowd, looking pale and bewildered. He mounted the stage and asked for the mic from Tina, who handed it to him.

Nate wasn't the type to ask for attention, so everyone knew something was up. Murmurs moved through the room, and tipsy party guests called out predictions.

"Nate's gonna say: *free buffet!*"

"Nate's going to sing us a beautiful lullaby."

Nate frowned, confused, doing his best to steady his shaking hands.

"The buffet is already free, Carol," he said softly, then urged himself to focus.

The room had quietened down by now, everyone watching to see what was going on. Nate spotted the faces of his friends—Christine's expression full of hope, Hannah's slightly preoccupied.

Nate raised the mic to his lips, and his voice rang out across the room.

"I'm really sorry, everyone. I'll keep this brief. I just—I didn't have the guts to say this a few hours ago. But now I've clocked off my bar shift and I've had three martinis. And a bit of someone's heart medication I think, to be honest. It was an accident . . . "

"Was it a green pill stuffed in a mini quiche?" someone shouted from the crowd.

Nate nodded. "Yeah!"

"It's magnesium! Sorry—you'll be fine!"

Nate resumed his focus, gathered his breath. "I just wanted to tell Zoey—wait, where's Zoey?"

Excited voices raced through the bar, and finally they found her.

"*Here! She's here!*" they shouted, and a space opened up in the crowd around Zoey. A confused smile danced across her lips.

Nate nodded at Zoey's outfit. "It's a nice suit."

"We love you, Nate!" said a loose, drunk voice, and others joined in, and Nate smiled, waved the attention away.

In the silence that resumed, one whispering voice: "Here's the lullaby, I think."

Nate let out a shaky breath.

"Zoey, I can't stop thinking about you. To be perfectly honest, speaking to you is the best part of my day. Every day. And if you'll forgive me for taking so long to ask you, I'd love to take you to dinner. This week. Or next. It's—I mean, either are good."

Gasps and claps ran through the room, whistling and excited laughter. The bar turned to Zoey to see her response.

She was beaming, blushing. She threw her hands up. "Yes! Of course it's yes."

The bar broke out in cheers as Nate stumbled down off the stage towards her. The two of them were quickly lost in the throng, and the music and the chatter started up again.

The excitement of Nate and Zoey had distracted Hannah for a few minutes. But once things went back to normal, and the noise of the bar picked up, a spark of anxiety made itself known.

Where was Luke? And where was Sophie? Hannah was out of step with the silly, electric atmosphere. That flicker of fear had returned, an unsettled trembling in her chest.

Some voice of reason in the back of her mind was telling her to find somewhere, away from everyone, to sit herself down and properly admit to herself that Sophie might not come—that at this point in the night, the chances were increasingly slim. The noise of the room made it hard to hear this voice clearly, though, and every few moments she was interrupted by well-meaning guests, for hellos and condolences.

Hannah picked a direction and moved through the crowd.

"Hannah!"

Hannah turned—Sophie? But it was Christine, reaching for her. "Chris."

Her friend's eyes were stormy in a way Hannah had never seen them. Christine's energy stirred the nerves already swirling inside Hannah, made her feel loopy, lightheaded.

"Can you *believe* Nate?" Christine asked. "I wanted to *kiss* him. I'm so fucking proud. Did you know he was going to do that?" Christine didn't wait for an answer. She tugged at the rings on her fingers apprehensively, the smile draining from her face. She leaned in close to Hannah.

"Something's happened," she said quickly. "I don't mean Nate and Zoey. Something else."

Hannah waited, dazed. "Chris—what are you talking about?"

"Someone's here. Rory. They're new—Esme told me. Hannah, they're . . . "

Christine searched for the words, her eyes racing around Hannah's face.

"Hannah, they're *so fucking* hot. *Look* . . . "

And Christine turned and pointed out into the crowd with a sense of emergency. The two of them paused, and they looked, but Hannah's brain was frazzled. Her voice was raw.

"Chris, I'll be honest, there are a lot of things going on in my line of vision right now." In fact, there was a woman mounting a buffet table, and a throuple trying to drink from one glass of wine.

"I need you to hold my hand on this one," said Hannah.

Christine nodded. Being discreet, she pointed her pinky finger towards Rory, a tall butch with a calm demeanour and a fiery grin. Their silk shirt was unbuttoned to the sternum, gleaming grey mullet catching the light. They were holding a beer and standing in a particularly rowdy conversation. They were—it was impossible to deny—so fucking hot.

"They're perfect, Chris. Go for it."

But Christine had frozen. Hannah paused. She looked Christine in the eyes—those eyes that had seen the inside of the Oval Office, and tanks rolling into war zones, whole cities swept away in floods. Finally, Hannah shook her head. "Chris. No. You've got to be kidding me."

Christine opened her mouth, closed it.

"No, no, no, no. You can't stand in front of me looking like *this*"— Hannah waved her hands up and down Christine's body, from her tall heels to her immaculate face—"and tell me—*me!* An invalid on death row!—that you're afraid to go over there and speak to that person who looks honestly very nice."

Rory looked over just then, with a shy but burning look in their eye, and gave Christine the slightest nod. Then they turned back to the conversation and sipped their beer.

Christine was frozen again. Hannah took her hands.

"Chris, I'm gonna die tomorrow. It's too late for me for a lot of things, but it isn't too late for you. My final wish is that you walk up to Rory and ask if they'd be interested in getting a drink from the bar and then riding each other like ponies."

Christine breathed deeply. She shook her head. "You're so right. You're so right. I'll go."

"Go," said Hannah.

"Okay, but I have to pee first," said Christine and she hurried away.

As soon as Christine went, Hannah deflated, that spark of anxiety still present in her chest. She regretted not asking Christine if she'd seen Luke. Hannah considered moving through the crowd towards the toilets to follow her, but the task of pressing through the heat and the bodies felt suddenly too much.

All the action with Nate and Zoey, and then with Christine, should have been exciting, but it only left Hannah unsettled, aware of how much life was still going on, and how much there was to be lost. Everyone around her was loosening up, their moods lightening further with the music and the alcohol. But Hannah only grew tighter, her thoughts darkening.

Hannah felt in her suit pocket for Ricky's drawing, pressed her fingers on it now, taking comfort in its promise.

She'd been so confident about her choice since she'd made it three months before. But Ricky had sown a seed of doubt earlier this evening, and it expanded now. As the night wore on, the reality of tomorrow morning was crystallising before her, taking a solid, terrifying form. It was like she'd been scheduled to go on a trip—a horrible, painful trip—and someone had said she could cancel it, that she didn't have to go.

The temptation to stay, to be cared for by Ricky and her other friends, was overwhelming. But she knew it wasn't that simple. She wasn't thinking clearly. And there was so little time left.

Hannah's pulse was speeding up uncomfortably. She clenched her jaw and set a task: find Luke and go somewhere quiet. They could go to a spot away from the lights and the noise. They could pretend they were kids again, could have a gentle few hours in the crafting clubhouse, make something with cardboard and glue, just like they used to. They could drink hot chocolate, and bring her parents' urns to have beside them. If she chose to, Hannah could play with pipe cleaners for the remaining hours of her life.

She felt suddenly that she might cry.

"You're beautiful, Hannah!" someone shouted now, pointing up at the enormous screen that hung above them all—a parade of images had begun, showing Hannah at nearly every year of her life. Some of her friends had prepared the slideshow, and Hannah spotted them now, below the screen in a row—Esme and the Eileens catching her eye, grinning, pointing up.

There was Hannah, on the screen, at six, in an orange snowsuit, holding a tiny snow shovel above her head like a barbell. Her dad shovelled beside her, his laughing face blurred at the edge of the frame.

There was Hannah at seventeen, riding her bike down a leafy July street, wearing a t-shirt she'd ripped the sleeves off. Her hand was raised, her knee bent, a smile breaking across her face, eyes squinting against the sun.

There was Hannah at twenty-seven, on a New York City subway train—all shine and grime and orange. Hannah, shaggy with leftover youth, mid-sentence, her eyes lit-up in a caffeinated way. Behind her, a Jack Russell in a duffel bag. Station lights blurred as they passed.

There was Hannah, thirty, next to Sophie, their smiles as wide as the forested road behind them. A photo taken in the sunbeam of another life.

Hannah was winded by the image. She turned away from the screen, but not before her friends spotted her reaction, their faces falling as they realised their mistake. Esme hurried to catch up with her, but Hannah was moving through the dense crowd, breathing deeply through pursed lips, and soon Esme lost sight of her.

On the screen Hannah was seventy-four, at a Palm Meridian holiday party. She was splayed across a couch in the library, holding a beer and wearing a plastic Christmas tree on her head. Small Eileen galloped behind, a horsey blur.

On the stage, the DJ had arrived and was setting up her decks. The next chapter of the night was buffering in the air. And all around, faces loomed towards Hannah—people she didn't know very well, now drunk enough to feel emboldened, to do the impolite thing and ask:

"Hannah, is she here yet? Your ex?"

"Do you know what time she's coming?".

"I'm really rooting for you, Hannah. I hope it turns out well."

Hannah smiled weakly, stepped away from them, but she kept getting stopped at every turn.

Clips of gossip rose up, but she was too distracted to overhear them:

"Did you see that guy Luca? Luke? He's all worked up—he's completely freaking out."

"Yeah, he's out on the lawn. Like he's seen a ghost."

Above them an image of Hannah and Sophie loomed on the wall, their smiles blurred, in front of the glittering lights of Las Vegas.

Hannah insides lurched forward. Sophie's face made her woozy. She thought for a moment she might be sick.

"What time is it, please? What's the time?"

Hannah groped at the wrist of the nearest person, discerning that it was nearing eleven.

"Thank you," she said as she squeezed on through the crowded space, feeling a panic rise in her chest.

What if Sophie hadn't *wanted* to come to the party? How had Hannah ever believed, truly, that she would be there? Forty-three long years had passed. Hannah was probably long forgotten.

Now time was hurrying along, even as Hannah willed it to stop. The night was slipping away from her. There it was—there it went . . .

The caterers had cleared away everything, the tables folded and chairs moved aside to make room for the dancing. A light was tested on the disco ball that hung from the ceiling. The smoke machine and strobe lights had been set up.

It all felt horrible and urgent, now, in a way it hadn't before. Sharp tears sprung to Hannah's eyes, a stab in her sinuses.

"*Palm Meridian Retirement Resort!*"

A voice boomed, suddenly, over everything, and all lights and eyes turned to the DJ—her pixie cut was phosphorescent in the disco lights, yellow jumpsuit edged with racing stripes. Her chin was up, shoulders back, smile growing. She was the captain of the ship, ready to stir up a storm and steer them through it.

"My name is DJ Inflammation. And I have just one question for you . . . "

The room's energy thickened, voices rising, lights flashing across Hannah's face as she pushed towards the terrace door.

DJ Inflammation revved the engine. The flags were up.

"*Are. You. Ready. To. Party?*"

The room lit up in cheers. A dancehall siren, a drumbeat rising in volume. A crush of noise, and bodies slowly beginning to move. The music filled their ears, buzzed into their brains, flicked some switch in their chests.

"Need a breather!" Hannah shouted to no one, her heart falling through her throat as she staggered out into the night.

21

FLORIDA
2024

Sophie peed for the seventh time that day in the Porta Potty at the edge of the swamp, and the plastic door snapped shut behind her as she emerged back into the humid morning.

The first two times had been at home in Montreal, two on the flight, and two at their motel up the interstate, where palms waved over flaking paint and sun-bleached vending machines.

Now, a fog spilled over the clumps of earth and dense vegetation. A familiar wave of nausea rose up, and Sophie steadied herself until it passed. She touched her stomach with a tenderness that grew larger and deeper every day, a love that thrilled and terrified her in equal measure.

Rotted wooden fences ringed the sprawling property, and they'd been told of the gators that lived beyond. Returning through the shade of the trees, Sophie imagined the gator families—wriggling babies, and watching, big-toothed parents—and felt her throat swell with emotion. How could she have predicted this affinity with reptiles? Pregnancy brought strange and unexpected things.

Sophie stepped along the path, and there was Hannah in the sunshine. Like Sophie, she was wearing a yellow hardhat and a borrowed pair of steel-toed boots. Hannah was chatting with Frankie, a tall, sharp-eyed woman of about sixty-five, with a contagious grin. After her conversation with Mina by the lake, the day before Esme's wedding, Hannah had made sure that she and Frankie were put in touch.

Now, stirred by thoughts of the gator babies, and flush with hormones, Sophie admired how Hannah looked in the light, the openness of her face and the kindness in the way she spoke to people.

"You okay?"

Hannah reached for Sophie's hand, and Sophie squeezed it. Frankie continued their tour.

"I'll show you where I'm thinking for the central pool."

Frankie's land started from the lush interstate and spread towards the horizon, a mix of thick groves and sprawling open spaces, ringed with palms and dotted with natural ponds.

"It was too good to be true," said Frankie, of discovering the land for sale. But it wasn't, of course. The discount price tasted of doom. The land had once been a cut-rate golf course, and its owner was liquidating property. Surrounding residents were slowly decamping to safer climes. In a couple of decades, the place would be ripped through with regular storms, a home sinking into the earth.

Frankie had spent the morning showing them around the grounds. Rented diggers rested on huge piles of earth, halfway through excavating sickly trees and tearing down the last of the golf course's meagre buildings.

As they walked, she sketched out her vision for the retirement community, waving her hands where buildings would one day be. She'd aim to start with a dozen residents and hoped to reach one or two hundred in time. Those who could afford it would pay a monthly maintenance fee. Those who couldn't afford it would be subsidised by a fund fed by wealthier residents. Buffets and squash courts would teem with life.

"The one thing we have to have," Frankie said, "is a bar."

Frankie nodded towards the horizon, where the lawns rose into a hill.

"I think up there"—she squinted against the sun—"would be perfect."

After their tour, Frankie poured glasses of orange juice, and they took a seat on a trio of lawn chairs, the sunlight playing on their skin, chequered by palms.

Frankie started her pitch.

"I know you understand my challenges here. It's a huge space, and the climate's only getting more and more punishing. To have older people living here, safely, we need an efficient way to cool it."

Hannah put her glass of juice down. She spoke softly. "There's no need to convince me, Frankie. I'd like to do it free of charge."

"That's too generous," said Frankie. "I can't—"

Hannah smiled, shook her head. "Just show me where to sign."

Stepping back across the property, they felt time stand still, watched birds chatter across the endless sky. They were somewhere perfect, Jurassic.

Sophie held Hannah's hand, placed her other hand on her belly.

Hannah thought of their child growing, right there, inside. She thought of her dad, somewhere she couldn't understand, but still close by. She was sure of it now.

They crossed the lawn, and the sun poured citrus onto everything.

22

FLORIDA
11 p.m.

*H*annah hurried through the deepening dark, the scent of earth filling her nose. She cut across the back lawns and away from the party.

A karaoke session had started in a faraway gazebo and flashing disco lights danced across the tops of the trees. The music and laughter fell away behind her. The sound of slapping water carried through the darkness—an unseen swimmer doing late-night lengths in the pool.

Heart slamming, Hannah headed towards a palm grove. Her eyes hadn't yet adjusted to the moonlight, and everything loomed in threatening shapes before her. At this time of night, it was like trekking through a jungle: the darkness, the creeping vines, the squelch of swampy earth and thick humidity.

If a Florida panther was stalking the grounds, should she let it kill her? Or should she summon the life in her shaking limbs to run, and live out her remaining hours?

Nausea rose hard in Hannah's throat, and she swallowed it down. She knew where she was going.

She emerged on the other side of the grove and turned left down a path that was crowded on all sides by thick vegetation. If she stopped there, everything would be still: the wide leaves and the sleeping flowers, the sky boomy black above. But she didn't stop. She couldn't stop.

The path curved and opened onto the main lawn. The food hall lay dark nearby, and mosquitoes danced in the security light of the welcome building. Hannah headed towards the open entrance gates, her footsteps sending lizards scampering into the dark.

What did she hope to find? The answer was there, if she let herself think it. But she didn't dare. She passed through the gates and stepped through the long grass, mud splashing up her pant legs. The road stretched in either direction through the gloom. Ants, their red bodies translucent in the moonlight, crawled up the edge of the ageing sign: PALM MERIDIAN RETIREMENT RESORT.

Hannah staggered through the grass at the edge of the road. Trees loomed on either side, their leaves hissing in a sudden breeze.

"*Sophie!*"

Hannah's voice broke through the darkness, brittle and wet.

"*Sophie!*"

But there were no approaching cars, no footsteps rustling through the grass around the bend. She stopped, and stillness reigned. She was alone.

Hannah gritted her teeth against a draining feeling. She wanted what she'd had earlier in the night: a gratitude, a warm-hearted acceptance, a hard-won calm. Belief that Sophie would come, would balance her fears with something joyful and redeeming.

How had she been so naïve? *Of course* Sophie wouldn't come. She'd long ago moved on from Hannah, and how embarrassing that Hannah hadn't moved on from her. They all knew this—all her friends, all the people at the party. They were too kind to say it, too gentle to deny Hannah her happy delusions in the last weeks of her life.

The thought of it made her feel sick, the humiliation like bile in the back of her throat. Hannah's stomach clenched and turned. She bent and threw up, her insides splattering in the grass.

She wiped her mouth with the back of her shaking hand and caught her breath. Feeling the darkness loom on all sides of her, she hurried back the way she'd come, heart pounding.

She had one more option. One more thing to check. Then she'd give up all hope for good.

Passing back through the gates, Hannah headed for the welcome building. She pushed down on the handle and the door opened, letting her in to the silent space, with its couches and cheerful lighting. Ricky's mug sat behind the counter, his forgotten coffee long gone cold.

Hannah keyed in Ricky's code and let herself into the security area, a dark room behind the check-in desk where a bank of screens showed live footage from the handful of security cameras that still worked around the resort. Apart from the petty theft of birdseed from the custodial kiosk, crime wasn't a concern—the cameras were mainly a way to spot residents with dementia who might be wandering at night.

Now, Hannah headed for the hallway that lay beyond. Headed for the mail room. She planned to scour every envelope, to scrape her hands along the insides of every mail bag she could find. She needed to do it for herself—to prove, for certain, that no word had come.

But as Hannah hurried through the security room, her leg bumping against a swivel chair, she spotted motion on one of the screens. She paused, unthinking, then stopped. Goosebumps rose on her skin.

The black and white footage showed a figure walking down a pathway. Hannah recognised it—the path outside the welcome building. This building. The figure had their hands to their face in distress.

"*Luke*."

Hannah ran out the way she'd come, pushing through the door of the security room, rushing through the foyer of the building, out into the night.

Luke looked up, startled, locking eyes with Hannah, his face wet with tears.

"Luke! What's going on?"

He opened his mouth, swiping at the tears on his face.

"I'm sorry—I can't . . . "

The words escaped him, and he strode off quickly down the path, leaving Hannah alone in the dark, the door to the welcome building slamming shut behind her.

23

MONTREAL
2024

*T*he mouth of the oven was charred and gaping, the stone around it blackened by tongues of heat.

How was everything suddenly hellish?

Behind the counter at St-Viateur, stocky men in aprons hauled out huge tubs of dough. They pulled it into ropes, and tugged and shaped, and now their movements seemed evil, somehow. Now the bagels were like flesh, loops of it, treated like soft candy.

Standing by the fridge stocked with cream cheese, Hannah felt a sickness rise in her stomach. She could no longer feel the people around her, that happy jostle of bagel patrons. She had to leave—had to leave—had to—

The street was hot and blinding: one hell replaced for a brighter, breezier one. Cheerful summer people passed by, licking ice creams and each other. They were on their way to the park to sip beers and heckle frisbee players, on their way to their homes to fuck, and feel calm.

Hannah stood in the way of these people, unseeing, feeling the sun press onto her skin, the hottest September the city had ever seen. She couldn't move on from the dough, so soft, it was awful, like gobs of skin, the tugs and twists and—

Suddenly Hannah was walking up her front stairs, had found her way home. The trees on their street provided shade, bringing hell down by ten degrees.

Inside, Sophie was in the bath again, the door closed, the dull sound of the extractor fan going. The one that didn't turn off any more. It sipped and sipped at the air, even though no one was asking. That green bathroom where they'd spent so many effortless hours together, closer to any person than they'd ever been before.

Now Hannah padded past the closed door, saying nothing, the floor-boards creaking in the quiet space. In the kitchen, she dropped her keys on the counter, spun as if there was something to do, stopped—there was nothing to do.

She stood in the centre of the room and felt the quiet move towards her.

The chatter of kids outside. The click of a passing bicycle.

Their home, dark and cool.

At the other end of the apartment, Sophie splashed in the bath. Hannah looked towards the hall, waited.

The peal of a cicada on an electrical wire. The hum of the extractor fan, sucking everything away.

Hannah went to the bedroom and lay on the bed. She'd meant to bring bagels back as a surprise for Sophie, with her favourite cream cheese. A kind of salty bridge, a gesture of—she wasn't sure—a gesture of something.

Now, that bagels were bagels again and not hellish loops of flesh, she suddenly felt sad to have failed to get any. But it was too late. Hannah was too tired, the prospect of the heat outside too much, and she lay on the bed, waiting for another splash from Sophie, feeling the hours pass as the sun set in orange against the wall.

In the weeks since they'd lost the baby, life had been like this.

Before, their love had been easy. Now it was a poorly directed play, the actors distracted and sometimes distraught. Every scene was clipped, or delayed, the lines not reaching their lips. The audience rustling, disappointed, creeping away.

Everything that used to be smooth was choppy. Ease was gone, replaced with worry and anger. In their grief, they should have felt fused together, and yet they felt pried apart. Something had broken between them, and all the love they'd held in the middle there had spoiled, had been made sad. The pain was too much, and so they stayed away from each other, afraid to get too close, to see the sadness reflected back. They each held their own half, and managed it, pretending that was all there was.

"We shouldn't have tried," Sophie said finally one evening, standing in the kitchen with dirty hair, watching the soup on the stove.

Hannah felt the words like heat. They expanded through the room, bringing sweat onto her skin. She couldn't be near them. She left her book on the table and went to bed. She thought of her dad, already gone. Of their baby, gone before them. They were stranded in the middle of a cratered landscape. How could anything feel steady?

They'd been flush with all this love, had rushed to make something with it. Now their child had gone, and so had that good fortune. They should've just held their love between them, maybe. They shouldn't have asked for so much.

After a month, Hannah went back to work, taking meetings from home, filling her calendar as thick as she could. Sophie had lunged through the kitchen again, coaching skiers, her brow furrowed, ear to the phone. Together, they tried counselling, bought books, took courses with three dozen modules. They returned to the sofa each night to compare strategies and notes. Their love was an animal they were trying to revive.

This was all very normal. This was common, they learned in those months.

That made it worse.

There came a point one night when Hannah couldn't bear things as they were. It had been building all along, this aching that grew stronger until it threatened to overwhelm her. She didn't recognise them any more, and it scared her—if they carried on as they were, they'd only drive each other further apart. Their love would become irretrievable.

Sophie was reading on the sofa, her shoulders hunched. It was early December, but their Christmas decorations remained in the boxes under the bed, unspoken of. Hannah was at the kitchen table, sketching in a notebook—on the page were the skeletal winter trees outside the window, gaunt and awful and grey.

"I can't do this."

Hannah's voice was even, too loud. Unfamiliar. Sweat had risen on her palms.

If Sophie's eyes hadn't lifted from the page of her book, Hannah would have thought she hadn't heard her.

Hannah kept speaking, hating her own words. "I need to take a few months."

The next morning, while Sophie was out for a run, Hannah packed a small bag and called Esme, asked if she could stay with her and Theo for a couple of nights. Twenty minutes later, they welcomed her in, Esme holding Hannah while she cried, her sobs breaking in waves. She was full of shame for pushing Sophie away. But she hadn't felt she had another option.

In the dark of the previous night, apart from one another in bed, Hannah and Sophie had agreed to take three months apart. Sophie would go to Vermont, to be with her mom. There was a coaching job in Europe she'd kept turning down, because of their plans to have a child. If she felt up to it, she might try that for a while. After three months, they'd check in with each other. They'd lay their lives out and discern what direction to go.

The joy of everything they'd had before had broken like a dam, and the grief surged in. Here they were, treading water with aching limbs. They couldn't see a way forward, and so they'd take a step out.

Maybe if they were quiet, maybe if they walked away, their love would repair itself in the silence left behind.

Two days later, Hannah returned from Esme and Theo's to her and Sophie's empty apartment. She dropped her bag and went out immediately. She walked to the mountain, up its winding paths, the cold air sharp on her skin. The city and its chalky smoke lay beneath her, the St Lawrence bending wide.

Eventually, Hannah went back to work full-time, travelling to meetings in the US and beyond. The distraction was good, but the same aching rumbled below.

Luke was the biggest help, sitting and listening and anticipating Hannah's needs. He made her laugh. He was kind. In fact, he was himself again—the kid version that Hannah had loved first, and loved most.

Business was good, too; business was helping. The business was changing peoples' lives, keeping them cool and warm. Keeping them safe and happy. But as the three-month mark approached, Hannah felt herself eyeing her phone. She felt the time like another loss between them.

How are you? Hannah texted one night after hours of deliberation, fearing both a reply and no reply.

A day later, her phone lit up:

I'm okay. I miss you. Not ready to talk yet, if that's okay.

Hannah was surprised to feel numb.

She booked more travel, doubled down on work. She did her best to ignore the time that was passing, the gulf growing wider between them.

Six months after they'd separated, Hannah was in London, stepping across the marble foyer floor at the Royal Opera House. She was arranging for the pipes to be upgraded there, for their systems to be installed alongside grand, gilded fixtures.

The engineers were chatting, and Hannah was thinking. Her phone rang and she answered, stepping into a square of sun that fell through the soaring glass roof.

It was Luke, at an airport, a world away.

"Han! I was just in Whistler. Some friends from undergrad wanted to hike. Fuck, I'm out of shape . . . "

Something hovered in his voice. A hesitation. Hannah watched through the doors as a London cab passed down the street.

"Han, I saw Sophie. She was at our resort."

He paused. Hannah's breathing stopped.

"I couldn't believe it," he said.

Something growing.

"Han. She's . . ."

The heat from the sun, through the glass, like an oven. Hellish, all of a sudden.

"Han, she's married."

24

*T*he future arrived on the lawn, where everything had spilled: party guests, glasses of wine, the sound of deafening bass from inside the bar.

In her rush from the welcome building, Hannah had slipped in the grass and scraped her hand, her heart thundering from what she'd seen. What was going on with Luke, and why had he run away from her?

Now Hannah hurried towards the lights and sounds of the party, wiping dirt and grass from her palms.

On the back lawn, smaller groups had splintered off and formed sub-parties, there in the tucked-away corners of the evening. A trio of smokers sat on a wooden pallet by the side of the bar, laughing in a halo of light, unbothered by the mosquitoes. Nearby, in the dark of the trees, an amorous pair sat in chairs that they'd pulled away for privacy. They shared a glass of whisky, their knees slotted into one another's.

Hannah climbed the path to the back terrace and its teeming landscape of conversations, everyone shouting to be heard over the music that drummed from inside. Through the fogged-up windows, the dancefloor was a smudge of strobe lights and moving bodies—some bodies slow and others fluid, whichever their joints would allow.

"Hannah!"

"Where've you been?"

"Have a drink with us, Hannah!"

Hannah faked a smile and waved what she hoped was a friendly hand in the direction of these voices. But she wasn't listening. She was looking for Luke.

"Have you seen Luke? Hey—sorry, have you seen my friend Luke? He's in the suit. He's the one who—"

"Hannah!"

Hannah turned, and Esme's face materialised in front of her, eyes wide with concern, hair frizzed with humidity.

"Ez..."

She hugged her friend long and tight, her body slowly relaxing. Now Hannah could feel the pain on her palm from her fall.

"I hurt my hand," she said, holding the scrape up to show Esme. "I fell. On the grass."

Feeling small and ridiculous, thick emotion clogged Hannah's throat and she started to cry. Esme pulled her close again, squishing her cheek into the top of her head.

"We were *worried* about you, babe. You completely disappeared, and then someone said they'd seen you go down the back lawns in the dark. We thought you were running away."

Hannah stepped back from her friend.

"Ez..."

Hannah's face was itchy with tears. She wiped them away with the back of her hand, searching for the right words. Maybe Esme knew something about Luke, about whatever was going on. Suddenly, though, the exhaustion of all of it was too much. She felt weary to her bones.

If Luke was upset about her dying, she didn't blame him. But Hannah couldn't handle all of this—not right now, not when she was still aching for Sophie, and when the hours were ticking down.

"Never mind," said Hannah to Esme. "Sorry. I'm just tired."

Esme took her hand. "Come on. Let's tell everyone we've found you safe. The Eileens are still looking for you. Christine and Nate, too. Marina's at the Eileens', looking after Ricky. We can meet them there."

"What's wrong with Ricky?" Hannah asked, fear jumping into her voice.

"He's—nothing, he's totally fine. I shouldn't have said."

Hannah held Esme's hand tighter, and they moved through the party, searching for and rounding up their friends. Each of them pulled Hannah close as soon as they saw her.

"You fucking scared us," said tall Eileen, as her wife hugged Hannah close. "There are *panthers* out there."

"Come here," said Christine, relief washing across her face, Nate beside her.

Soon Esme was guiding them away from the party, not trying to find Luke as she'd done with the others. Esme seemed to be pretending that he didn't exist.

"Wouldn't mind a few minutes away from Quinn, to be honest," Esme murmured to Hannah as they moved down the dark paths. "She's been following me around all night, wanting to talk things through. She wants me to change my mind, or something. Or maybe she's just trying to punish me. Sorry—I'll stop—this isn't the time."

Hannah thought of the strange things Quinn had said earlier, wondering what they had meant. Maybe Quinn had been talking nonsense, just trying to stir the pot? Hannah could ask Esme right now, could get everything out in the open. But she kept quiet—she had the increasing sense that whatever was going on, she didn't want to know about it.

The room was a balm when they reached it. The door was open, and a warm light spilled onto the path.

"Hannah!"

Marina was sitting on the bed, consoling Ricky. When Hannah appeared, Ricky quickly wiped away his tears, and came to her.

He seemed to want to say something to explain himself, but he finally shrugged it away.

"I don't want to lose you."

Hannah reached up and hugged him tight.

Spotting Hannah's soiled suit, the Eileens fetched her a clean t-shirt and sweatshirt and pair of jeans to wear. She found comfort in the clean scent of their laundry detergent as she pulled the clothes on in the bathroom, taking care to transfer Ricky's drawing from her suit to the pocket of the jeans.

"Let's get you some water. And some wine," said Esme, putting a hand on Hannah's shoulder when she returned.

Hannah settled into a seat at the table, feeling the exhaustion of the night seep further in. She breathed deeply and looked around at the room where she'd spent so many hundreds of hours.

Outside, the resort was flush with tropical plants and pastel colours, but inside the Eileens' room, you had the impression you were in a mountain lodge nestled in the Rockies. They'd long ago transformed the plain space with wood beams, wood furniture, knitted blankets, heavy rugs. Across the walls were photos of themselves and their son—rock climbing, swimming in a gorge, alpine cycling. Beside their bed was a photo of their wedding day, in a wooden frame: two young women beaming beneath a towering sequoia, red blotches on their arms and legs.

On the wall by the door was a slim, almost unnoticeable panel that regulated the temperature of the room. The same panel that was on the wall of every room in every building of the resort. Designed and engineered by Hannah.

"Thanks, Ez," said Hannah, accepting a glass of water and a goblet of wine. Small Eileen arrived at her side, taking Hannah's injured palm and wiping it gently with a wet cloth, then covering it with a bandage.

The group had poached extra chairs from outside and set them up around the table, nearby lamps emitting a soft, yellow glow. Now, tall Eileen excavated the mini fridge and brought the spoils over: a twelve-pack of beers, a bottle of tonic water, a pack of salami and a block of hard cheese. Glasses were laid out for everyone, and Nate poured whisky and wine from one of the many bottles they'd brought from the bar.

Hannah sipped her water, watching her friends chat and settle in

around the room and the table. Esme went to the bed and flopped backwards, her legs dangling off the edge. That was all of them, assembled.

Then there was a knock on the open door. Rory ducked their head
in, sheepish.

"Sorry to bother you. Is Christine here?"

Hannah looked to Christine, an incredulous smile jumping to her
face as Christine stood up from the table and went over, kissed the new
arrival on the cheek.

Hannah stood and shook Rory's hand. "I'm Hannah. I've seen you
around, I think."

"Rory. It's really great to properly meet you. Sorry, I shouldn't in-
trude, though. Just wanted to check on Christine. I'll leave you all to
it . . . "

Rory made a start towards the door, but Hannah shook her head vig-
orously. "Don't be silly—stay! Let's enjoy. Let's get you a drink."

Smiling, Rory introduced themself to the others and settled in at the
table.

Hannah leaned towards Nate. "All good with Zoey?"

He blushed, smoothed his pant legs with his hands. "Really good.
We're taking it slow."

"SLOW, MY ASS," called Esme from the bed. "I saw you two by the
DJ booth. Tonsils everywhere!"

Nate laughed with his head back, tossed a pillow at Esme.

Hannah quickly finished her glass of wine and refilled it. For a few
bright minutes, their makeshift party had got Luke out of her mind, and
she tried her best to lean into easier feelings. But soon tall Eileen noticed
someone was missing.

"Where's Luke?" she asked.

Hannah opened her mouth, considered looking away, pretending
she hadn't heard the question. Finally, she managed an answer.

"He's been all over. I think he's made some friends at the bar. I'll go
find him in a bit."

Some part of Hannah knew she *should* be looking for him. But a larger part was afraid of what he would say, afraid of what would come out. Something was going on tonight. She wasn't stupid. But the look in his eyes—shocked on the dark of the pathway—filled Hannah with dread. She was too tired. And she was running out of time. She took a long sip from her glass of wine.

As they drank more, the sadness that had suffocated them let up for a bit. Their conversation picked up again, and Hannah did her best to let go, to forget about Luke and Quinn and the rest of the party for now. She embraced a feeling of floating, listening to the voices of some of the people she loved most in the world.

"I swear if they scanned my brain, it'd just be jellybeans. Just forty thousand jellybeans. And a pair of socks."

"I'd always thought a panopticon was a kind of Italian dessert."

"No, that's panna cotta."

Then small Eileen, to someone else, like she was speaking to a child: "That's okay, babe, we'll get you your cheese. We'll send you off to the cheese parade. That's all right."

Hannah talked to Rory, got to know them, spoke with Marina and Nate. The agitation in her chest grew quieter as she finished off more wine.

A while later, feeling drunk, Hannah moved to the now empty bed, lying down on top of the faux-fur bedding. She closed her eyes, rubbed her hands along the material.

"Eileen, I'm not joking, this is the softest thing I've ever felt."

Small Eileen laughed, climbed onto the bed next to Hannah, and lay down, sighing. For a long while they stayed like that, side by side, listening to the laughter of their friends drift over them.

Eileen turned her head to Hannah, only slightly. Her voice was soft.

"What're you thinking about?"

Hannah's eyes were still closed. She wiped the residue of a tear that had fallen down her face and pooled in her ear. She opened her eyes and turned her head.

"Sophie."

Small Eileen took Hannah's hand and held it tight.

Hannah was shaking her head, looking up at the ceiling now. "I see what you and Eileen have. It just—"

Her voice broke.

"It hurts me that we never got to have that."

Small Eileen sat up, slapped the bed with her hands. "You *did* have that—sorry . . . " She lowered her voice, propped her head up on a bent elbow. "You *did* have that."

Hannah saw in the dim light that Eileen's eyes were wet. She wanted Hannah to understand.

"Just because it didn't last forever doesn't mean you didn't have it. You've stayed a part of each other, all those years since then. And that's important."

Hannah looked at small Eileen, the sadness sinking deeper. She wished so badly that the night had ended differently. But she couldn't tell that to her friend, not now, not in the right way. So instead she just nodded, slowly sat up.

Hannah's voice was hoarse when she spoke again. "I should really go find Luke. I think he's upset. I don't know what's going on."

With the wine swirling through her head, it seemed so wrong to Hannah, suddenly, that Luke wasn't here with them. That he'd come all this way, and they had so little time left.

Esme was sitting at the end of the bed, taking a large gulp of pills from a bottle in her purse, washing them down with a glass of water. She put her hand firmly on Hannah's knee.

"We'll look for him in a bit, babe. Let's just sit."

By the time they all headed back outside, more party guests had decamped to the lawns. The bar was suddenly too small, the terrace too crowded, and the vast, inviting space of the resort was like an ocean where everyone wanted to swim.

Stepping through the grass, its wet, earthy smell all around them, people were slipping off their shoes and drinking wine from plastic cups, holding the open bottles in their fists. The scent of chlorine wafted from the pool. The sky was inky black above, splattered with stars.

The groups were quickly growing bigger and bigger, people sprawled out on the dark lawns. A fire had been started in a portable fire pit. Disembodied voices came out of the blackness, faraway peals of laughter, the sounds of golf carts starting up.

Hannah and her friends were drawn towards the fire, which made their features orange and urgent.

In the centre of the lawn, they found some chairs, and the drunkest people around them used their energy to search the nearby area for even more chairs. A satellite party set up in the night.

Hannah's mind was racing. She sucked cool air through her nostrils, and tried to take comfort in the presence of her friends. Esme was there, beside her. Nate and Ricky and Marina, too. Christine and Rory were shy and laughing. Both Eileens, who had since shed their formal outfits and now wore only their matching undershirts, slick with sweat.

Everyone's voices rose and the smoke grew thicker, obscuring the stars. New logs were tossed on the fire, and sparks flew up—a bright, spiky violence. A breeze picked up and smoke pushed into Hannah's eyes, the choking scent of ash. Her throat was dry and she thought of cremation.

Hannah felt in her pocket for Ricky's drawing. She pulled it out, unfolded the creased paper. The details remained the same, rendered in delicate pen: a hospital bed in place of her own, a bounty of cheerful flowers. But now, in the flickering light of the fire, the image just looked frightening—like a room engulfed in flames. Hannah let the breeze pull the paper away, and it floated along the ground.

Something was straining behind Hannah's sternum, threatening to break through the bone. What was there to lose? She let it out of her mouth, addressed to no one.

"I don't think Sophie is coming."

But her words were lost in the noise all around her.

The moon had moved in the sky again. A glass broke nearby, and a laugh went up, the fire hot and sputtering, and every person in the world, it seemed, tumbled around Hannah, except for one.

25

The same lonesome pain had followed Hannah through all four seasons now. Maybe it shouldn't have been surprising to find it here, too, inside this cheerful sapphic snow globe.

The fire crackled and jumped in the fireplace, reflecting off everything: the shining red baubles on the tree, the big windows bordered by night-time evergreens and edged with snow. This party taking place across broad rooms furnished with handsome carpets and Arts and Crafts lamps. Bing Crosby, the soft clink of cutlery, the creak of wood floors.

It was so cosy it approached obnoxious, and the joy of it all gave Hannah a headache.

"Hannah! So glad you're here. I've been dying to meet you."

All night it had been like this: wonderful, bright, curious people, accosting her with their kindness. And all night, Hannah had met them feebly, with vacant eyes.

"Hi," she'd say, heart sinking, as she made a big project out of eating an hors d'oeuvre from a napkin, each puff pastry requiring her undivided attention.

Hannah had done everything she could to make herself a pariah at this party—skirted around the walls hoarding huge cubes of cheese, pressing a finger to her nose to check on her long-blocked nostril—and still they came, these people with infallible social skills, with a genuine interest in meeting new people. But Hannah could not understand them. She would never, she truly felt, be one of them again.

The invitation had come by text from Esme's friend Frances a week before, while Hannah was working through rounds of meetings in New York. Hannah had met Frances many times, including at Esme's Boxing Day party in Montreal a few years prior.

From Frances's text, it was clear Esme had told her Hannah was in the area, and that she could use a push, a pick-me-up. A Christmas party full of beautiful queers fit perfectly.

The winter sun had been out when Hannah had received the message, and the coffee in her veins had made everything seem a bit lighter. Had made it easier to feel brave.

Today, though, catching the Amtrak, Hannah had been sluggish with regret. The sky was overcast, the world leaden and coated in winter grit.

Things had improved only mildly when Hannah arrived in the town where Frances's parents owned an old farmhouse. Out the windows of the cab, the main street twinkled, as if cut from a Christmas film: a tiny grocery store, a glowing coffee shop, a historic water mill with an informational plaque.

Hannah ached to find comfort in all of this. But she was tired, and she wanted to turn back, to catch a train home to Montreal and curl up on her mom's sofa.

Standing by the fireplace now at the party, Hannah became aware that her legs were sweating from its heat, and that her mulled wine had gone cold. Everything was out of whack, and her nostril still blocked, so that when she breathed, she gave out a whistle. She was like a little steam train, depleted of dopamine.

Hannah tuned into the conversation circle she was in, that she'd barely been aware of, then excused herself as politely as she could. At the refreshments table, she busied herself with eggnog, wishing painfully that Esme was beside her. Esme would've been at the party—would've been the lifeblood of the party—but she was in Montreal, finalising her divorce with Theo. Afterwards, they were getting dinner and drinks.

And so Hannah stood by herself at the edge of the party, a lump rising, stupidly, in her throat. Needing something to ground her, she focused on the pine boughs that twisted up the railings of the stairs, but they made her dizzy. Then she tried the top of a woman's hair, a bun jumping as she spoke, like some shiny-coated animal.

"Hannah!"

It was Frances, shimmering in a deep green dress, that signature red hair spilling from her head.

Hannah startled at the surprise.

Frances's joy was incomprehensible, a smile suffusing her voice: "Are you ready?"

With a sickening stab in her heart, Hannah remembered what she'd agreed to earlier, when she'd first come in the door. Frances had pulled her aside, voice low, eyes sparkling.

"I've got a friend here tonight," she'd said. "No pressure. And I promise I'm not saying this just because you're both single—I think you'd really like her. And I know she'd really like you."

In her stupor, Hannah had barely understood what Frances was saying. She'd nodded—sure, sure, sure.

Now, faced with the prospect of a living, speaking person—undoubtedly lovely, undoubtedly wonderful—Hannah didn't know what she could say. How could she explain it? These people meant well. They meant *more* than well. But it was *after*, now. It was *after*. Didn't they see?

They'd known her *before*, and they'd known her *during*. But in this after, she could not—as much as it broke her in half—ever be the same.

Hannah opened her mouth to explain this, but nothing came out, just a whistle from her nostril.

Choo-choo. What's happening?

Frances's smile faltered only slightly. She squeezed encouragement into Hannah's wrist.

"I'll go get her—you stay right here—I'll be right back."

And Frances waded back into the party.

"*Fuck*."

Hannah turned away, squeezing between circles of conversation to reach the kitchen, a warm room with homey furnishings. Party guests stood in clumps around an island, their laughs grating Hannah's ears.

"Excuse me—do you know where the bathroom is? Do you know—the bathroom?"

A woman pointed to a hallway.

"Thanks."

But a line had formed outside the bathroom door, more people chatting and laughing. Seeing Hannah's spooked expression, one man pointed further down the hall and whispered:

"There's another one upstairs if you need it badly."

Hannah thanked him, thoughts flashing, and hurried on.

The noises of the party muffled behind her as she padded up the stairs. The bright overhead lights were on up there. The stylish curation of the party felt far away.

Hannah passed the bathroom, following the sound of the branches that knocked against the windows at the back of the house. The wind picked up and died, picked up and died.

Hannah had never been in this house before, but she knew the room would be there. She'd developed a homing instinct, in the past year, for these tucked-away spaces. She sniffed them out without even trying, in airports and parks and train stations.

This room was especially perfect. Hannah felt a merciful bit of peace flood through her as she stepped out of the bright hallway and into the dark.

It was a screened-in sunroom, its thin winter windows letting in a draught. It looked over the back of the property, a broad lawn blanketed with two feet of snow and ringed with pine trees.

In the dim of the room there was a couch against the wall, and a TV from the 90s, dusty and bulbous and grey. At the far end was a shelf of VHS tapes, a cluster of boxes, an ancient exercise bike.

Hannah sat on the couch and pulled a scratchy blanket up to her stomach. Though she shivered in the draught, she felt her heart finally slow. Her eyes adjusted to the half-dark, and she watched the backyard in its wintry quiet, its moon-lit pines.

The muffled clatter of the party came up through the vents—someone had called a toast. They were making a speech, and thanking Frances for hosting them. Out back, a chunk of snow slid off the roof and made a knocking noise on the drifts below.

Hannah wiped a tear from her face with her palm before it could wet the blanket.

She had let Sophie go twelve months before. She'd made a mistake. But Sophie would always come back to her, in a way, with the snow. The winters would return her, or at least the feeling of her. The bittersweet winters with their bittersweet gloom, comfort prickling Hannah's skin.

For a long time, Hannah looked out at the yard, and then she looked closer, at the screens themselves on the outsides of the windows.

In the warmer months, the glass of the windows would be slid aside, and the screens would protect against flies and mosquitoes. The summer heat would bake its way in.

How uncanny they felt, these summer screens, in the blue-dark dim of winter. How impossible to envision one season of life when you were sunk so deep in another.

26

The fire had grown, its flames licking up to the sky. Its heat pulled sweat onto their skin, the whole group of them rollicking around on the lawns.

Luke had been gone a long time now, and Hannah's brain took stock of the possibilities—that he'd left, and was walking down the dark road. That he'd gone to bed, too sad or too scared to speak to her. That he was back at the bar, drinking with the rest of the party.

With the wine, Hannah's worry for him had soured into resentment. If Luke wanted to come and explain himself, then he could. But Hannah didn't have much time left. She didn't want to go looking for him, didn't want to entertain whatever was going on.

As the fire roared in front of her, now, Hannah's mind was stuffed up with Sophie—with the loss of her, the ache. And under the weight of it, something that had been bending in Hannah's chest finally broke. With so little time remaining, every need felt sharp, immediate: must live. Must jump. Must run. Must dance like I'm the worst winter storm in sixteen years.

Hannah hooked her thumb into the neck of her t-shirt and pulled, her stomach glistening with sweat beneath.

"Let's fucking jump in the pool."

The group, loose with wine and tight with grief, cheered, and items of clothing were peeled off without another thought and discarded in the grass. The fire illuminated wrinkled skin, jubilant stomach rolls, constellations of varicose veins spread across softened legs and tough, lithe torsos.

"Let's fucking go!"

Suddenly a wobbly mass migration was taking place, a decamping from the bonfire and a ramble across the lawns. Most were on foot, but others led the charge in mobility scooters, everyone taking off clothing as they went—a strip-show on-the-go.

Shouts broke up through the palms as they neared the pool deck. Joyful bodies in boxers and briefs, lacy bras, and then nothing—skin bare, grey pubes triumphant. Soon the turquoise surface of the pool was shattered by a series of splayed limbs, lit up from below.

Hannah was shaken awake by the slice of her body into the cold water, the surface churning as everyone slipped in and splashed around. A pink-haired woman with enormous breasts floated by on an inner tube, while members of the cycling team swam lengths underwater and came up gasping, grinning.

Those not inclined to swim brought the party to the pool deck, hoisting bottles and sprawling on loungers, playing music through portable speakers. The wavering light of the pool reflected across all their faces, the fire still flashing beyond the trees.

About a hundred yards away, the other side of the pool was ringed by residential buildings, and Hannah could see party guests passing along the outdoor corridors there. They were laughing and drinking and chatting, dipping into one another's rooms, their voices delayed by distance.

At the side of the pool, small Eileen peeled off her undershirt and cannonballed into the water. Nate was close behind her, his chest gleaming with sweat as he jumped into the air. On the deck, Esme, Marina and tall Eileen set up at a group of loungers and were pouring drinks for themselves and a large group of others who'd joined them.

The broiling atmosphere had brought libidos to a frenzied peak. Many people who'd glanced at each other over the buffet several hours ago now had their tongues in each other's mouths. Christine and Rory laid their bodies against the steps of the pool in the shallow end, trading bashful kisses, half naked and wet. A cry rose up from the far end of the deck— someone had unlatched the clubhouse to fetch more towels and found a resident and the catering manager in the middle of vigorous lovemaking.

Nearby, Nate swam coolly towards Zoey, who'd stripped to her bra and underwear, her wet hair slicked back on her head. She beckoned him with a finger, laughing. Soon their lips met, mouths smiling hard, as the water licked hungrily at their shoulders.

Hannah's head swam with wine. She dipped beneath the water, looked around at the kicking legs and tangled bodies with chlorine-blurry eyes, all the noise muffled with the heavy glug of water in her ears.

With her nose sticking out of the water, Hannah paddled slowly, soaking everything in. She watched the people she loved splash around her, their shouts rising up to the dark sky. There they were—alive, all around her.

A bittersweet feeling swam through Hannah's veins as she let herself imagine Sophie there now, sitting at the edge of the pool, legs in the deep end. Hair soaked through, skin beaded with water, smiling. Waiting for Hannah. This whole time, waiting.

Hannah kicked her legs. She sputtered water. Felt Sophie's absence like an ache in her gut. She willed herself to let it go. The hours had run out. It was time to let it go.

Finding the pool suddenly very loud, Hannah paddled to the stairs and heaved herself out. She went to Esme, who offered a fresh towel. Hannah slowly dried herself, draped the towel around her shoulders and sat between Esme and tall Eileen, in a circle of half a dozen others.

Hannah watched the scene, all the sloshing and shouting. She squeezed her eyes shut. Jumping into the pool had been a good release, but now the sharp and uncomfortable awareness of the end—of death— had crept back, even stronger than before.

"Can you pass my pill bag, babe?"

Hannah reached for a small purse beneath the lounger, handed it to Esme. She watched as Esme took a second large smattering of pills, a dozen or more, in all shapes and sizes.

"You okay, Ez?" she said quietly.

Esme nodded, sipping them down.

In the circle at the loungers, their conversations had turned to the spiritual, the psychedelic and unexplained. Someone named Fritz described a run-in with aliens in 1990s Michigan, recounted the light beaming in through her bedroom window in the middle of the night at six years old.

A woman named Nic shared a near-death experience, when she'd slipped down a sharp cliff on a hike in her twenties and hit her head on a boulder. She said she'd felt a love *like a deep, warm soup* and had travelled down the nearby highway in her mind, could later recall place names and landmarks to doctors that she should not possibly have known.

One of the caterers described his experience taking DMT in his forties, after a difficult divorce. Sitting in his Manhattan apartment, he'd watched the artifice of reality peel away, had felt his consciousness exist apart from his body, had felt he'd died and that dying was fine, that in fact dying was not dying as we understood it. That there was something waiting beyond the end.

Hannah wanted to listen, wanted to share, but her mind was fixated on Sophie, tormenting Hannah in her final hours.

"Is there room for me?"

This was Christine, wrapped in a towel. She took the place beside Hannah that tall Eileen had just left empty, heading off to fetch more food and drinks.

Hannah rested her head on Christine's shoulder. They both listened as everyone around the circle guessed at what it felt like when you died.

"Apparently it feels like being sucked through a vacuum."

The darkness made them think like this. Their theories about death spanned sensibilities and settings: they imagined eternal drive-thru windows, hotel check-ins, highway tollbooths, zeppelin rides. Some felt their souls would explode, while others were sure they would melt.

Hannah spoke softly, privately, her head still on Christine's shoulder.

"Where do you think I'm going tomorrow, Chris? When I die?"

Christine moved Hannah's head from her shoulder, ran her hand once over the back of Hannah's wet hair. Hannah looked her friend in the eye, terrified at how much she needed comfort, suddenly. She needed an answer that worked.

"I think you're going where Sara is."

Christine held up her hands, gathering her thoughts, beginning to explain.

"It's here, but it's different. It's like a present placed on top of a present. A place on top of a place." Christine laughed. "Look, I don't want to sound nuts, talking about other dimensions and everything. But I'm completely serious. The knowledge and the science that we have now would've seemed like magic, like the supernatural, two hundred years ago. I think there are all kinds of things about consciousness and energy that we don't have the tools to understand right now. Things that will be self-evident in the future. And just because we don't understand them yet, doesn't mean that certain things aren't so."

Hannah saw the tears in Christine's eyes, the smile rising on her lips.

"I know it makes me sound crazy. But Sara's still here, Han. I feel it all the time. I can't explain it." Christine struggled to get the rest of her words out, as her throat tightened with emotion: "And you'll still be here, too."

Hannah hugged her friend, pressing her face into Christine's shoulder so she couldn't hear the squeak of tears now escaping.

She pulled away and tried to collect herself, looking towards the hectic churn of people in the pool. Rory was laughing on the opposite deck, dripping in a pair of shorts.

Hannah nodded towards Rory, sensing they both needed something lighter. "Are you getting laid tonight, Christine?"

Christine wiped her eyes, and put a hand on Hannah's leg.

"Oh babe, I already did."

Something in the air changed after that. The confessions began to slip out, each one emboldened by the last.

"Guys, you know Toyota? My ex-girlfriend? I made her up. I named her after my car."

"I never had shingles, really. I just wanted to get out of the silent disco."

"I don't know what salad spinners are for."

Small Eileen, walking by, offered her own confession, wiping her wet hair back off her face. "I've been cheating on Eileen for twenty years."

Then she splashed into the pool, leaving shock and horror in her wake. She resurfaced, grinning. "I'm only kidding!"

Hannah was drinking from a glass of water when a pained voice came from nearby.

"Hannah?"

Hannah turned on the lounger to find Ricky behind her. He'd pulled himself out of the pool and was dripping in his boxers. His eyes were purple and raw. He'd been crying, hard.

"*Rick*. Come here."

Hannah's heart tugged painfully as she stood and wrapped him in a fresh towel. She pulled him aside to the bushes that lined the pool deck, where a shuddering sound went up, a kind of mechanical straining. The landscaping hid one of the generators that kept their home running.

"Rick. What's wrong?"

Hannah's own voice caught her off guard—she sounded pleading. She was exhausted, and she couldn't bear to see Ricky's young face contorted with grief in the way it was now.

He spoke with a choking throat, waving his hands around at the pool. "I don't know how everyone's partying and laughing, Han. This is horrible. This whole thing is sad and horrible. People think I don't understand, but I do. I've seen people who've just had heart attacks. I've been the one to go into their rooms, to check. I've held people's hands while they're dying. It's *final*. The whole thing. That's why I don't want you to do it. And you're gonna do it. I know. But, just—don't do it, Han. Just don't do it."

Hannah pulled him to her, held the back of his head, stroked his back. He dwarfed her, this young man with so much life in him.

"Rick, come here—we've all been drinking—"

"You can't, Hannah, you *can't go*." His voice was ragged now, and his body tightened against hers as if bracing for loss.

Hannah clung to him, squeezing hard, as though she could wring out his sadness, like water from a sponge.

What could she possibly say to this person who she loved? What could make him understand her?

Don't you think I want *to stay with you?*

Hannah thought of the plans that Ricky had made, that sketch of her room. It was still lovely, unbearably lovely in its own sad way, but its promise seemed flimsy now—not nearly enough to match this horrible thing that was barrelling towards her.

"Don't do it, Han," Ricky said, muffled, into her hair.

Hannah was crying now, and her voice warbled as she spoke. "Rick, I have to. I have to. You wouldn't want me to stay. Not really. I'd be a wreck."

He pulled away from her.

"You could wait, Han. You could give it a few months. See how you feel. Maybe the doctors are wrong, and you'll live for *years*. You saw the research. And you know we'll all take care of you. I can stay with you all day. I can drive you around in the security cart, if you're up for that. Make you really comfortable. If you go blind, I'll describe things for you. I can get some really good painkillers. There are guys who sell stuff like that, all up the coast . . . "

Hannah pushed her fingers against her forehead, shook her head.

"Ricky, it's not that simple. This is a choice I've made for myself and—"

"But it's *not* just yourself, Hannah. It's all of us, and—"

"Esme, can I speak to you? Please?"

Hannah glanced over, spotting Quinn by the loungers. She had walked up to Esme and bent low to speak with her. Esme's face was tight, but she stood, and they moved to a quiet corner of the pool, where Quinn spoke animatedly. Hannah didn't have space in her brain right now to keep up with this. She looked back at Ricky—this young man standing here, begging her to live. She took his hands. She wanted him to understand what she was feeling.

"Look, Rick. I know you know this already. Probably more than most of us. You've sat with people while they're sick and they're dying. You've seen that life isn't always good. Life, for life's sake, isn't always worth it. It's not sad—or no, it *is* sad—but it's just the truth. And I can't thank you enough for offering to help me. But I can't run from this. I can't defer it. Things end, Ricky. Things end."

Thoughts of Sophie rose up in Hannah's mind. She focused on Ricky's face to hold it together.

"All of us here, at the resort, we've all seen some people suffer on their way out. And *I don't have to do that*, Rick. I'm choosing not to. I'm choosing to be strong till the end, and to go out when I'm ready. Do you understand why I want to do that?"

Ricky choked on his tears, nodding his head.

A voice broke above the noise of the pool:

"You think you're *perfect*, that's what hurts me. You think you're perfect, but you broke my heart."

The conversation between Quinn and Esme was getting heated. Hannah glanced over, then back at Ricky.

"I love you, Rick. But you don't need me here. You've got your whole life ahead of you. And you're going to be fine. I know you'll be absolutely fine. You have Marina. You have the others. You're—"

Suddenly something moved nearby. Hannah glanced over.

It was Luke, his suit stained with soil, his eyes wide, frozen.

"Luke."

Hannah's heart jolted painfully at the surprise.

"Sorry Rick, just give me a second . . . "

And she hurried towards Luke. Her voice came out hoarse and angry. "Luke, *what's going on?* What's wrong? Where *were you?*"

But he just shook his head. Dazed, he sat down on the nearest lounger, beside the circle of conversation that was still loudly confessing its sins, unaware of anything.

Fritz, emboldened by her UFO story, let another one slip out:

"I killed a man. Twenty years ago. He stole my car."

The crowd balked.

"Well, I stole his first." Fritz took a sip of beer. "This was in Santa Monica."

The group wasn't sure how to respond, but they didn't have to. Quinn's voice rose above all the others, coming from the other direction:

"*There* he is! Why doesn't he tell us himself?"

Hannah turned. Quinn was rushing towards them, Esme chasing behind her, eyes wide.

"Quinn—*don't*—Quinn . . . "

Hurt and anger flashed in Quinn's eyes as she planted herself in front of Luke, whose head was hanging in his hands. He looked up, his face pained and weary.

"Luke, Esme here seems to think she's perfect. But I know she's not. Hannah, you'll be interested in this, particularly."

Hannah looked to Esme, bewildered.

"Esme's not a perfect friend, you know, Hannah. And neither is Luke. There's something they didn't tell you."

Hannah became aware of the faces watching them, of the rowdiness slowly quietening down. Her friends were listening—the Eileens, Nate, Zoey. Christine and Marina. They were dotted around the pool deck and throughout the pool. Ricky stood dripping beside them.

Esme's voice was sharp. "Quinn, *stop*—we'll talk about it. Don't be selfish. This isn't worth it."

But Quinn just waved her hand at Luke. "Luke, you know what I'm talking about, right? Why don't *you* tell us all, since everyone's in the mood for confessing?"

The pool was quieter now, most of the group watching, listening.

Luke shook his head, avoiding Quinn's eye.

"I'll tell her myself then." Quinn locked eyes with Hannah.

"Quinn, *stop*—"

But Quinn ignored Esme, stepping closer to Hannah.

"Hannah, Luke confessed his love to your ex-girlfriend. Sophie. Forty years ago. Esme *saw* him—she saw the whole thing, with her own eyes. And she never told you. Even once your relationship had fallen apart."

The sound of blood was rushing in Hannah's ears, her face hot.

"What the hell kind of person does that, Hannah? Keeps a secret like that from her closest friend?"

Hannah turned away from Quinn, not understanding. She turned back.

Her throat was so tight she was surprised she could speak.

"Is that true?"

She looked at Esme, at Luke, wetness rising into her eyes.

Luke's head was back in his hands. Esme was pleading.

"Hannah, I made a mistake. Your dad died that day, and I didn't know how to approach it later. It never seemed worth it—the pain it would cause. It never seemed like the right time. I wanted to protect you, Han. You have to understand that."

"I lied to you, Hannah." Luke's voice was loud and hoarse, cutting over everything else. Esme stopped, turned. There was a long, horrible pause.

Hannah's skin flashed hot, cold. Luke looked up, his face wrecked, eyes wet.

"The other thing is true. What Quinn said. There's something else, though. I've been lying to you this whole time."

Hannah felt her insides clench. Her reflex was to pull him up by the arm and push him away. To send Luke away right now and never see him again. She only had a handful of hours left, and she was ready to leave it, to let it go.

Hannah sucked in a breath, wiped tears off her cheeks that she hadn't noticed were falling. She looked around at the half-naked bodies, the worried eyes watching her. Some others carried on, across the pool, the drunkest ones. They were climbing stiffly out of the water and daring each other to run and jump in, their bodies splashing violently into the deep end.

Whatever Luke had to say now, Hannah didn't want to know.

But she heard her voice coming out of her mouth.

"What, Luke? What do you mean?"

Luke was shaking his head.

Hannah leant down and put her hands on his shoulders, dipped her head to look into his eyes, shook him.

"Luke, fucking speak to me . . . "

He shook his head, shook his head, shook his head.

"Luke, please fucking explain. What did you lie about?"

Hannah repeated her question, harsher now, blood rushing uncomfortably to her head.

"Luke, *what did you lie about?*"

The generator shuddered louder now, crackling in a way it hadn't before. Luke avoided Hannah's eyes as she towered over him.

Esme took Hannah by the arm. "Han, let's go to your room. Let's just—"

"No, I can't *fucking stand* this, I—"

Hannah's voice broke, and Luke sat up straight, put his hands up to stop her. Slowly, shaking, he let his hands fall.

A pause hung in the air until it was nearly unbearable, Luke's tears rolling off his face and into his lap.

His voice was quieter when he finally spoke:

"I called you, Han. From Whistler. I told you Sophie was married. But it wasn't true."

The pool fell away, for Hannah, all at once and was replaced with a ringing in her ears.

"*What*—what does that even *mean*—Luke—"

But Hannah's voice was interrupted by a scream, a smashing of glass, a dozen more screams.

On the other side of the pool, someone had crashed into a low table of drinks while running heavily, drunkenly, across the deck, aiming to jump into the water. They'd smashed many bottles, and the glass of the table itself. There was quite a lot of blood, quite little clarity about *whose* blood, and many frantic people.

As they all watched, stunned, someone else fainted at the sight of the spreading puddle of blood, and hit their head on the deck with a stomach-curdling *thunk*. Everyone in the pool was now screaming.

"Call a paramedic!"

"Someone help!"

Hannah held her hands up to Luke and Esme, unable to process all this at once.

"I have to go . . . Just give me . . . "

The bonfire was still raging on the lawn. Now, the worried hum from the generators rose loud enough that it could not be ignored. Everyone brought their hands to their ears in pain.

"*What is that?*" someone screamed, and in one booming, draining surge, all the lights went out, the resort around them lost in some ancient darkness.

27

JFK INTERNATIONAL AIRPORT, NEW YORK
2026

The stark light of the terminal reflected in the night-time windows, obscuring the tarmac beyond, where luggage carts slithered and icy planes lumbered to their gates.

"How was Frances's party in the end? I didn't ask you last week."

Luke checked his hair in the reflection of the airport window—pulled his fingers through the front, tilted his head to check the sides.

Hannah's voice came through his ear bud.

"Oh god. I didn't tell you. That was a low point."

She let out a defeated laugh, and he heard her turn on the kitchen tap. The sounds of her mom's apartment came through the phone to him—the kettle boiling, the chatter of the TV from the living room.

"I couldn't stop thinking about Sophie. It was . . . like, it was worse than it's been before. Frances tried to set me up with someone, but I sort of ran off. I didn't . . . " Hannah trailed off.

"Anyway, I came straight home the next day. This week's been better. We bought the biggest gingerbread house they had at the store—it's massive. And I finally beat my mom at Scrabble."

Hannah's mom's voice rang through from the other room: "I let her have the French spelling of banana, Luke! Because I love her!"

Luke was finding it hard to focus on the conversation. He was perched at a bank of seats, and his knee bounced anxiously as he watched the mundane commotion of the airport—gate attendants making garbled announcements, a toddler climbing a duty-free display, a slow-moving courtesy cart and its flashing light.

"How were your parents?" Hannah asked.

Luke's attention returned. He frowned automatically. "Not great. I stayed out of the house a lot. Did a lot of walking. A few days feels like a long time there."

Luke had, understandably, not had much to do with his parents in adulthood. They'd moved to Ottawa years before, and he'd only held himself to one promise: to visit them once a year.

"Anyways. They're alive. They're all good."

Luke wiped a speck of lint from his crisp, white shirt and took a deep breath. He checked his watch. It was time to get moving.

An announcement rang through the terminal, reminding passengers that unattended items would be removed and destroyed. But Luke didn't have any items—just his suit jacket and his wallet. He felt light, light, light.

"Where are you going again? Oh, hang on, the pizza's here."

Hannah's voice moved away from the phone as she opened the front door to collect their delivery from the top of the steps. There was the swish of cars passing down the street, then the door closing.

Luke strode through the terminal, his pulse quickening. "St Lucia. Just for a break."

"Jesus, cool. Put on some sunscreen."

Luke breathed out a nervous laugh. There was the clatter of plates as Hannah set up the pizzas in the living room.

"Anyways, I'll let you guys eat." He hesitated, added, "You're feeling okay?"

"Sorry, one sec, Luke—Mom, I'm just getting napkins."

The sound of the TV receded as Hannah returned to the kitchen. Her voice was low, contemplative.

"Yeah, I'm okay. But I'm gonna take the new year really seriously. I spent the last year mourning me and Sophie, and that was fine. But now she's *married*, for fuck's sake. I can't do it any more. I have to move on."

Luke boarded a moving walkway, and the world sped up with his stride.

"I never thought I'd say this. And I don't want to say it . . . " Hannah paused, and Luke could hear a heavy resignation in her throat. "I think I have to accept that I'll probably never see her again."

Luke side-stepped a family on one side of the moving walkway, who were laden down with backpacks and rolling bags. He was flying, soaring. He was terrified.

"Anyways," said Hannah, not waiting for his response, "I'm sick of thinking about it. I'm sick of talking about it. I'll see you in a week, yeah? Have a good trip. Be safe."

"Thanks, Han. See you later."

Luke hung up the call and stepped off the moving walkway. He passed a handful of boarding gates, a shop selling neck pillows and potato chips. He spotted the sign for the bar and resisted the urge to wipe his sweaty palms on his pristine pants.

The space wasn't fancy, but it was airport fancy, the dim lighting meant to make it feel like a real bar and not an artificial little enclave next to gate 34D. Luke stepped across the carpet, searching the tired, travelling faces that were dotted around at tables and stools.

"Luke."

A flash of heat rose from his skin when he saw her. He smiled, his mouth suddenly dry.

"Soph."

She stood to hug him, and the familiar, forgotten scent of her knocked him in the chest. He sat down quickly, dazed.

"Warm," he said, for something to say, pointing to a fake electric fireplace on the wall beside them, which of course wasn't warm at all.

Sophie took it in her stride. Before Luke could compose himself, a very tall college student with a notepad was looming at his elbow. A boy like a wavering green bean, oozing boredom.

"Drink?" he asked, his eyelids heavy.

Luke picked up the laminated menu on the table, flipped it over inef-
fectively. "Are you . . . ?" He asked Sophie, but she raised her hand, all
good, a tonic water already before her.

"A Chardonnay, please," said Luke, and the boy wavered away.

While Sophie was closing her laptop and moving her things off the
table to make room, Luke took the chance to take her in: her dark hair tied
up in a ponytail, the gut-punching softness of her face, her quiet strength.

She tucked her laptop into her bag and straightened up, and he
nearly buckled under her direct attention. There was something tired in
her usually bright eyes.

In the beat of silence that followed, Luke let out a breathy laugh,
ready to speak, but Sophie beat him to it. Smiling, she seemed to allow
herself something.

"It's nice to see you," she said.

A surge of pleasure ran through him, but the moment was ruined
when the boy returned and thumped the glass of wine onto the table.

"Thanks," Luke said, taking an eager sip. He fiddled with the stem
of the glass, feeling foolish. This meet-up had been his idea, and all his
words had left his head now. He grasped at an image, at anything.

Switzerland.

"You're going to Switzerland."

Sophie nodded. "I've got a coaching job that starts in a couple days.
I've been living out there for the last few months. Was just home with my
mom for Christmas. A lot of jigsaws. Walks. A lot of Scrabble."

Stifling guilt, Luke took another sip of his wine.

"You're good, though?" Sophie asked.

Luke swallowed hard. "Yeah, good. Really good. Busy."

Sophie didn't seem to listen. She was thumbing a napkin, avoiding
his eye. She was readying a breath.

"How's Hannah?"

Luke's heart raced but he licked his lips, shrugged. "Yeah, good. We
don't really chat that much, you know, here and there . . . "

Sophie lifted her head and frowned, confused. "But, like—even with
the business . . . ?"

Luke laughed awkwardly, waved this away. He was flailing. "How have you been? You're okay?" he deflected.

Sophie thumbed the napkin again, her eyes wandering the bar. "Honestly, not really. Like—I'm fine, but . . . Just having a rough time of it." She looked back at Luke, and he could properly see the pain in her eyes for the first time. "When Hannah and I first broke up, I felt so insane. I wanted her *so badly*, but I felt like I couldn't even bear to hear from her, or text her, let alone see her. Everything just felt so sad. And then the months kept going on, and I wanted her more and more, but so much time had passed, and it just kept feeling more impossible. I kept picking up my phone and wanting to reach out, but I was totally paralyzed by it. I still kind of am, I guess." Sophie sucked in a big breath, fixed her eyes on Luke. "That's why I'm glad you messaged last week. Hadn't heard from you since we bumped into each other in Whistler in the summer. I guess it's just nice to . . ." She hesitated, laughed sadly. "You know, see a familiar face, and all that."

Luke opened his mouth to reply, faltered. Sophie seemed to collect herself. She continued.

"Where're you going anyways?"

Luke let out a nervous breath and smiled. He stared into his wine glass, gathering his words.

"Soph, I need to speak to you about something."

Her face clouded with worry as she put the napkin down. "What is it?" she finally asked, sounding weary, like she didn't really want to know, like she couldn't handle more.

Luke wiped his hands on his pants, his pulse roaring in his ears. Finally, she was right there. Finally, it could all be real.

His voice was even and strong when he finally spoke—good.

"Are you seeing anyone? Because I—"

The oxygen left the airport bar. The faux fireplace went out, the menus shrivelled up into squiggles of laminate, and the bean boy fell with a thud on the carpet as Luke's heart stopped—because he knew in that moment it was over.

An announcement rang through the terminal, but to Luke's ears it was far away, like he was underwater.

Then the oxygen returned for one surging, deafening moment, just so Sophie could take an eternity to say, so low, so small, he almost couldn't hear her:

"Is that what this is about?"

A pause, where he lost everything, all over again.

"You have to be *fucking kidding me*." She stared at him, her face screwed up in repulsion.

"Soph, don't—just listen . . . "

But she was already gathering her things, her face disbelieving. Suddenly she spun, looked down at his feet, at the floor. She clocked his lack of luggage. Her anger was quiet, turned to disappointment by the time it left her mouth.

"You're not flying anywhere, are you? You just bought whatever ticket you needed when I told you I was flying today. 'Oh my god, that's so crazy, I'm flying out too. Same terminal!' You tried to pass it off as coincidence."

Luke tried to reply, but nothing came out. He held up his hands, seeing it all slip away. He said whatever he could get out of his mouth in that moment, knowing it would be his last try:

"Sophie. I love you. I loved you at the lake. I love you today. I came here because I needed to tell you again, properly. When you're not with Hannah. I needed to know how you felt."

Sophie was standing over him now, duffel bag over her shoulder. She tried to keep her voice down, but it came out frantic, exasperated. "You *know* how I feel, Luke. I told you, *last* time."

The bean boy came to collect their glasses, but veered away, sensing danger. Sophie searched Luke's face for sense. "I lost *Hannah* last year, and you're sitting here trying to—fucking—what, step in in her place? Are you out of your mind?"

Luke didn't have a response. It had gone so differently in his head. He stood, but Sophie strode out, and was gone, the tarmac beyond blinking in the night.

28

FLORIDA
2 a.m.

For a few minutes, the county was wiped clean from the map. Any aircraft flying above saw only an inky spill on an already sparsely lit state.

When the lights clapped back on again, they revealed a sombre and soggy tableau: small Eileen tending calmly to someone's shredded, bleeding leg. Tall Eileen tending calmly to the unconscious person. Hannah kneeling between the two.

The swimmers in the pool climbed out in silence, feeling ridiculous and sorry and grim. Across the deck, Luke watched, stunned, beside Esme, who held him by the shirt sleeve as if worried he'd run away. Quinn stood beside them, her hands shaking.

Nate, Zoey and Ricky sat knee to knee at the edge of a lounger, their faces stoic. Marina joined them, taking Ricky's hand. Christine and Rory sat down nearby, wrapping towels around themselves.

Everyone assembled was silent. The music had cut off with the power and the only sounds were the murmurs of the Eileens to their patients, the swish of the breeze through the tops of the palms.

They all did their best to ignore the pool of blood.

"You'll be okay," said small Eileen gently, reassuringly, finishing up the bandages on Cari's leg, having cleaned and assessed the wounds in a matter of minutes. Nearby, Leah, who'd fainted and hit her head, came to. Tall Eileen spoke calmly to her, kept her still. They murmured back and forth for a few minutes, then tall Eileen looked up and around at everyone assembled.

"She'll be all right, everyone. She'll be just fine."

A ripple of relief ran through them all. They let out nervous laughs, and quiet conversation bubbled up. Tall Eileen turned her attention back to Leah. Hannah went to her, held her hand. Then she checked on Cari, kneeling by her side. She thanked small Eileen and hugged her.

Finally Hannah stood, shaking, and looked across the pool to Luke. She headed towards him, breathing deeply.

"Hannah . . . "

Esme tried to intercept her, but Hannah strode right past. Her voice was quiet when she spoke.

"What the fuck do you mean she wasn't married? What does that *mean?"*

Luke was wiping tears away. It took a long while for him to find the words he needed. Everyone was silent again, watching. Quinn had backed away, horrified by what she'd caused.

"I was jealous, Hannah. I loved her. I loved Sophie the whole fucking time. And when you two were separated, and I ran into her in Whistler, I really figured it was over for you guys. I thought the lie could maybe help you move on. That's how I justified it at the time . . . "

"You fucking *bastard* . . . "

This was Esme, storming towards Luke, but Hannah grabbed her wrists and held them tight.

Luke did his best to ignore Esme, looking directly at Hannah, his eyes pleading. "Han, you don't understand how it was for me. I was so jealous of you, for so long. You had this perfect, happy family who loved you. And then you got Sophie, on top of everything. It was all so easy for you. And I was *so in love* with her. It was like, without you, we were perfect for each other. I know it doesn't make sense now. I don't know what the *fuck* was wrong with me. But you have to understand how I was feeling."

Luke paused, choked out the rest of it:

"I saw her another time. About six months later. I wanted to see her, and I wanted to—I don't know, I wanted to try. I reached out to her, and met her at JFK. And I humiliated myself . . . "

Luke kept speaking, but Hannah wasn't listening any more. She let go of Esme's wrists, which she'd forgotten she was holding. Horror pushed up in her throat, the taste of bile. She was winded.

"I'm so sorry, Hannah. I'm so sorry . . . "

Hannah couldn't calibrate what she was hearing. All the hope and the anticipation of the night that she'd kept trying to discard. This anguish and defeat that she'd tried to heave off for the last few hours . . .

Luke's eyes were wild. "Hannah, I'm so sorry. I'm sorry. It was wrong and I'll regret it for the rest of my life . . . "

The magnitude of what he'd told her pressed onto Hannah's brain, adrenaline pumping through her, the loss expanding. She spat out her words, reeling, unbelieving. She was losing control. "Luke, I *could have had a life with her*. I could have . . . "

Hannah's voice broke, and she shook her head, unable to stop the tears from falling down her chin and onto the pool deck. "Luke, you took *forty-three years* from us. Forty-three fucking years. I have six hours left." Hannah stared at him, imploring, anger roaring in her ears. "Why did you come, Luke? Why did you even dare come, when you knew you'd done that to me?"

Luke threw his arms out, pleading. "I wanted to *see you,* Hannah! You're *dying*. You're my oldest friend. Of course I came. I didn't know you'd invited Sophie. I didn't know you still loved her. Hannah, to be honest, I thought you and Esme would end up together. I always thought that."

Hannah looked at Esme, who was standing beside her, distraught. All around the pool deck, their friends watched silently, stunned. Hannah looked back at Luke, his hands still flailing.

"Look—when I came today, I knew we'd talk about Sophie. I knew she'd come up. But I didn't think you'd still miss her after all these years."

Hannah's pulse pounded. Her face was burning. Words were insufficient, but they were all she had:

"Well I *do*, Luke."

Hannah spun around, breathed deeply. Esme touched her back, tried to calm her down.

Luke gestured at Esme. "Han, I've been trying to speak to Esme all night so I could explain myself. About what she saw, with Sophie. I totally lost Esme as a friend after that. We never spoke properly. I thought I could make amends tonight, maybe. I didn't . . . " He faltered. "I didn't plan on telling you the truth about anything, Han. There's just—there's too little time left."

A pause, and the sound of the breeze slapping at the pool. Everyone's shivering, dripping bodies were all around them, silent and still.

Luke looked at Hannah, his voice stronger than it had been before. "This doesn't excuse what I did, Hannah—what I did was unforgiveable. But I *loved* her. I can't explain how painful it was to watch her love you so deeply. So close to me. For years."

Esme scoffed, but Luke kept going.

"Hannah, what I'm saying is: I know she loved you. She *adored* you. And you know she got the invitation—you have the confirmation from the post office. Hannah, you know her better than I know her. And even *I* know that if Sophie gets an invite like that, she goes."

Hannah's throat was dry and tight, her head throbbing. She felt suddenly wiped, like she'd been hit by a golf cart and dragged across the lawns. She sat down slowly on the lounger closest to her, and the realisation dawned on her.

Luke was right.

For as long as Hannah had known Sophie, she'd never turned down a chance at adventure. She'd boarded that plane to Vegas with Hannah, fourteen hours after they'd met on the street in Manhattan. She'd flown to Tokyo to surprise her, wired and rattled through with love. She'd barrelled down hills and launched herself into the air for a living. She had hungered for travel and change.

They knew Sophie had got the invite. And if Sophie had got the invite, then, barring some disaster, she would come.

"Luke's right," said Hannah quietly.

Esme nodded in agreement.

A long, heavy pause. The bass from the party at the bar came tinny across the lawns.

Hannah said what everyone was thinking:

"So where is she?"

Esme shook her head. "I'm sorry, Hannah. I don't know."

Everyone on the other side of the pool started over to Hannah's side. Ricky sat beside her, and took her hand, whispering an apology for earlier, and Hannah held his head to her chest, kissed his soggy curls.

Nate, Zoey and Marina came over, then Christine and Rory. Quinn lingered at the side of the group, wide-eyed with shock.

Esme glowered at Luke, and he stepped away, sitting down nearby. The rest of the party circled around Hannah, and for a while, everyone was quiet, murmuring and watching the Eileens care for Leah and Cari, watching the bonfire light up the palms nearby.

It was Nate who spoke first. "Sophie definitely knew the party details?"

Hannah nodded. "Everything was in the invitation. I said I knew that she might not want to come, but in case she did, I gave her all the info she'd need."

They took this in, everyone watching, or thinking.

Ricky spoke next, his face still puffy with tears but his expression clearing. "She'd be coming from Switzerland, right?"

Hannah nodded.

"Yeah, Zurich. Apparently she's still a big skier, so she's been living out there. She'd be coming via New York, maybe. I don't know."

Ricky nodded.

"So the little airport, then," considered Christine.

"We were there yesterday!" volunteered a member of the cycling team, gesturing to her wife beside her. "Our daughter was flying out after a visit. It was nearly empty—a guy at the baggage carousel said they were having signal problems because of the blackouts, and a lot of inbound flights had been delayed."

"Yeah, I heard about that too," said another.

An energy picked up in the group, a rustling.

"That's it!" cried small Eileen, from across the deck, having helped Cari onto a lounger.

"That's it?" asked Hannah, feeling her head spin, feeling herself already dead, feeling the energy drain out of her.

Small Eileen threw her hands in the air, her arms wet and splattered with blood, her voice carrying across the night to the group assembled. "Her flight was probably delayed! She probably only got in tonight, and the whole grid's crapped out. She's probably at the airport right now, frantic, still trying to figure out a way to you. No signal. No internet. Not many places to catch a bus or a cab around here. She's probably distraught, thinking she'll miss you."

The crowd was buzzing now, everyone agreeing this was possible. Luke looked on, his face exhausted and open, desperate for hope.

Hannah's mind was spinning. Esme whispered in her ear: "Han, I think the nice people might genuinely have a point."

Hannah looked up, into Esme's eyes. Eyes that she'd known for longer in her life than she'd known most. Esme held her gaze, soft and steely.

"How long have you got?" asked one of the baseball players.

Hannah looked at her, and her heart picked up pace, thumping to remind her she wasn't dead—not yet.

"Till eight in the morning."

"What time is it now?" someone asked.

"Two-thirty!" another replied.

They looked at Hannah. The soggy bunch of them, their bodies wrinkled and sunken and bloated and spent.

Hannah was suddenly steeped in one of life's greatest feelings: unexpected relief.

Nate, normally sensible, stood up. "Well let's go!" he said.

"Well let's go!" Hannah said. Standing up, she felt life rush into her veins in a way she hadn't believed she would feel again.

"*To the carts!*" cried Esme.

"*TO THE CARTS!*"

The exodus was messy. Drinks were slugged, towels donned, clothing sought in bushes, flip flops thrown through the air. The swimmers, the loungers, Fritz—who'd maybe committed murder. Hannah and all of her friends.

Shaken, Quinn was slinking away in the shuffle of everything, and Esme caught her, pulled her close. They spoke quietly, quickly. An apology, or the start of one.

Alone, Luke strode away from the pool, towards the lawns.

The century had seen many things, but it had not seen exactly this: a fleet of golf carts, sweeping with speed out the gates of the resort, commanded by a battalion of the half-naked elderly—towels flapping, eyes bright, pedals flat to the floor.

Both the carts and their drivers were reaching speeds they weren't designed to reach, but still they held on, refurbished parts and all. The noise was enormous, and the crickets in the trees seemed to swell with it, hearts catching onto the sound and rising higher.

"*LET'S GO!*"

Christine drove a cart with Hannah, while Rory, Nate and Zoey perched on the back. They held onto the roof with desperate hands as the cart hurtled down the road.

Here it all was, as real as it had ever been. Hannah tasted the sweetness of the air in her mouth, the thickness of this place, willows hanging either side. The swamps lay beyond, the gators, the airboats. The ancient ponds and beloved homes, sinking into the earth. Out here, there were simple things: the grey road, its yellow line; the black sky gaping, inviting, above.

How could you leave a home like this?

"*TRUCK!*" cried Esme, out front, warning of a tanker coming the other way, carrying food and water downstate. The carts behind, who'd zipped into the wrong lane, lurched over. Some pool noodles were scattered in their wake, and the last carts braked to collect them.

Hannah craned to look behind her, the wind whipping her hair. She watched Esme speed beside them with Ricky, Marina, both Eileens. Behind them, the passengers of five more golf carts were yelping and shouting into the wind. Some of them were too drunk to have followed the recent developments in any detail, but this didn't diminish their enthusiasm.

"WE'RE COMING, SOPHIE!" cried small Eileen.

By the time the band of them neared the tiny airport, twenty minutes away, the carts were straining for gas, but they persevered. The wind on Hannah's face was cool but she felt her skin hot with anticipation, her stomach cramping, the fuzz of alcohol fading into clarity.

The carts made a hazardous turn, emerging off the interstate and north towards the airport, the trees thick and black against the sky. The dead of night was a big, unfathomable thing, until they saw the command tower, the strips of light, the chain-link fences, the green highway sign with a white airplane:

REGIONAL AIRPORT

Esme tore right, then left, through bare concrete roads lined with scrub brush, hobby planes parked in the distance. There were homes in Florida bigger than this airport.

"That's the terminal!"

"The entrance!"

Hannah braced herself for seeing Sophie as the cart came to a screeching halt.

"Go, go, go!" cried Christine.

"Go!" cried all the others, who'd brought their carts to slamming halts by the entrance and hurried to join Hannah beyond the sliding automatic doors.

Hannah's heart was hammering as she arrived inside, her feet

carrying her faster than she'd thought they ever would again. The silence
hit her: the tiny terminal, its bright fluorescence.

Sophie!

The carts were left scattered on the pavement outside as Hannah's
friends rushed through the door to join her.

Here it was: The quiet turn of a baggage carousel. A closed car rental
kiosk. A security guard, a hundred yards away, sitting on a chair, yawning, sniffing.

"Sophie," said Hannah.

She ran to the end of the space, stopped. She looked out the windows,
saw the abandoned parking lot, with not a passenger in sight.

Hannah turned back, walking now, towards her friends, seeing the
hope in their eyes, in their hearts.

"Sophie," said Hannah, dizzy with pain.

Sophie wasn't there. Of course she wasn't there.

Hannah watched the last of the stragglers tumble into the terminal,
their towels dripping on the hard, glossy floor. She saw the light leave
their eyes as she felt it leave hers.

The pain sliced through Hannah like a blade on the baggage carousel.

"It's okay, guys. It's okay," she said, with a faraway voice, watching
Esme come towards her.

Hannah couldn't close her eyes, even as they filled up with tears, even
as Esme's hair mashed onto her face, a hopeless hug.

Hannah saw the group of them for what they were now. So recently
flush with life, they'd been flattered by the light of the sunset, the forgiv-
ing dimness of the lawns. Now, under the fluorescent strips of the terminal, they appeared differently: smaller, their skin more mottled, their
veins garish, their wet hair mussed by the wind. They all stank of whisky
and wine, the sour bite of chlorine—herself included.

"Let's go home," said Esme. "Let's go home."

29

FLORIDA
4 a.m.

*I*n the harsh light of the food hall, even the hash browns looked grey. Their potato bodies—once golden, once a source of solace and life-affirming joy—were just splodges of grease.

The whole group of them who'd rushed to the airport sat slumped around a cluster of tables. The rest of the food hall was empty, a sea of tabletops with a lonesome shine. Everyone's forks scraped against their plates. Outside, the slightest shade of blue changed the quality of the black sky.

Damp and defeated, their surge of energy had drained away, the energy that had propelled them down the interstate at impossible—perhaps miraculous—speed.

A heaviness bore down on them, a sensation of comfort and hope receding for good.

Their chatter was low:

"Can you pass the toast?"

"You've got vodka Jell-O on your swim trunks, babe."

"I think I told the frisbee team I was adopted."

René—head chef and a twenty-year resident—had anticipated an extra early breakfast rush, given the party. When the group of them had returned, depleted, through the gates of the resort, she had already been unlocking the food hall, ready to soothe them with coffee and eggs.

Now, Hannah let her head rest on Esme's shoulder beside her. Her plate was heaped high with food, lovingly prepared, but she couldn't eat. She let Ricky and small Eileen reach over and take what they wanted.

Where was she?

Hannah saw Sophie's face in the curve of a fried egg, her smile in the slices of honeydew melon stacked on one side of her plate.

Hannah didn't know where Luke had gone, or if she'd ever see him again. His words by the pool—his ragged voice—still rang forcibly through her ears.

There was no replacing what he'd taken from her. And no time left to redeem it at all. The thought was annihilating, and freeing, in equal measure.

And so Hannah gave up.

Across the table, now, Nate and Zoey made a tower of tater tots on the plate between them. Christine and Rory compared hands, thumbing each other's knuckles softly. Ricky was eating, eating, eating, and Marina picked a piece of scrambled egg out of his hair.

Hannah reached out and touched Esme's hand.

The next day, once Hannah was gone, Esme would pick up her ashes from a facility near the hospital. As a group, her friends would drive out to the Atlantic Coast to scatter Hannah's and her parents' ashes together, to be licked up by the icy foam while the heat baked down on the beach.

Death was still coming. It had always been coming. The weight of that was indescribable, the heft of it so great. Sitting at the table, Hannah still felt she was being crushed. But watching her friends, she felt the weight shift by a tiny measure—a millimeter, maybe.

She thought of the party, of the lawns. Of the one or two Florida residents, up late in their homes by the interstate, who would have seen the group of them roar by.

Hannah felt herself smile.

She'd had so much fun being alive.

30

awn broke for Hannah one last time, and the colour seeped back into everything: the parking pylons (gut-punch orange), the palm leaves (deep-breath green), the stucco walls of the residential buildings (yellow and pink), the egrets (diamond white) scattered through the shrubbery like seasoning, and the pool noodles (a kaleidoscope of colours favouring lavender and blue).

Birds fluttered through the trees as the light poured gently into the world, illuminating the lawns, dewy and scattered with party detritus, plus the odd party guest taking a tranquil nap in a roller kayak, a siesta in a sand trap. When the day's first activities began, these people would be lightly nudged away with an oar or a putter and sent in the direction of their rooms.

Hannah and Esme made their way across the grass with huge mugs of coffee, a blister pack of painkillers, and a Ziploc bag full of soybean bacon, gifted by René the chef.

Loopy and drained, their chatter was the same as it had been for decades:

"Look at that slug. Fucking huge slug."

"That bird looks like my ex-husband."

With their heads swimming, Hannah and Esme climbed a gentle incline at the western edge of the resort. They sat down, allowing their joints to crackle as they lowered their bodies onto the cool cushion of the grass.

For a while, they shared a quiet moment, crunching on Ziploc bacon and gazing out over the lawns, lone streamers and empty bottles of wine.

At the food hall, Esme had apologised again. About what she'd seen that afternoon on the beach, the day before her wedding, all those years ago. About seeing Luke speaking to Sophie. The reasons she had kept it from Hannah. Maybe she had been wrong to try to protect her friend, Esme had said—it wasn't her place. But Hannah had just hugged her tight, waved this away. There was no point regretting anything.

Now, on the grass, Esme sniffed, and Hannah saw she was crying. Esme turned her head away, wiping her nose with her thumb.

"Sorry—I'm sorry . . . "

Hannah wrapped her arms around her friend, pulled her close, Esme's head falling onto Hannah's shoulder.

Esme's voice came out as a rasp, contorted with grief. "*It hurts*, Hannah."

Hannah clenched her jaw and squeezed Esme closer. She was sick with these goodbyes.

At the food hall, Hannah had said goodbye to her friends, their voices choked with tears. Small Eileen had squeezed her close, forcing a smile onto her face as she sobbed. She spoke as if Hannah was going away on a long trip. "You be safe, okay? Be safe for me."

Christine held Hannah's hands in front of her for a long time, gulping down tears. "Remember what I told you. About Sara."

Hannah nodded, nodded, pulled her close.

"I'll be right here. I'll come visit, tomorrow."

They laughed, and it seemed it might break their bones.

Hannah felt the strength of tall Eileen's arms. She soaked in the smell of Nate's aftershave and Marina's shampoo. Even though these memories would be wiped away in a matter of hours, it felt important to absorb them now.

Hannah held Ricky for a long time. He was the one she worried about the most. He pulled away, managed a lopsided smile.

"I'll miss you, Hannah."

"I love you, Rick."

Luke had been hovering nearby. He'd reappeared after breakfast, looking broken. Now Hannah went to him, exhausted.

"I don't have time left to hate you."

He nodded, eyes cast down.

She hugged him stiffly, then softly. She spoke before they pulled away, so she didn't have to look him in the eye.

"I don't blame you for loving her, Luke."

They had let go and Hannah had strode off.

Now, on the grass with Esme, Hannah clenched her jaw tighter.

There was nothing that Hannah could say now to make anything better or to ease any pain. They both knew this, and they bore it. They sat together and they cried, and Hannah listened to Esme's ragged breathing until it calmed.

Finally, Hannah spoke:

"Someone was talking about the procedure last night. They said it's just like falling asleep." Hannah hesitated. "But how could they know?"

She blinked through her tears at the green vista before her, felt the humidity rising already, with the dawn. The dew would soon be scorched away.

In one gasping breath, Hannah could feel fifty-eight years ago: her and Esme riding their bikes down the curve of Parc at night, the mountain rising in the dark beside them, the air whipping their skin.

And now:

Esme beside her, still alive, in the hazy dawn light. Hannah watched her—hair tossed down her back, lipstick faded from last night, her beauty still there, accentuated by wrinkles, tugging at everyone who saw her.

Hannah saw Esme's twenty-year-old face in this face. The same brightness. The same joyful hunger.

Esme looked up at Hannah, the same memories swimming in her

eyes, and for a moment they regarded one another, a new electricity rising in the air. Fifty-eight years of it, rushing up.

Esme's lips were softer than they had been. How could that be? As they kissed, they were young again, rushed mad with infatuation, feeling it multiply within them and tumble out of their throats. Careening around the winter streets of Montreal, the ice and the pain and the beauty. Their skin flared with warmth, mouths pulling closer.

Everything Hannah had already lost was returned to her, in that kiss, and she was made newly aware of everything she was losing again, and how lucky she was, to have them to lose.

With a hand still on each other's necks, they pulled away, and checked each other's eyes, searching for reluctance or regret. But there wasn't any. They sat back up, wiping away tears. They laughed, feeling twenty.

A long pause, the swish of the grass.

"I really loved you, you know." Esme touched Hannah's hand.

Hannah nodded. She knew.

"I know I ran away a lot," added Esme, and they both laughed quietly, squeezing hands between them.

"I know."

It was not lost on Hannah that Esme, more than anyone, had turned out to be her most enduring love.

In the distance, a golf cart clipped along between trees. Soon, the croquet players would start, and the tennis players—activities for a day that Hannah would not see her way through.

Hannah and Esme composed themselves, took deep breaths, savouring the peace of the dawn, the gentle slap of the pool.

"I don't know if this helps, Hannah . . . "

Esme stopped herself, weighed her words carefully.

"But she knows that you love her. That doesn't change because she didn't come."

Hannah looked away, bit her lip. She nodded, unsure—then stronger.

She wasn't certain she'd made her peace, but she owed it to Esme to pretend.

31

FLORIDA
2057

A heavy rain fell on the parking lot, the water slapping the leaves of the palms and splattering on the pavement.

Hannah thanked the motel owner and dropped off her keys, then dashed out to the car, opened the door and thunked it closed behind her.

Inside: the rushing patter of rain on the roof, the wash of it across the windshield. The delicious, anonymous scent of a rental car, factory fresh.

Last night Hannah had sat on a plastic chair outside the door of her motel room, drinking a soda from the parking lot vending machine. In the humid dark there had only been her and the crickets, the faraway swoosh of an unseen car in the night, the primordial gurgle of the swamps that spread beyond the willow trees in the blackness.

On the drive down, she'd passed sunken clapboard houses and abandoned shopping malls. She'd smelled the sweet night air, felt the shiver of something new, and had known this was right.

Now, Hannah waited for the rain to ease up before pulling onto the road. The car was piled with her boxes of things. Her parents, in their urns, were snug in bubble wrap.

It was very early morning—just past dawn—and when the rain cleared, the blue sky was wisped with pink and orange, and mist rose off the pavement. A heron stalked the side of the road, and palm trees sprouted up everywhere, slumped towards one another in lazy conversation.

An hour later, Hannah was sitting on the terrace of the bar, overlooking the resort and drinking a coffee. She admired her new home—its shining pools, its bright buildings, the birds flapping over the broad sky.

Palm Meridian wasn't new to her, of course. She'd visited before it had even been built, had stepped amongst the piles of earth with Sophie and Frankie. Sophie had been pregnant and both of them had been young, their lives a broad lawn before them.

Just as she'd promised Frankie, Hannah had funded the cooling systems that had made it possible for the resort, and its residents, to survive. Instead, the place had thrived.

Decades later, when they were nearing retirement age, Esme had moved down before Hannah. Once Hannah and Luke had sold their company, it had felt only fitting that Hannah should retire there, too.

On the day she'd signed up and made her first payment, Hannah had also made an anonymous donation, enough to fund resort fees for everyone for a very long time to come.

Drinking her coffee there now, on her first day, Hannah closed her eyes, felt the sun on her face. Minutes later, there was the chug of a golf cart climbing the hill. Hannah craned down to look—it was Esme, brazen and lipsticked, her scarf billowing in the wind.

It hadn't been home yet. But now it was.

32

FLORIDA
6 a.m.

*I*t was six in the morning on the last day of Hannah's life, and she and Esme had made it up the slope to the bar, bleary and salted with Ziploc bacon.

Inside was a happy carnage of streamers and lost orthotics, stacked glasses and scattered disco ball pieces. Hannah collected her parents' urns from behind the bar.

With her mother under one arm and her father under another, Hannah stood at the head of the dancefloor, watching its glossy surface shine in the growing dawn light.

Outside, Esme was waiting by a golf cart. She helped Hannah load the urns into the storage compartment.

"I'll take us," said Hannah. She stepped into the driver's seat, waited for her friend to settle, and tapped her sunglasses down onto her nose. They crunched through the gravel and curled back onto the path. The way was clear, the resort still empty at dawn. Hannah pressed the gas pedal to the floor. She took them soaring across their home, carving the paths with ease, hearing the laughter tumbling out of Esme's throat.

Closer to their rooms, Hannah slowed and wound down the paths. The shrubbery was thicker here, and it rubbed their arms as they passed.

Outside Esme's room, they agreed without speaking that they needed to downplay the moment. That they could not bear another lurch in their chests, another step towards goodbye.

"I'll come and get you," Esme said.

Esme would pick Hannah up from her room in just over an hour, would drive her to the hospital for her appointment. Hannah had asked to go into the appointment itself alone.

"I love you, Han."

"I love you, Ez."

Esme went inside and shut the door. In an hour, she would take another round of pills from the bottles in her purse. The leukaemia was spreading through her blood, cells multiplying madly in her bone marrow. She'd make her own peace in her own time.

She'd never tell Hannah that death had come for her, too.

Soon Hannah was parking the cart outside her own room. She let herself in, stepping around the packed-up boxes, and put the urns on the table by the door.

Hannah stood for a while in the centre of the room, feeling the crush of it all release from her. On the bedside table were the drinking glass and toothbrush, untouched. Her green windbreaker on the wall, with the letter for Sophie in the pocket, and the land deed smelling of Nevadan desert dust.

Hannah ran her hand along the bedsheets, crawled beneath them. She tucked herself in while Florida shimmered outside.

The sun rose higher, the warmth nosing through the window.

It had been snowing the day that Hannah's mom had died. It blanketed the mountain, covered the sidewalks, reflected the street lights— red and yellow and green. It made the city quiet: quiet enough for Hannah to hear her mother leaving, as she knelt beside the bed.

There had been sorrow in this—of course. But could you ask for much more? A mother, once coursing with life, leaving all of it to her daughter. Safe and happy. There, and warm.

Now, lying in bed, Hannah watched her mother pack soil into the flowerpots on their Montreal balcony, the snow having melted and spring arrived again.

She saw her father on his bicycle, approaching their apartment, jacket flapping, a smile rising on his lips. It was Saturday, and the bagels were fresh in their brown paper bag.

Pain was going to come, sometime. Hannah had always known that. What we love will be taken away. And when we, ourselves, go, she thought, maybe we'd find it wasn't like sleeping at all, but like waking up.

As Hannah lay in bed, in a wedge of sunlight, an understanding flooded her: she would never know where Sophie was. What she felt. What she remembered of New York and Vegas, of Vermont or Montreal.

She gripped the sheets and imagined Sophie, her skis slicing through the air, the slope lost beneath her.

Where had their baby gone? Hannah knew it now: he was in the lake water that lapped at their legs, in the shudder of a night-time airplane, in the slot machines and the vinyl booth at the diner. He was in their end and their beginning, in the dripping springtime trees.

Here you go—this boy is yours. He always has been.

Crossing the state line from Georgia into Florida ten years ago, something had brought Sophie back to Hannah. It hadn't been hard—Sophie had hovered over most days since she'd left, bringing Hannah a sad kind of happy.

The vegetation had grown thicker, and Hannah had sped on into Florida, towards the resort that would soon become her home.

She'd remembered Sophie on New Year's Eve, at the diner, a lifetime before. They'd all crowded around the TV at the counter, where the numbers slipped down.

A trucker—a regular—had rushed into the diner with only seconds to spare. The owner had flicked her apron-veil over her shoulder. Laughing wildly, she'd welcomed him in:

"Why do we always seem to meet right before the end?"

33

The driver had lived in the area for all of his sixty-five years, had watched the state sink into the ocean like it was settling down to sleep.

He described how many people had fled, moving west and north for dryer lives. How at first it had been devastating. Communities were depleted, and those who'd stayed lived lonely lives. After a while though, he saw the truth of it: the apocalypse was strangely beautiful. He'd watched nature push through the floorboards of his neighbours' homes, watched wildlife roam freely through the strip malls and IHOPs that had once been sprinkled with litter, the air around them choked with car exhaust. He'd watched the palm leaves turn a shade of green more vibrant than they'd ever been. He'd seen an end allow a beginning.

The driver pressed his toe on the gas and sped them both along the interstate, the ghostly ruins of Disney parks poking above the trees. It was morning, and the day's humidity pushed in through the open windows. The breeze rattled the air freshener that dangled from the rearview mirror: a pine tree laden with cartoon snow.

"Gosh, I really hope you get to see her. If I could see my girl again . . ."

Sophie's heart raced in her throat in the passenger seat as she tried to control her breathing. She was already scheming a way to thank this man, whose name was Glen, and the three other strangers who'd helped her hitchhike from New York since yesterday morning.

She'd flown from Zurich to London and caught her second flight, which was meant to fly from London to Orlando. But when the blackouts rolled through Florida, airports large and small had diverted flights. Crossing the world wasn't as easy as it had once been—with less fuel there were fewer flights and more disruptions. The Atlantic, which had once felt small, was a yawning chasm again, and Sophie had found herself stranded at JFK when she was meant to be in the thick of a Florida forest.

It was the kindness of strangers that had ferried her down the Eastern Seaboard, a white-knuckle twenty-four hours full of southern storms that threatened to flood the roads and stop her trip. She ate fly-by meals in roadside diners with her drivers, traded stories in the glow of the dashboard, watching the highway lines, her hope flickering in the dead of night.

Sophie told every one of them her story, and as she spoke, their feet nudged harder on the gas pedal.

Now, it was morning. Sophie had dreaded the dawn, knowing she'd missed the party completely, and knowing Hannah would think she hadn't come. She had found the resort's phone number and tried to call, but nothing would go through. Signal, each of the drivers said, got thinner and rarer the further south you went, with connection dropping off completely once you reached the bottom of the state.

Leaving Zurich, Sophie had packed nice clothes, a bag of make-up, a pair of her dressiest shoes. She'd meant to look her best for Hannah's party, on the other side of the ocean. But now, more than a day after she'd lifted off, Sophie had forsaken all illusions.

If she was lucky enough to reach Hannah in time, Hannah would find Sophie as she really was: grey, aged seventy-seven, lightly withered, soaked with sweat in a pair of shorts and a t-shirt. She still had an athlete's body, coiled with masterful energy, her arms and legs marked up with sporadic scars—a record of a life spent bounding outdoors. She'd long ago cut her hair, the waves now shoulder-length and tied away from her face. Her soft features, washed with wrinkles, were unmistakable, a burning behind her still-bright eyes.

At the last and final pit stop, Sophie had brushed her teeth in a gas station bathroom, scraping off the residue of the airplane pasta, the burgers in Philadelphia, the rogue cigarette she'd shared with the last driver, Linda—the two of them passing it back and forth in the front seat, knocking the ashes onto the interstate in Georgia. The country seemed to creak and fall apart as they roared south.

Now, Glen and Sophie sped past a superstore with a sprawling, cracked parking lot, the morning sky bursting above.

"Nearly there."

Sophie had stopped wiping her hands on her shorts and just let them sweat. Her eyes ticked along the trees, anticipating the sign, remembering the design that Frankie had proudly shown them, sipping orange juice, forty-three years before.

Ten minutes later, Glen lurched the car towards the entrance when they saw it:

PALM MERIDIAN

RETIREMENT RESORT

Sophie hugged Glen as she climbed out with her duffel bag.

"Take care!" he shouted, and he drove off.

Sophie approached the resort, unseeing of anything, aware of the breeze in the trees, the sound of a swimming pool and laughing voices. The gates were open, the whole place slightly overgrown, rolling lawns squared by bright buildings beyond.

Her words were ready in her throat as she strode forward, in search of a security guard, a greeter:

Hello! My name is Sophie Welch. I need your help. I'm looking for . . .

But in the corner of her eye, Sophie saw them—a group standing in the grass by the entrance. Something about the way they stood, mournful beside a line of golf carts, told Sophie everything she needed to know.

The woman in the centre of the circle turned, her eyes bleary with tears, as if she sensed Sophie there.

"Esme!" cried Sophie, desperation spilling out of her throat.

The face was more than forty years older than when she'd last seen it, and still could not be mistaken.

"Sophie!" Esme was already running towards her. The others, who'd been consoling one another, were bright faced with shock.

Sophie was flooded with everything. She couldn't hear herself speak: "Where is she?"

Esme didn't waste a moment. She leapt into gear. Sophie understood immediately: time was ticking down.

"Get in the cart! Get in the cart! I'll drive you!"

Sophie discarded her bag in the grass, and ran to the nearest cart, Esme slamming into the driver's seat, cranking the key, and screeching out.

Sophie turned and waved to the group she'd interrupted, all of them waving back, skipping towards the road—the joyfully shocked and dazed faces of people that Sophie knew Hannah loved.

The interstate that had been tranquil in the morning fog was now alive with the sound of the golf cart's screeching tyres, a motor straining beyond its limits, birds breaking up from the trees. Sophie held on tight to the seat, feeling the wind whip away tears she hadn't realised were falling from her face. Beside her: Esme, hands cool on the wheel, scarf flapping.

Esme shouted over the noise. "There's a phone in the glove compartment! The second emergency number calls the hospital. Phone them and tell them they have to wait! We're coming!"

Sophie fumbled with the latch of the compartment, rooted around in the clutter of maps and first aid equipment, found a phone that must have been thirty years old. Nearly falling out of the cart, she stabbed at the phone screen, was startled to find it come to life. She tabbed to the speed dial numbers, pressed to ring.

The phone pulsed, trying, trying . . .

But the century had fallen through completely. The signal couldn't reach beyond the height of the trees.

Esme glanced over, her eyes wild. Sophie shook her head.

They'd have to chance it.

Esme pushed her foot as hard to the gas as it would go, the cart tearing along at a speed it had never reached, not even the night before on the way to the airport.

The greenery racing by above them, the air slapping their skin, they understood that it could be over.

Esme jerked the wheel, let it slip smoothly through her hands, navigating towards the hospital down smaller roads, bumping over uneven ground, no longer maintained by the county.

A smile had grown on Esme's lips, and she glanced over to Sophie, then back at the speeding road.

She shouted over the roar of the wind. "I always liked you, you know!" Esme was grinning. "You made Hannah so happy!"

The hospital was visible above the trees—a white *H* on a blue background, battered by storms. With two more jerking turns, where the cart threatened to topple and send them skittering onto the street, Esme pointed them towards the entrance. She bumped over a curb, then a grass median, crashing back down, revving across the parking lot and landing them at the sliding glass doors.

"Thank you!" Sophie called.

Esme waved from the cart.

The reception desk loomed in front of Sophie.

"I'm looking for Hannah Cardin. She's in this ward."

The receptionist pointed the way, and Sophie found herself running through white corridors, the wayfinding signs swimming in front of her eyes, her heart floating somewhere out of her body, out with the palm leaves and the sunshine on cracked bits of parking lot.

There was the room—Sophie slowed as she neared. The door was open, a green windbreaker hanging on a hook just inside. In the pocket, an envelope, addressed with the curl of an "S."

Sophie staggered towards the door, feeling the blood rise up through her ears, deafening her into a kind of quiet.

Just through the door, she saw the bulk of the bed in the light blue-dark, an arm with a patient's bracelet . . .

By the time you read this, Soph, you'll be sitting in my bedroom here at Palm Meridian, and I hope I've given you a drink and maybe a cheesy breadstick. Don't worry, there's fresh food at the party. I just had to empty out my fridge this morning, because they don't let you take perishable food where I'm going. (Ha ha.)

I know we haven't seen one another in a very long time, but I hope you agree it doesn't matter. I hope you agree that "time" is a bit beside the point entirely. My time with you was a place. It was my home.

I know I look like a piece of wet laundry these days, as old as I am, and that my arms aren't what they used to be. My boyish good looks have gone and I'm more like someone's pet goat they're rehabilitating. Because of you, though, I've not had to reckon with age at all. Because of you, I've remained, in mind and spirit, exactly as I was the day I met you: twenty-seven, a mix of smart and stupid, my skin flushed with icy Manhattan air and two drinks buzzing behind my eyebrows. For fifty years, I've been there on that sidewalk with you. The hotel has not stopped burning. The snow has piled in the street.

Pain is going to come, sometime, for all of us. It came for us in Montreal. And we couldn't bear it.

Now it's come again. This time it's taking everything away. But considering how much I've been given, I can only be grateful for having had it at all.

I'm sorry I reached out so late, and I'm sorry that I won't be here much longer, but we've got tonight if you'd like it.

If I don't tell you this evening, I'll tell you now:

If I've got thoughts where I'm going, I'll think of you.

I hope, for a while, I kept you warm.

If Hannah had been around to tell her friends, she would've told them that in the end, it was everything they'd guessed it would be: a zeppelin ride, a melting sensation, a joining up of the brightest thoughts, a coming and a going, a sleeping and a waking up.

Hannah would tell them something stranger: that at the end, she felt someone beside her. Someone who'd always been there, even before they'd met. A familiar feeling. Later, a gasping, losing laugh. A press across the sun-baked parking lot, the sky licked by the everlasting palms.

ACKNOWLEDGMENTS

Some of the most fun parts of *Palm Meridian* to write were the parts describing the community around Hannah—smart, hilarious, kind, talented, too-good-to-be-true people. She cannot fathom her luck! *I* cannot fathom my luck! In real life, I am surrounded by people just like this, and so many of them have helped bring this book into the world. I will forever be grateful.

Firstly, my eternal thanks to Susan Armstrong for your belief in this story, your steady hand, your endless grace and skill and kindness. To be paired with you is a wild privilege. Thank you for choosing me.

Thank you to Gráinne Fox and Kelly Karczewski for shepherding this book into the US in the most mind-bogglingly extraordinary way— and all with a mix of humor and formidability I could not write. Every day I aspire to match it.

Thank you to Christina Demosthenous and Margo Shickmanter for not only being the kinds of editors that people dream about, but for being walking embodiments of the resort—razor sharp, full of passion, and always up for a laugh. This book is boundlessly better because of you. Thank you for taking a chance on this story.

Thank you to Brittany Lavery and the whole team at S&S Canada for so brilliantly caring for this book in my cold, beautiful home country.

For your support in bringing this book to life, thank you to Catriona Paget, Madison Hernick, Mary Pender, Orly Greenberg, Celia Albers, Millie Seaward, Emily Moran, Mia Oakley, Caitriona Row, Eleanor Gaffney, Gabrielle Chant, Charlotte Stroomer, Sharmaine Lovegrove, Amy Guay, Rhina Garcia, Eva Kerins, Meredith Vilarello, Caroline McGregor, Alison Forner, Clay Smith, Toby Triumph, Allison Green, Jessica Chin, and the entire teams at C&W, UTA, Dialogue, and Avid Reader. Thank you also to Brett Popplewell, Frania Hall, Alice Furse, Henry Fry, Catherine Cho, and the T&H Comms team.

Thank you to Nez, my first and most loyal reader. I write mostly to make you laugh.

Thank you to Jenny for our home in Peckham, when this story began.

Thank you to Montreal, which I carry around with me.

This book is dedicated to my family. Mom, Dad, and Alice, every bit of joy and hope and humor in this story comes from you.

And to incomparable Sophia: I am yours. I always have been. Let's grow old and jump in the pool.

ABOUT THE AUTHOR

GRACE FLAHIVE was born and raised in Toronto, Canada. She studied English literature at McGill University in Montreal before moving to London, UK in 2014, where she's lived ever since. *Palm Meridian* is her debut novel.

ARP credits page tk